the CLINCHER

the CLINCHER

A HORSESHOER MYSTERY

Lisa Preston

Skyhorse Publishing

Skyhorse Publishing books may be purchased in bulk at special discounts for sales promotion, corporate gifts, fund-raising, or educational purposes. Special editions can also be created to specifications. For details, contact the Special Sales Department, Skyhorse Publishing, 307 West 36th Street, 11th Floor, New York, NY 10018 or info@skyhorse-publishing.com.

Skyhorse® and Skyhorse Publishing® are registered trademarks of Skyhorse Publishing, Inc.®, a Delaware corporation.

Visit our website at www.skyhorsepublishing.com.

10 9 8 7 6 5 4 3 2 1

Library of Congress Cataloging-in-Publication Data is available on file.

Cover design by Erin Seaward-Hiatt
Cover photo credit istockphoto.com

ISBN: 978-1-5107-3272-8
Ebook ISBN: 978-1-5107-3274-2

Printed in the United States of America

Chapter 1

THIS GUY WAS ALWAYS SUCH A faker, acting like I'd killed him, broken his leg, whatever. I bit back my growl, because he's the over-sensitive type. With some, it works to improve manners but with the fakers, and I have a few on my list, I have to keep my *grrs* inside. I'd whacked him in the ribs twenty minutes earlier, but it taught him nothing. With his leg over my thigh and a freshly driven nail sticking out the side of his hoof, it could be so unhealthy to add serious kicking to the mix. He'd already scraped a layer of flesh off my inner wrist when I trimmed this hoof. Now he was rocking, swaying back and forth as though he lacked the God-given balance anyone with a leg in every corner has. I just hate it when they rock. Did he hear music under those big ears? Need his skull wrapped in tin foil? I gritted my teeth and twisted the nail point off in the apex of my hammer's claws.

My client pursed her lips together, looking prissy and pissy while fiddling with the lead rope. Always fussing with the rope. And she'd about fainted when I slapped her boy. Patsy-Lynn Harper doesn't buy her clothes in a big enough size and she has that ridiculous white-blonde hair piled up over thin, dark eyebrows. And now she had those silly eyebrows pinched up in pointless worry. It's easy to see the overgrown Paint comes by his flair for fretting honestly.

But today was worse than usual. Patsy-Lynn had been in a tizzy from the moment I walked into her immaculate barn. She'd been on the phone saying in her southern drawl what a bad idea something or other was. She'd hung up pretty quick when she saw me. On this visit, I saw Spartacus had a scrape on one hind leg. It wasn't enough to worry about, just a little skin missing, but Patsy-Lynn had dabbed ointment all over it. She said that she thought he'd hurt himself, kicking out some of the pasture fence. Earlier in the week she'd found a broken board.

The horse leaned again, putting so much weight on me that he was basically asking to get the flat of my rasp across his ribs. I don't know how my legs held both of us or how I found the fortitude to not beat the daylights out of him. The footing helped. One fine thing about the Harpers being on my client list is their setup, that's got to be said. The barn is sunrise-pretty and well-built, with these brick-looking rubber cushions lining the aisle. I could see the heels of my boots biting into the flooring and I told my knees to hang in there, drove two more nails home, then twisted off the points quick as I could.

Wearing what Guy calls my Wood Plank face, I told myself I'd be out of there in fifteen minutes. I drove and wrung the last nail then released the hoof from between my knees. With one hand, I reached for my clinchers and rasp while the other brought his foot forward to my hoof stand. Soon as I did his clinches, I prettied things up with the rasp and lied to Spartacus as I patted him.

"You're a good fella." I turned to put my tools in the truck.

Patsy-Lynn hollered for her barn-help to come fetch her baby and take him back to his stall.

I hate it when clients call critters "baby." My dog, Charley? He's not my baby. My horse, Red? Also not my baby.

Barn-Help brought his blue-check-shirted, bow-legged self up from where he'd been mucking stalls, rolled his eyes, and shot me a glance to see if at least I appreciated him. He was a new guy, I was pretty sure. Patsy-Lynn Harper does go through the help.

She fiddled with a cross-tie like she had the whole day to kill and I guess she did. These people who don't work, I don't know how they can pass all the hours on their hands. It seems like she must have filled quite a lot of time buying stuff. The Flying Cross started looking pretty snazzy after Mr. Winston Harper married Patsy-Lynn last year. She set to marking her new territory by purging the help and redecorating. She'd scored big, marrying a rich older fellow whose only kid was already raised. Even the barn was repainted, with lots of fancy new touches to impress the horses. They now have mud-free paddocks all year—and that's a real accomplishment on the edge of the Cascade Mountains—because she bought those grids-over-gravel things that cost about a gajillion bucks a square foot. The new stainless steel mini-fridge at the far end of the barn aisle where she kept vaccines and cold drinks glimmered.

The stall down there had its top door shut so some new horse couldn't stick its head out. Patsy-Lynn hurried past it with a couple sodas and raised a Diet Coke in my direction like an offer, but I was humping my anvil up to the tailgate and didn't exactly have a free hand. If I ever drop that mother on my foot, I won't be able to work for a month or two.

She studied her barn-help as he latched Spartacus's stall door. "You have to watch them every minute," she whispered to me. "That last guy got my new hedge trimmer."

Just as the barn-help hung Spartacus's halter on the stall door hook, the stud kicked. Patsy-Lynn looked gratified that her horse shared her opinion.

"Your last barn-help made off with your hedger?" I asked.

"A day labor fellow I had in here for pruning the orchard and a few other things." She shook her head and popped her gum. "Well, Rain, six weeks from today to re-shoe, 'kay, hon? And let's make it first thing in the morning, 'kay?"

When she started calling me Rain was when I shortened Patsy-Lynn. And I'm not her hon. And not everybody can be first thing in the morning, for crying out loud. She hadn't liked today's afternoon appointment when we scheduled it the month before last. Seems she's used to being first.

"'Kay, Pats." I ignored her frown and penciled in the next date and time—it did turn out to be first thing on a Monday morning, six weeks to the day—in my appointment book and then on a card that I gave her even though she tried to wave it away. To survive, I need to be more business-like in this thing, so I got these cards and the appointment book and I might get a sign for my truck doors. It's hard to picture Ol' Blue with a sign on the doors, but it'd be some cheap advertising.

Patsy-Lynn entered the date in her phone, then wrote it on the big hanging barn calendar—for the hired help, I reckon.

I finished putting up my tools then used my cooling bucket's water to rinse my hands and arms. In a fit of helping, Patsy-Lynn had once dumped my bucket while I was putting my anvil stand in the truck. It has to go in a certain way. Before I could stop myself, I'd given her a whole lecture about how I liked to wash off my hands and arms in my bucket, last thing. Never, never dump a horseshoer's water bucket.

Patsy-Lynn acts like it makes her all kinds of cool to have a woman shoer. When she babbles about women getting to do all kinds of jobs, I just ache to ask if she's ever done any at all.

This afternoon she about shocked me by asking if I wanted to stay for a coffee and chat. She offered this up like it was some sort of rare gift. She'd gab all day no doubt if I could stay and stand it, but this is how I feed myself and make my rent and truck payments and I can't hang around jawing with some bored, rich housewife.

She chirped about how welcome I was to hang with her for a bit. Said she could show me the catalog picture of the new paneling she'd ordered for the tack room. Does her husband know how much money she wastes on decorating? I made it plain to

Patsy-Lynn's pinched face that I had another client scheduled. Confussed—Guy calls it "confussed" when someone acts confused and fussy—might have been her state of mind. Seems all she needed was some girl time. All I needed was to get the Flying Cross in my rearview mirror.

I drove Ol' Blue through the ranch gate onto Oldham lane. Down the road a piece, a vehicle straddled the centerline, going around a pretend-cowboy in a brown leather hat who was walking down the road. This is ranchland, with shoulderless roads. I pulled Ol' Blue all the way to the side as the shiny, black-windowed truck nearly took me out, grinding the gears with every shift, right down the middle of the road even after he'd passed the dude afoot. I called him a foul name before I remembered I'd sworn off cursing in my pledge to become a better person.

My last client of the day, Abby Langston, lived with her daddy across the highway from the Harpers. This is hilly country where black basalt ribs through the grass. Over here in the west part of Butte County, every coastal evergreen grows, just not as tall because we have less rain than the coast. We have the pines. Lodgepoles, Ponderosas, Yellow and Sugar pines shed their needles on the forest floor, making for soft trails amid the spruce, fir, and cedars. This is the trick of central Oregon—it doesn't know whether to be like the rugged, thick-treed coast or the high east deserts. A few quiet dirt roads on the outskirts have the land looking more like green brush, and the meadows in there are mostly man-made. It makes for wonderful trail riding and a lot of one-horse places, like the Langstons and their neighbors.

Keith Langston is a banker in our little town of Cowdry, a divorced guy raising his daughter. I get the idea that Abby isn't swapped between the parents every year or two like I was.

When my back's aching and the day's been full enough—mid-afternoon can feel tired when I've done four full shoeings, especially right after finishing a stud like Spartacus—my mood will always improve upon clinching the last hind foot on the last horse.

Ol' Blue rattled over the cattle guard that put me on the semi-rural street where the Langstons live, and I smiled big.

Abby Langston is one of those cutie preteen girls that make the horse industry. She keeps her little Arabian in the field back of the house and thinks it's the smartest and most beautiful horse in the world. Her tack room's decorated with pictures cut out of magazines, flashy Arab shots mostly. Arabs at the Nationals, an Arab climbing Cougar Rock at Tevis, lots of other endurance pictures, a few shots of Ride and Tie, the whackadoo team sport that combines trail riding and running.

Abby rides bareback and sometimes without a bridle. She's polite and so's the mare. Liberty's always clean, bug-sprayed, and stands quietly when I'm doing her feet. I was looking forward to an easy appointment.

A hex was what I put on myself. Liberty twisted around and whinnied across her pasture over and over. It was like shoeing a drunk pogo stick.

"No," Abby told her mare, snapping the lead rope. "You stand still." The kid's face puckered in consternation and she growled at her horse, just like I'd taught her.

Good girl. If Abby doesn't get stupid as she goes teenybopper, she'll be less like I was. We could have been sisters if I could go back to pre-teenybopper times. My braid's longer now, but at her age I'd had that same shoulder length, straight brown hair, thick as any mane, bangs, and brown eyes with teeth that might have wanted braces. In the last couple years, I became a trim one too, like Abby is already.

At the Langstons', there are no rubber mats and no covered barn aisle for me to work in, but Abby has the place swept up and a manure fork's at the ready in case Liberty lifts her tail. No shoer wants to stand in a fresh pile of horse apples.

Abby gets a nod from me because she does all her own barn chores. She's one of those little girls who'd ached for a horse, thought them and dreamed them and loved them with her every breath before she ever scored Liberty. I'd been one of those girls and I understood the need completely. When I was with my mama, I'd had to fill that hole with the *Black Stallion* books, *Black Beauty*, *National Velvet*, the *My Friend Flicka* trilogy, *Misty of Chincoteague*, and the like. I still picked up beater copies and gave them to Abby, getting the girl properly book-equipped, and she pretty well worshipped me for the favor, especially for the last find, one every little lover of Arabians needs, *King of the Wind*.

Liberty has big feet for an Arab and the horn quality is nice, not those brittle, shelly hooves like my first horse of the day. That Thoroughbred had needed shoes but the owner just wanted a barefoot trim. A lot of horses don't pick their people too careful, but little Liberty chose fine. The mare's always been a good weight. Abby doesn't give in to the temptation to equate food with love. She keeps treats down to a few carrots and feeds sensibly. Plus, obvious from the fact that I can never reset, but always have to shape fresh shoes for Liberty, Abby rides the dickens out of her mare.

Standing back now, I could see this dancey horse was getting a belly.

"Abby," I said, "what—"

She waved furiously with both hands for me to quiet down, looking around quick like someone might hear us. There was nothing to see but maples, cottonwoods, and evergreens one direction. The other way stretched neighbors' pastures, then the distant buttes and hills. Still, Abby shot a guilty look all around and hissed for me to shush.

I don't like kids telling me what to do. I was a kid too recently to give up the scrap of respect I have for being a decade older than Abby. She saw the growl coming up my throat and looked apologetic quick enough.

"I can't say anything yet," she whispered.

I gave her a solid You're Full of Crap look.

Abby's face was desperate, pale. "He'll kill me."

"Huh?" I reached for her shoulder, but she clammed up and went to wringing her hands, staring at the faraway hills of Black Ridge.

"Really, Rainy. He'll kill me."

If drama's what I wanted, I'd have stayed with my mama the last bit I lived with either of my folks. Truth is, I was enough of a disagreeable badger in my teens that neither of my parents could hardly stand me, and the feeling was mutual. Looking back, the real problem was that I couldn't stand myself and I viewed anyone with the bad sense to be related to me as highly suspect.

Mama said I made her look old and that could hurt her career, such as it was. As if she was ever going to go from shampoo and food commercials to a big screen star. I used to call her "Mama" every chance I found, just to watch her wrinkle.

None of that's Abby Langston's business and maybe her suddenly misbehaving mare being pregnant's not my business, so I shut up and shod the horse.

Chapter 2

Pulling Ol' Blue up to the little one-bedroom house on the last acre of Vine Maple Lane, that's me coming home these days. It's a well-named lane, braced with old cottonwoods that dwarf the scraggly vine maple shrubs. Come fall, the brush is the first thing to turn bronze, distracting us from winter's approach. All's green now. The dangling chains of yellow flowers from the big maple in the pasture mean that May's here.

The house doesn't look like spring exactly. Guy probably wasn't the first owner to let the garage be a spare bedroom, seeing as how there's also a carport hitched onto the north side of the house. The winter rains mold or rust anything standing still, so any kind of a roof over the head is helpful. The house has clapboard siding with peeling paint, letting everyone know that though it's blue now, it used to be yellow. The trim looks like it was always white. The little front stoop's steps and railing are just gray-weathered wood. Soon as I pulled up, someone came down those sagging steps.

A tall, lanky-built guy with a cold drink and a smile is a real nice sight. It's scary sometimes, like I don't know whose life this is. This is a better person's world, not mine, but it's kind of working for now. I shut off Ol' Blue, easy in the fresh silence.

9

Guy handed me his drink while Charley bumped at his heels to get a greeting in, too. "Your lettering is here," he said, drying his hands on the tail of his rugby jersey. He has this group of friends with names like Biff and Chip and Buddy for poker and rugby. The first hobby explains why he hardly ever has to use an ATM and the second explains his crooked nose.

"My lettering is here," I said, because when it's hard to understand Guy even though I got every word, well, one way of letting him know he needs to use more words is to repeat what he says so he can hear he's making no sense.

"Come see." He went up the steps and held the door open for me. In the corner where the dinette sits lay a wide sheet of letter decals he'd ordered from someplace online.

In a big arc over the house phone number, the decal read: DALE'S HORSESHOEING.

"Oh, the lettering you were thinking about ordering, to go on the truck door." I was generally a C student, except for the four hundred or so days I skipped.

When we'd kicked around the idea of getting lettering, I thought it would go on the door and Guy thought it should go on the camper shell. I'd told him it was called a topper and I hadn't even bothered explaining to him there's topper people and there's camper shell people. Anyways, he'd gone ahead and bought the size to go on the door. Now Ol' Blue would be a rolling advertisement for my business.

Guy got himself a glass of iced tea. We're likely the only two-legged critters to come out of the Texas panhandle not liking sweet tea. It's an amazing thing that we found each other here near the end of the Oregon Trail. Amazing we're together anyways, me shoeing and eating his cooking, him cooking and helping me get set as a shoer.

Was it just convenience? A sexy, good guy with a pasture and empty garage to use as a bedroom, a hookup that didn't unlatch?

Fixing to tell Guy about Abby's mare and the kid going skeezy, I thought back. He'd gotten me that client, too. Keith Langston had bought the pony a few months before Guy and I met up. Guy knew Langston from the bank in town.

Now Guy got dopey-looking and sort of beamed at me before he got busy confussing me again.

"The truck," he announced.

"Mmm." I closed my eyes and took a long pull of tea. The cold glass soothed my hand.

"Why did you call it *the truck?*"

I opened one eye and gave him a look that was supposed to mean Because It's A Truck. But he wasn't grabbing, just grinning, so I gave him another eye and another look. This one meant Because It's A Truck, Stupid.

Still, Guy stood there all expectant.

If he wanted to be thick as mud, he could do his own stirring. It's hard to think of a reason why I should have to beg a man to make himself clear. He knows I wish he'd just speak his mind.

Then it seemed like he all the sudden remembered my yearning for clarity. "It's just that I think most people would use the possessive pronoun. Most would say *my truck* and I've noticed you're saying *the truck* and I'm wondering when that started and what it means."

Eyeballing him some more was my best option.

Guy grinned, looking chock full of delight, then popped his eyebrows up and asked, "Do you know?"

"No idea."

When Guy talks like this, I don't even have any idea why I'm in the room with him. If I wasn't already puppydog tired, it would have been a fine thing to slay him with my old rounding hammer, pop his eyes out with my hoof level, do dentistry on his molars with my clinchers and any other good new uses for my trade tools I could think up.

Guy was ready to discourse. "It might be that you're not thinking of property in terms of yours or mine. You're thinking of us and the future. Maybe you're finally relaxing a little bit about living together and—"

For one thing, we don't live together, I just rent his garage for a sleeping place. I was all set to congratulate myself on the awesome power of my scowl, 'cause he shut up like he'd slapped himself. But it was just a new subject.

"Oh," Guy said. "Look, something happened. I should have told you right away. It's upsetting. I don't know how I managed to get distracted. You looked cute, as always, and you're adorable when you're dirty from work and there I go again."

We nodded together, 'cause, yeah, there he did go again.

Guy took a serious sip of air. "Well, I'm sorry, this really is bad."

I waited, since that seemed to be the only thing I could do. We were both pretty quiet while Guy's mood got softer still.

"The police were here," he said.

"Po-lice?" I said it proper, like the two-word way it was pronounced in my part of Texas.

"Po-lice." Guy nodded. "Well, Mrs. Harper, Patsy-Lynn Harper, she's . . . they said someone found her body."

I set my tea down and realized my hand that hadn't been holding the glass was cold, too. Maybe I looked confussed because Guy said it again, in another way.

"Your client, Mrs. Harper, is dead."

Chapter 3

GUY MADE LIKE TO HUG ME, but I was having none of that. There was stuff to know and I gave him a look to say so.

He put his hand over mine.

"She's dead?" My mind spun hard to get wrapped around this thing. Death was a specter bad enough to say twice. "Really? Dead?"

Guy nodded.

"How'd she die?"

"I think she killed herself."

That didn't fit with Patsy-Lynn sprucing up the ranch she married into.

Didn't fit with her being so chatty with me.

"Why?" I didn't mean to ask out loud.

"Well," Guy said, taking his time here, "I don't know. People have issues, stuff you don't know about them. Problems or demons or things of that nature."

He was dead right, but I shook my head anyway. Guy's mother teaches people how to analyze others and his father is an economist who lectures on incentives. I kind of hate it when I can hear their learning in him. Makes me glad that he turned away from that professor life after his bachelor's degree, followed his heart to cooking school.

"But, Guy, you said you *think* she killed herself, like you don't know for sure."

Again, he nodded.

I thought of Patsy-Lynn making an appointment for me to re-shoe Spartacus in six weeks. "Then why are you jumping to the conclusion that she killed herself?"

"The deputy who was here said that she was in a garage with the car running. There's—"

"In her garage with the car running? Guy, I don't think they have a car. It's all trucks and quads and maybe a Jeep-like thing over there." It's a vehicle my daddy would call a Jap Jeep, but I'm not going to be like him.

Guy waved his hands, looking exasperated with me, which is silly, because I'm as clear as clean water. I've explained to Guy the difference between cars and trucks, and he claims to understand. I've also made clear the difference between car people and truck people. That, he doesn't get.

"Car, truck, whatever," he said.

"Why would she kill herself?" I fussed.

Thinking about what a death leaves behind gave me the heebie-jeebies. Now there was a widower and, come to think of it, a step-son left behind, though he was away at college or traveling or some such. I'd never met him and I'd seen awful little of the old man. Patsy-Lynn had been the reason I got the Flying Cross account. The old man had used another shoer, but when he married her, she'd moved in and changed most everything. The horses became a bigger deal—Spartacus was grown up enough to be marketed as a stud—when Patsy-Lynn hired me to shoe. Changing the help was just her making her mark, cleaning house, I always figured. Patsy-Lynn had loved her well-run new barn she'd scored with the old man, sure enough. Made me wonder now about her husband, and how the dust would settle. Would the old man marry again?

Imagine if my folks, like Mr. Harper, had remarried. Then I'd have me a couple stepparents. I shuddered at the thought of twice as many parents to disappoint.

Guy hugged me and we both repeated how awful and hard to believe Patsy-Lynn's sudden death was, then he gave me a side-of-the-neck caress like I was bereaved. That Guy's a genuine sweetie, in any case.

He picked up his huge wad of keys from the kitchen counter. He's got one for the Cascade Kitchen, the restaurant where he works, two for his so-called vehicles, and a storage unit, and who knows what else. I've made him stop keeping them in his pocket—they bruise during his power hugs—unless he's about to leave the house.

"I had been about to make a run into town when the police came by. Is there anything you want from town?"

"Red'd like a sack of oats." There had been some other reason I wanted to stop in town, but I couldn't summon the notion. "What do you need?"

"I'm going to buy a tool."

"Oh, dandy. What is it you want to make?" I asked, barely following the conversation. It was awful that Patsy-Lynn was gone, but why would the police come to tell me special?

"Hmm?" Then Guy sang, "If I had a hammer . . ."

He's got a voice like a god. Not a major god, but one with some pull, definitely. So he can sing a tiny part of some stupid old song and it's nice listening. But I'm a truth teller on almost all accounts now, so I said, "If you had a hammer, you might find you do less hammering than you think. Surely not in the morning and the evening and all night long."

Guy went on to a whole 'nother chorus, so it had to be said. "Quit singing that stupid song."

Silence, except his, "Well, fine."

"Could you possibly identify what tool you want?"

"I just thought I'd go to a tool store and get a tool. I'm not too particular on what kind."

"What, exactly, do you want to do?"

"Impress your father."

Oh, dandy.

Some months back, Guy had the bright idea that we should be introduced to each other's parents. My mama's too liberal to be a Democrat and Daddy's too conservative for the Republicans to claim him. I'd no idea where Guy's folks fit, but he'd gotten them on the phone from Amarillo and made a big bunch of noise, telling them all about me.

Given that Guy's parents teach college, they might not have been impressed that their son's girlfriend hadn't finished high school. His mother kept saying, "A fairy what? She's a fairy?"

"Farrier, farrier," Guy had hollered.

"Horseshoer," I'd said.

It went like that.

"Wonderful, darling," is what Mama said.

"I'll see about getting a run up that way," is what my daddy said. He'd done trucking along Interstate 10 for a long while, ever since he got too gimped up to make a ranch hand and took to driving truck for his wages. My folks split when I was five years old, and this is how I come to have the luck of being born Texan and the misfortune of being passed back and forth between California and Texas. But there is nothing my daddy can't fix, as long as it isn't a relationship.

We headed for the truck—my truck—to get to Cowdry. I'm not big on riding on Guy's scooter and his little car's an embarrassment, so we always go places together in the truck. In my truck.

Looking back, I don't know how Patsy-Lynn slipped my mind so quick, but I'm not proud of it.

* * *

Since Abby had paid me in cash, the ready money let me pull into the 24 Fuel on the way home. An old Ford Supercab with two men, both slightly familiar by sight—the driver in a blue cowboy shirt turned toward the passenger in a dark hat—pulled out as I parked at the diesel pump. I can't drive up to the 24 Fuel without thinking about my first time there, that night last year.

It's where I met Guy.

Ol' Blue had 80,000 miles and six years on when I got the loan. Part of this truck's appeal, in addition to the hand-sized longhorn hood ornament a prior owner had added, was it already had a topper over the bed. Having a topper lets me lock up my tools. I'm not one of those shoers with a fancy, special-built unit in the truck bed with locking drawers and compartments to store everything. I counted myself lucky in managing to buy a good used pickup truck. And the first thing I did with the new-to-me truck was go searching for Red, my old horse, planning to buy him back as soon as I found him.

My old man had sold Red ten years back. I wanted to make things right with him. With the horse, I mean. At that point, I'd just wanted to get one thing right and Red was the only piece of the past I could see to fix.

The people in West Texas my daddy sold Red to had moved to Arizona and later traded him away for a mare. Then Red's new people leased him out, eventually selling him again. Red spent time in Nevada. A farmer swapped him for a tractor. And so on, for hundreds and hundreds of miles. It took many months for me to figure out Red was up here in Oregon, but that's where the trail ended. I hadn't known this part of the country and didn't know what I was going to do once I got my hands on my horse. I was just taking one step at a time.

Although I'd climbed all over my young horse when he was two and three, I hadn't started Red; I had just planned and dreamed about when I'd make him a riding horse. But strangers got to break my horse. They took Red's prime, but there's still plenty of life left in a fourteen-year-old Quarter Horse.

Finding Red and buying him back took me all of a winter, but it was the best thing I'd done since graduating horseshoeing school.

And while I burned with shame over the bigger thing that I hadn't mended, I did patch things up with Red. First, I told him how sorry I was for his having been sold and traded. Horses have to say good-bye too much. I promised Red he'd never be sold again, and we'd have a good cry about lost years soon as we cleared that second-to-last owner's property. He agreed.

Loading Red was a bear. Then I saw that I didn't have enough diesel to get Red to the next county, much less across a western state or two, not that I had a destination. So, there I was under twittering lights at this all-night gas place, the 24 Fuel, debating with Charley, the old gold-colored Australian Shepherd I'd found on Interstate 5 just the week before.

The night we got Red back, the debate for Charley and me was whether to buy dinner out of the coolers and shelves in the 24 Fuel. He'd been hungry when I found him and I—hungry for good company—had been giving him half my food for the last week.

Then this fancy scooter-motorcycle-whatever thingy pulled in. A tall lean-muscled guy in a polo shirt and tan pants hopped off and bought himself a cup-and-a-half of gasoline for the zippy thing he rode.

Lordy, he was good looking enough to curl my ponytail. Straight blond hair, green eyes, twisty grin and a nose crooked enough to give him character. The beauty part was, this fellow studied me and clearly liked what he saw. His breath steamed in the cool night air, which showed just how hot he was, 'cause my exhales didn't make vapor.

"I'm Guy." He looked to be, like me, mid-twenties, and offered his hand.

I'm a gal, I wanted to say. But I didn't say anything.

"Guy Kittredge," he said, his right hand still waiting.

"Rainy Dale." I shook paws because I am familiar with at least some social norms.

"Filling up, Rainy Dale?" he asked, bright as a barn.

"I believe I will."

The scent of diesel rose as Guy started pumping my fuel, followed up with ammonia from the mighty fine job on the windshield. Ol' Blue had probably not had such clean glass since five or six owners ago, rolling off the line in Detroit.

Then the screaming started, along with those disaster-type noises that come from a shod horse striking his steel on the inside guts of a trailer. Ol' Blue swayed as the trailer groaned on its axles. This guy, *Guy*, froze mid-wipe, taking a break on the headlight-smearing job he'd given himself.

See, from day one, Red was one of those who sometimes has a switch flip in his head and suddenly a fine animal is only taking orders from Horse Planet. He's not a joyous gift from God when he's like this. That night, Red must have received a set of orders to behave like a lunatic and proceeded to go insane in the back of the borrowed stock trailer. The night was cool—spring is sharp and wet here—and Red's steamy horse-breath showed, oozing out the sheet-metal seams.

Guy's eyes went huge, then huger.

Patting my truck door as I switched the ignition partway and waited for the glow plugs, I said, "I'd better get Ol' Blue down the road."

"Ol' Blue." Guy sort of smirked, but the grin fell off his face when Red got a fresh set of orders and set to thrashing. All my horse really needed was to be moving down the road. I figured he wouldn't be so bad if the trailer was in tow.

"Red's not big on trailer time," I explained.

"Red." Guy looked ready to let his chuckle become a howl.

Charley wiggled at the window, cocking his head with questions, his uneven ears pricked up. Both his ears are shorter than when he was born, but the hair grows in long fringes that cover the old injury. He chortled his pre-woof, which seemed like an endorsement of Guy as a guy. I felt entirely safe on that front. In appreciation for Charley's dog quality opinion, I scratched his chest. Pale fur went flying.

"This is . . ." I started to say, then reflected that I didn't have much of a life if I was about to introduce my new pooch to some stranger at a gas station.

"Old Yeller," Guy suggested, a look of triumph on his face like he'd cured cancer or idiocy or something. "You have the primary colors."

The primary colors? Something was un-level in this guy's thinking, but for some reason I didn't feel warned off the man. Still, he needed to be set straight. "His name's Charley. I better go and get this whackjob horse of mine unloaded somewhere for the night."

"Where are you going?"

"I don't know. I just need to park and let him be on some grass for a while."

"There's a pasture at my place. I'm about two miles down the road." He pointed as though he really believed he was in two places at the same time.

But the thing of it was, I didn't know where I was going to park. I was just hoping for a grassy field somewhere. Red pickets okay— I'd taught him all his ground manners when he was young—and I was going to sleep in Ol' Blue's cab of course, but hey, a pasture a couple miles down the road sounded pretty soon. So I'd followed this Guy fellow down to his keep, looked it over, and knew we'd be okay for the night.

Red started screaming as soon as I stopped at Guy's place and the kicking recommenced, too. Then I made to unload.

"You're not going in there, are you?" Guy looked horrified. I wasn't so keen on it myself, but it wasn't my trailer and it was my horse, so them's, as they say, the breaks.

All this was before I knew enough about the man to see that some folks would later be inclined to call him my foo-foo boyfriend. It was before I knew he'd memorized every show tune and sings parts of every song, but with the wrong words. Before I knew I'd be living in his garage. Before I started digging myself into Butte

County in general and the little town of Cowdry in particular as a professional horseshoer on her own.

It was before Guy started trying to dig into my past, which I can't be having.

When Red's heels came shooting back at us, Guy whistled. "Check that out!"

It's true the horse's feet were way too long, a couple months overdue, hoof wall beyond the shoes with just bits of clinches holding on the keg shoes some yokel had nailed on when Red was under his last so-called owners. I waited to hear the joke about the cobbler's kid having bad shoes then remembered I had a clean slate with this guy. Guy didn't know anything about me except that I had a truck, a dog, and a horse. He didn't know I was a new shoer needing to create a client base so I could buy some hay and groceries. He didn't know I'd ached for my childhood horse for years and only had him back an hour. And Guy probably thought I had enough means to own a stock trailer, but that was his mistake for jumping to conclusions.

After spending the night on a cot in Guy's garage, first thing the next morning, I reshod my horse—a pure pleasure.

After graduating from horseshoeing school, I'd spent the next few years apprenticing. My first mentor was a Texas panhandle ranch shoer for the most part, so I got fast and strong at the sheer basics. We kept working horses working. Then I interned with a shoer in southern California who had a real wide range, pleasure horses and show horses of most kinds, even a little track work. When I found Red last year, I was plenty past interning, certified and ready to start my own business, but that first morning at Guy's place last year was my first time shoeing my own daggummed horse. I loved it.

As I was finishing Red's last clinches, Guy stepped out with two mugs of coffee and said he didn't know a thing about horses, but he knew his neighbor needed a farrier.

I'd started cheap—fifteen dollars a head less than average for the area. I kept sleeping in Guy's garage and he kept taking the rent money I paid in cash each month.

Since then I've been in Guy's bedroom and he's been on my cot. And as long as I'm making a list, we've done it in the pasture, the hay shed, the truck, the kitchen, the living room, and the laundry room with the washer on spin. Proximity and happenstance are what put Guy and me together, but that sure doesn't seem like a good enough reason to be with a fellow. Sometimes I figure we're not together anyways, not really. The plusses are hard to argue with some days. His hands, his mouth. Double on that last, because it's also the stuff he says and how he says it.

Guy asks. From the beginning, he asked.

Can I hold your hand? May I kiss you? Could I touch you there?

Chapter 4

A<small>T THE CO-OP, I CHECKED THEIR</small> bulletin board for my business cards. There weren't any left, so I put more under thumb tacks and then bought Red's oats, hoping some of those cards would mean new customers.

I'm a pretty shoer, and that's not referring to how I start every morning with my hair clean. Sure, my jeans are loose—three sizes smaller now than when I was a fat high school kid and they were tight-fitting—plus, about once a season, I use a little mascara and lip gloss. But I mean that I shoe pretty, driving every nail with the right power so they come out spaced perfectly, and I'm careful to make my clinches uniform. My clients who show—especially the halter class competitors and others graded for looks instead of performance—are way into having their horses' feet look pretty.

Pretty shoeing is part of what built up my clientele in the last year to the point where I can buy food and diesel and hay regular enough. I paid for Red's oats with the cash money left over from topping off Ol' Blue. The co-op is more than a feed store. There's racks of tools and automotive stuff and even housewares and some clothes.

Guy eyeballed every selection in the tool aisle, and got pretty taken with the range and wisdom of tape measures and those little

23

do-alls—multi-tools—that used to be just jackknives, but now have pliers and every such thing in them after they're twisted and folded around the right way. I have a dandy do-all on my belt, found it on the highway. I love road shopping.

Guy pawed every clever little tool and device like he'd really discovered something. That boy loves his gadgets. The kitchen has corers and curlicue slicers and a thing called a spiralizer. He even has a little butane torch to caramelize sugar.

I am not allowed to try using his kitchen torch for any kind of welding or soldering, though I have been tempted. I do love welding.

"Look at this," he said, after he hunted me down in the automotive section. He was holding a fat tape measure, a tape measure on steroids. "It's a recording tape measure. You push a button and say what measurement you took. There's a built-in microchip, no tape, of course."

"Of course," I said, giving him a look that didn't need defining.

He caught, good for him. "There's your Wood Plank face."

I kept wearing Wood Plank and didn't need to say a thing.

"I meant there's no recording tape, like a tape recording machine. The audio recording is done digitally. There *is* a tape to be a tape measure."

Guy pulled out the retractable metal tape and told me that we were two feet six and one-quarter inches apart.

Sometimes, we're a lot farther. Even standing shoulder to shoulder, we can be miles apart. When it comes down to it, we don't know all that much about each other. We don't know near enough.

"I," he said into the gadget, "am five foot eleven and three-quarters of an inch tall." He spoke with a baritone fitting the seriousness of his proclamation. Then he pushed another button and darned if the tape measure didn't play back his voice, his words.

He bought the silly thing while I studied on the car washing products that all but promised a brand new vehicle. Never mind, I can use soap and water from home to clean Ol' Blue.

Guy beat me to hefting out the fifty-pound sack of feed.

My truck was on Depot Road, right next to the railroad tracks at the side of the Co-op Feed & Seed. I guess way back when, town-folk thought Cowdry was going to be a lot more important in the beef market than it ever was. The train doesn't even stop here now, but they'd clearly once meant for a lot more feed and feed-eaters to be in the empty dirt lot between the tracks and the co-op.

We stepped onto the red cinders and sand that train people seem to like putting next to tracks. The ties and rails are bedded down on heavy black rock. Vibration told us about the coming freighter before the train's whistle sounded. I crunched across the cinders, ready to leave, but Guy set down the bag of feed and walked the other way, up the slope, near the edge of the railroad ties. He faced the beginnings of sunset as he watched the train. When he squints—and he does a lot 'cause he rarely wears sunglasses even though he always packs them—he gets little crow's feet in the corners of his eyes. The good-looking kind of crow's feet.

As the train rushed in, Guy quit squinting at it and stood there, too close. His shirt plastered hard to his chest, and his hair flew back. The steel wheels banged, the couplings knocked, and the railroad cars swayed into the curve.

Several feet below him, on safer ground, the train's power made me wince. So did whatever's in Guy that makes him tease trains. There's got to be something wrong with a man who won't step aside for a hundred steel freight cars.

Not 'til the last car passed did Guy come down the slope, grab the grain with one arm, and reach for my hand with the other. He didn't say a word, just looked happy. Driving home, I was picturing the lettering on the truck doors and wanted to get at the project before we lost the light.

We'd have made it home before dark if the deputy hadn't come after us.

Chapter 5

ANGRY PEOPLE MUST HAVE DESIGNED POLICE uniforms. It's all black boots, tan clothes, and sunglasses spat out of a white car with a shield on the door. My daddy, who covers more miles in a year than plenty of people drive in decades, told me to be polite, but quiet when it comes to getting pulled over by the police. There's a reason why "You Shoulda Shut Up" is my favorite song. Aside from being a catchy tune, it's good advice.

The deputy seemed solid at the same time he looked average. Wearing a bulletproof vest will do that for a person, and maybe the look is helped by the buzz cut and mustache. His left arm had the man-tan of a person who wears a short sleeve shirt and drives with the window open, even though a central Oregon spring doesn't exactly mean we've got sunning weather.

I figured he'd ask if I know how fast I was going. That's what they always start with, then they've got a person digging for registration and insurance cards out of the glove box.

Even if Ol' Blue had a working speedometer, which it doesn't, it's fair to say I wouldn't have been looking at it anyways. And if I had been, any relationship between my speed and what some road sign recommended would have been purely coincidental.

The deputy strolled up in his own sweet time and opened with, "Do you know why I stopped you?"

"No. Do you?" I encouraged him with part of a smile.

"Were you at the Harper residence this afternoon?"

I said, "Huh?" which didn't make me sound too bright, but here I'd been trying to decide whether to fake a guess at my speed or just come right out with I-dunno-you-tell-me.

"The Harper residence. You there?"

People leave out whole words and it's left for the rest of us to guess. This is not exactly fair and it makes my mind ping. Anyways, *residence* is a hoity-toity word for *home* and I don't cotton to hoity-toity. So I was still thinking what to say when he barged on like a bull getting at his evening feed.

The deputy glared past me and fixed Guy with a look that made it plain Guy should have been clear that the police wanted a word with me.

"Well, Miss Rainy Dale," the deputy said, "we'd like to talk to you. At the very least, you seem to have been the last person to see Patsy-Lynn Harper alive."

There was more than a little wrong with his words and I paused while my brain tried to fire up and identify the problem.

Pausing wasn't the deputy's thing at all. "Have you got any injuries, Miss Dale?"

"Everyone's got injuries." I don't know why I said that. Sure I've been injured, but I wanted no pity. Also, I don't want anyone knowing about my injuries.

The deputy wasn't looking at me as I spoke. He was looking at my arms, hung by my hands from Ol' Blue's steering wheel. He studied the long red scrape Spartacus had given me on the inside of my right arm.

Before I opened my mouth, the deputy said, "Miss Dale, do you have any fresh, recent injuries?"

"None to speak of." I wasn't giving the sheriff's man eye contact.

"Did you leave anything there?"

"There?"

He looked as annoyed as someone in sunglasses can. One thumb hooked in his gun belt. So, pretty annoyed.

"Yeah," he said again. "Did you. Leave anything. There?"

I thought of hoof trimmings I'd pared off Spartacus. Did that count? Probably not. "Nope."

"You sure 'bout that?"

"Yep."

"No tools? Nothing at all?"

I studied the deputy, 'cause he was going about it so, so careful. Bile rose in my craw. Picking through my brain before I answered again, I spoke slowly. "I left her my card. An appointment card for the next shoeing."

"You left her your card," he said right back.

"Yessir."

"How about you head on over to the station for a quick statement? Follow me, okay? That suit you?"

Yowie. Seemed like whether it suited me or not, it suited him. I looked at Guy and for once he seemed to be without words. I pointed Ol' Blue at the deputy's bumper and followed him on over to the sheriff's office to get it done.

Cowdry's not the county seat, so the sheriff's satellite station is just a few rooms in the beater strip of stores at the bottom of town. Even though it's not my stomping grounds—Guy's house is off Cowdry's north end—I do have clients to the south. I've driven by the sheriff shop at the strip mall, but I've never been inside. When I shoe for Sheriff Magoutsen, I keep my head down and try not to call him Magoo. He's a little guy with a big, round baldness up top, always squinting through his glasses so bad I expect him to bump into things. He keeps his ropers at a boarding barn, not at his home and certainly not near this west county office.

Guy was mighty quiet on the ride, but he walked inside with me. Then they wanted me alone for the statement, so he waited in the lobby and I ended up in a small room with an older fellow in a suit. He introduced himself as detective so-and-so, but his name left my brain as soon as it entered my ears. Stained-suit-fellow had some paperwork and an old-fashioned tape recorder. No mustache on this fellow and really short hair, grayed-up red. The short cut helped hide his impending baldness. The open sport coat and loosened tie helped hide the button-straining paunch.

Suit Fellow asked me a bunch of stuff I'm sure they knew, like who I was and where I lived and all, then he asked, "Are you here of your own free will?"

"Sure," I said. What I meant was: I guess so. But I hadn't really considered the question.

"I understand you told Deputy Paulden that you hadn't left anything at the Harper residence on your visit there this afternoon."

I felt a little choked about things. Couldn't say why. Nobody likes being asked questions by someone who doesn't really ask but instead makes statements that get a girl sweaty. And Suit Fellow was worse than Paulden about too few words.

"It wasn't a visit," I said. "I was there to shoe her horse. One of her horses. And I told the deputy that I left an appointment card."

"No tools?"

"Nope." My tools are my living.

"Didn't leave a file?"

"A file? Nope." Picturing a big wad of papers that go in a filing cabinet, I gave the man a look of pure confussment. He was a lot better than Guy at grabbing onto the meaning of looks. Maybe his suit bestowed some smarts.

"You didn't leave a file." He stood and went for the door. Leaning out of the little interview room, he hollered at someone he had hollering privileges on. "Bring me that evidence from the Harper garage."

Something else got said in the hall, but I couldn't make it out.

Suit Fellow fetched me a can of soda without asking. He carried it by the rim, set it down and stood over me. "Here's a drink for you. Thought you might like it."

"Thanks." I kept my hands to myself.

"You a blood donor?" he asked.

The door latched hard, like it meant business.

"Huh?" I twisted my ponytail hard to one side.

"I asked, do you know your blood type?"

Several seconds is how long my jaw took to get working. "That's not even close to what you asked me."

He raised his eyebrows and hurled out a monologue about the case developing and them requesting a number of samples from a number of people to rule out possibilities. A knock sounded on the door. Someone cracked it open and handed Suit Fellow something in a clear plastic bag with official-looking tape on the bag's edges.

Inside that evidence bag was something I'd know at a distance even if I didn't know whether it was mine. It was long and flat, less than a quarter inch thick, about two inches wide by seventeen long. One side is for coarse work and the other's for fine smoothing. And the last three inches of one end bears a wicked point.

I twisted my ponytail the other direction. "That's not a file. That's a rasp." My mama would have hollered at me to quit playing with my hair. She always got after me for it, like it was the worst thing I could do.

She learned.

"A rasp," Suit Fellow said. "Okay, is it your rasp? Did you leave it at the Harper residence earlier today?"

"Look," I explained, "I use up a rasp in about thirty animals. I go through them pretty often and carry quite a few in my truck. When they get more worn than I'll use, I often give them to clients so they have one for emergencies. I may have given one to Patsy-Lynn. I think I did, some time back."

He looked like he was trying to decide whether to believe me. And he set the bagged rasp down on the table. The unnatural feel of indoor offices, with thin carpet and fluorescent lighting, is not my world, but under the unnatural lights, I could see the rasp in the evidence bag a lot better. It was a used rasp, the brand I used.

There was blood on the rasp. Lots of bright red blood, and maybe some skin snagged in the teeth.

Chapter 6

THAT RASP IN THE DETECTIVE'S EVIDENCE bag? Yeah, I was pretty sure it was one of my old rasps. And I felt cold as the north side of a cedar forest in December, where the frost stays in the shadows, the sun never warms the ground. My voice had trouble.

"Guy said she killed herself in the garage."

"Mrs. Harper," Suit Fellow said, making it real clear who'd be asking questions, "was found in her garage. And this tool, this rasp as you call it, was with her. And we'd like more information about that." He looked set for me to spill some beans.

I was fresh out of beans. "Did you ever think there might be another way to go about this?"

Muscles in Suit Fellow's jaw tightened as he gave the wall a good looking-at, then checked his notes. While I got the silent treatment, it did occur to me that I might not be quite as cool as I pretended.

Even though my daddy ran afoul of the law more than he should have, I thought I was considered rehabilitated in the eyes of who-ever did that kind of accounting. Sheriff Magoutsen being one of my clients didn't seem to be helping me here though. I don't know how many deputies there are in this county, but I'd think they'd all know the sheriff keeps a few good Quarter Horses with a buddy in Cowdry for weekend roping. Even though he himself lives at the other end of the county, Butte's not too awful big and Magoutsen's horses would have to get shoes somewhere. If this detective fellow thought about it, he might have been able to deduce that I could have been the sheriff's shoer.

When I landed that account, Guy made up new words to an old song and tried to get me to sing, "I Shod the Sheriff." It went on and on, eventually allowing as to how I shod the sheriff's horses, not the actual sheriff.

I felt a surly coming on, but this Suit Fellow was one of those rare men that can see a surly settling 'round my shoulders and make nice before I soak in it.

He now looked all pleasant and interested and good stuff, bringing both his hands to clasp friendly-like on the tabletop. "Miss Dale—"

"Rainy."

He made a gentle little wave with his hands. "Sure. Rainy. I don't want to upset you and I sure appreciate you helping us out—"

"No problem," I cut in, even while warning myself it wasn't nice to interrupt. My heart's new goal is to be nice. My mind chose that moment to remind me I was supposed to have bought my mama a Mother's Day card when I was in town earlier.

Suit Fellow nodded, pretending I was being as nice as he all the sudden was, letting me get away with a snitty bit of folding my arms across my chest.

"The thing is," he said, "we're wondering why this rasp of yours might have been at the Harpers' place."

"Well, first of all, why do you think it's necessarily my rasp?" I asked. "And B, exactly where was the rasp?"

More little calming motions. "Now hang on. How about you tell me precisely where you were at the Harper residence. Can we start with that? I'd like to know about your visit there, in detail. Tell me everything you noticed, everything you did."

I gave an accounting of my afternoon at the Flying Cross, drowning the man in such detail that my talk could have been used as a lecture for beginning shoeing students, including how sharp freshly rasped—perfectly level to receive a shoe—hoof walls are. I flashed my scraped arm. ". . . And then Spartacus was a real pill for that fourth foot, swaying and aggressive. I was fixing to whack him again but I didn't . . ."

While the detective's eyes glazed over, I gave an excruciating recital of doing those last clinches. Gorgeous clinches if I did say so myself. I needed to wash my whistler after my speech, and downed half the soda in a few good swallows.

This detective was a methodical note-taker. When I finished drinking my soda, he said some quick words about it being the end of an interview and clicked off a tape recorder that had been holding down the table. He pushed papers like so, and checked some forms on a clipboard, then stepped out to murmur with a couple men in uniform and came back in to purse his lips before he said he didn't have any more questions at that moment.

He was, I decided, like a warmblood. One of the good, big European breeds like a Trakehner or an Oldenburg or a Hanoverian. Warmbloods have the size and strength of a Thoroughbred but are less flighty. Guy is athletic and rangy-muscled like a race horse, but of course, looking at him, palomino is what springs to mind, because he's such a light blond and has that skin that's barely tan.

Faking a friendly, Suit Fellow, my own personal plainclothes deputy who spent the last half hour of my life, said, "So you weren't inside the Harper house at all?"

I shook my head. I thought of Patsy-Lynn's unlikely invitation for coffee that I'd turned down.

"Great, it'll be easy to eliminate you then. Would you care to give us a set of your fingerprints?"

My knee-jerk reaction was feeling not at all sure I cared to give him any such thing. "Do I have to?"

"No, you do not have to give up your prints at this point. I am asking for your consent."

"But I don't have to." I meant to ask, but it came out a relieved statement, 'cause I just wanted to go home.

"No, indeed." He reached for the soda can, gripping it lightly by the rim again and whipped it away. "I can just lift them off of this."

Jeez Louise, I thought, unable to come up with a more brainy notion.

Next they wanted to photograph my arm, which was a first. They shot it plain, then with a ruler held against the abrasion Spartacus had blessed me with.

Golden Boy was waiting for me in the station lobby and I drove us home, which felt like it would be the last of my anything for the night. I wasn't ready to talk about any of this police stuff.

Guy let it go. All the way home he told me about some stuffed onions he was going to try out on me. He'd done what he calls *prep* earlier, so in about fifteen minutes, the little house smelled like scent heaven. He chopped cheese for Charley's dinner bowl, then finished our grub. Wild rice and walnuts and apples and squash, barely cooked, added to black beans and corn, then roasted together in the onions' shells with cheese broiled on top. It is a thing to behold with the nose and eyes and mouth, an onion like this.

Red onions, of course, because Guy likes color in food. He lectures on it if given a chance, but I'm pretty stingy doling out those kinds of chances. I guess the cooking school where Guy got his training harped on using local produce as some kind of gotcha. Anyways, he goes on a bit more than a body can stand about fresh, local bounty and color and flavors. And he blabs about the intrinsic value and protein potential of combining squash and corn and beans. The man makes pumpkin soup, for goodness sake. I mean, it's good, real good, and sticks to the ribs fair enough, and, in truth, I'd never eaten so good in my life.

But, no matter how healthy a person tries to be or eat, bad news could always be lurking. Look at Patsy-Lynn Harper. Did she know that afternoon was going to be her last? She was alive and thinking about paneling for the tack room, holding a cold soda pop, able to feel it all.

Actually, when I thought back, Patsy-Lynn seemed edgy-clingy, like she really wanted me to hang out with her at the Flying Cross. I frowned. The man serving me dinner noticed.

"We can talk about anything," was his first try. "Anything and everything."

That was too silly to merit me making my lips move in response. Charley and I passed a look that let me know my dog's the only one who understands. Guy will never get it like Charley does. Charley and I know there's chunks of everyone that stay apart from the world and that's the way it has to be. Guy thinks people can talk about anything. Just the idea ticked me off and I had half a mind to light into him for a diversion.

"They don't actually say she killed herself," I blurted. "They're investigating."

"Isn't that just routine though? I mean, that they ask all kinds of people for statements and things like that. Really, what is there to investigate?"

"I s'pose . . ." I thought about them wanting my fingerprints, wanting to know if I'd been inside the house.

"If she didn't kill herself," Guy asked, "who would kill her? Who do they think did it?"

"I wonder," I said, creeping myself out with what seemed logical.

"What do you wonder?"

"I wonder if they're wondering if I killed her." They did suspect me, didn't they?

He laughed. "You're a gentle soul. You're not capable of murder."

Of all the stupid things to say. I'm part-Texican. Of course, I can kill. Does he check his noodle at the door?

"You don't know me," I told him. "You have no idea what I'm capable of."

He looked edgy, like he always does when I go black on him, but honestly, he brings this on with his dumb talking. If he knew the truth about me, he'd likely run screaming right out of the county. So, of course, I've never told him and, of course, that's a lump between us that'll be ugly always. Starting with a scar, so to speak, so where can we go from here? I try not to think about it because the headache gets so bad so quick it can make my eyes wet.

* * *

Later, reaching for my hand and rubbing his thumbs over my palm, Guy asked in that entreating way he has, "Come to bed with me tonight?"

A blur of fast fur hopped up onto the back of the sofa. Made me flinch. Spooky, Guy's cat, hisses and scratches, and throws up on people's shoes a lot. If he didn't, he would be kind of pretty to look at with his chocolate coat. I don't take trash off cats. I've called him *Pukey*, but Guy isn't having that.

I know, I know, what kind of a guy has a cat anyways?

Still, when I don't sleep on my cot in the garage, Spooky the Pukey doesn't get to sleep in Guy's bedroom, even though that's where the cat lives when I'm not there.

Other than not seeing eye to eye on the Guy issue and the shoe-vomiting thing, Spooky and I do okay, I guess, and Guy tries to be a good sport about having hooked up with a dog and horse gal who doesn't get cats.

When I nodded my agreement to going to his bedroom, Guy started shedding his clothes as he headed down the little hallway.

I followed Guy to Spooky's sanctuary.

The double bed is pushed against the wall, so there's more floor space for the exercises he does on the rug, but it means one person's sort of trapped in the bed. Guy watched me pop open the snaps on my shirt. He'd rather do it himself. He looks like a kid at Christmastime and says he'd like to be the one to undress me, like unwrapping a present, but it makes me tighten up, so he's learned to hold off. That man can undress himself quicker than anyone else in the world. It's amazing. He pulls his button-down shirts right over his head and his jeans drop like he's standing over an intense pocket of gravity.

Yep, lean, rangy Thoroughbred, if they came in palomino. He has defined, flat muscles in his arms, chest, and belly. Then I saw he had a rough mark across his side, bruised, red, and decorated with little bits of fresh scab.

"Yowie," I said. "How'd you get that?"

"What?"

I pointed. He glanced, then shrugged.

"But don't you remem—"

"Shh," he whispered. "Come here, will you? Couldn't you use a back rub?"

Chapter 7

COME SUNUP WHEN THE FIRST MORNING rays kissed the seed-heads of the brome growing wild, I dumped a handful of oats, top-dressed with the vitamin and mineral supplement I favor, in a bucket for Red. He was doing those muted whinnies where the nostrils wiggle out throaty little nickers. His rump showed a fresh scrape, maybe from a rough rock when he rolled. Like any healthy horse with a minor injury, he needed no doctoring. The wound was dry and half-healed already. Still, Red nuzzled me, appreciating my inspection and returning the attention. He's a doll in the mornings.

The ache of having lost my horse, taking years to get him back, and the rest of it—of how I could pick one thing and not another—all boiled up. I brushed it away by currying Red, loving his strong horse scent.

We'd been several days without rain, so I used my aquarium net to strain the water trough clean of gunk. After sturdying up this old lean-to at Guy's place, I'd added a gutter and made it run into the trough, so rainwater is what keeps Red's palate from parching. Guy thought I was almighty clever and—being's he's way into conservation-type things, all but lip-locks trees—he praised my water collection system no end.

38

To me, it was just a quickie, inexpensive improvement to Red's living situation. I wanted my horse to have a good home. The worst thing about it now is that he lives alone and horses really shouldn't. They're social, herd animals and they need their own kind for company. No, I didn't like Red living alone.

Charley trotted up and wanted to know if I'd be riding.

"You bet." I slipped Red's hackamore on, hauled myself onto his back, and gathered the mecate reins.

It's a work of art, my mecate is, a whole twenty-two feet long when not doubled up to be reins, made of hand-braided horsehair. The fiador steadying the braided rawhide bosal to the latigo head-stall is horsehair, too. The works had been a gift from the people who'd owned Red's mother. The mecate and the foal I named Red were the best presents any ten-year-old girl could ever receive. I'd ground-worked Red for all my tween years, swore I wouldn't start him 'til he was four. But by then, I'd lost him.

Getting Red back honored the kindness of the folks who gave the colt and the mecate to me, but I really reclaimed my horse to mend myself. And it was only patching, because in one big way, what I did by getting my horse back—in light of what I could have been trying to do instead—was the most unworthy thing in the world.

Still, riding out is when I'm happiest. Horseback, followed by my dog, I'm as happy as I get.

Charley is invisible when I ride, because he positions himself right on the horse's heels. Red has had to learn to live with Charley's heeling. A herding dog is either a header or a heeler, and there's no arguing the point with the dog—it's hard-wired. Charley heels, getting right on the end of the livestock he's moving. Early on, Red tried to solve the annoyance by creaming Charley's corn, but herding dogs are the most agile beings on earth. Red never managed to do any good taking shots at the panting little Australian shadow. My gelding learned to live with it. Maybe aging is all about getting used to things or trying to fix them. I'd woken up that morning burning to make right, to pay condolences, remembering that I had Turned Over a New Leaf.

Through pastures, state land, and undeveloped tracts, there's a
way to ride dirt almost to the grocery store at the edge of Cowdry.
Landscaping trees in the parking lot are mighty handy since there's
no hitching posts.

"Wait here," I told my pretty good horse.

Charley wavered, deciding whether to watch my horse or follow
me, but he planted his stub tail when I told him to wait. He would
wait forever.

Inside the grocery store, I found the sympathy cards and wiped
my wet eyes. Well, isn't one of the saddest things about a person's
passing that someone else grieves? That wasn't quite right, but the
thought of Patsy-Lynn dying ate on me. I felt for Mr. Harper.

The first card seemed okay—condolences for your bereavement
on the cover and all about treasured time and memories inside—
so I got it and a matching envelope, then a card for my mama.
Walking past the Milk Duds with determination, I got in line.
Then who do I see but Cherry Edelman.

Cherry will probably always be someone who reminds girls like
me why we never got picked for cheerleading. She must braid her
hair every night to get that crimped look. Wasn't that a thing a
generation back? I've been in schools in LA and it kind of cracks
me up how you can drive a thousand miles away and it's like going
back in time. Country folk are not up to speed with how people are
dressing in fancy places, but some of them, like Cherry, think they
are, yet they're decked out like the Californians were forever ago.

Her nails are always long and polished and her clothes are
always coordinated-looking, with colors and everything going on.
And always, always, she's clean. For mercy's sake.

But her displaying the hots for the man I keep company with
was the best reason for me to give Cherry little time.

She looked up from her little bag of goods she'd just bought.
"Rainy!" She's a gusher. I just eyed her and she prattled on, com-
menting on my card—ooh, someone got a birthday or did someone
die?—like she had to get a word quota in for the encounter. When

I allowed who the card was for, her eyes got wide. I had the unkind thought that she'd just realized there was an opening for the job of rich widower's new wife.

"So, hey, how arrrree you doin'?" Cherry asked.

She sort of coos and trills. She'd have made an excellent pigeon.

I allowed, "Fine," before stopping because she clutched her hands to the base of her neck.

Cherry looked out the store window to where Red was tied. "You prefer that thing to Guy's motorcycle, huh?"

"He has a scooter," I told her. "Guy couldn't ride a motorcycle to save his soup."

She fell in step with me as I walked out. "Scooter, motorcycle, what's the difference?" Cherry waved her hand and rolled her eyes then started rummaging in her purse. There's purse-women and then there's gals like me. That's assuming there's other gals like me though. Maybe I'm alone.

Not that she was really asking, but I'm for educating where it's needed, so I said, "A scooter doesn't have a clutch in your hand and a gear shift under your toe. It's more like a plastic bike with an automatic transmission. All you do is twist the thingy and it goes." I'm pretty sure that's how it works, anyways.

"Twist the thingy?" Cherry looked coy, like we were talking about our sex lives. She found what she was looking for in her purse and made the lipstick rise up out of its case in a way that about made me blush.

I cleared things up for her. "The throttle."

Okay, I ride neither scooter nor motorcycle myself. Fell over the one time I tried Guy's scooter-thingy and swore off for life, but that's not really the point. The point is—

"Well, I wouldn't pass up too many rides on it if I were you." Cherry blabbered on even as she wiped lipstick, whorehouse red, on her mouth and a bit beyond.

Guy taking me for any kind of ride is about none of her business. I got out of there pointing across the parking lot with, "Say,

Cherry, looky. There's a man yonder must need a woman all over himself." And I tried not to mind her scowl. Anyways, she looked where I'd pointed and I just loved that. Nothing but asphalt and a few cars between us and the next building.

It's the only brick building in town, the vet's office, stately-like and nice looking with plants in curvy paths around the edge. Vass, the old vet, retired not long after I started getting known 'round here as a shoer. I liked the old vet a lot and he'd still see my critters if I had need.

A new vet, Nichol, came to town not long after me and took over Doc Vass's office and clients, again a large animal vet who did a mixed practice, seeing dogs and cats as well. New Vet and I first butted heads when he left me bristling over orders for a shoeing job on a foundered horse. And I was right, did it my way and the horse was better off. The thing is, I know New Vet realized I was right later on, but he wasn't a big enough man to say so.

So I wasn't impressed with him, but his looking like a genuine stud-quarterback and having a naked left ring finger, no bird band so to speak, meant a few gals in town were sniffing around as soon as he showed up. Cherry herself was likely a breeze shy of spreading her legs in front of New Vet the first time he stepped across the sidewalk last spring. He smacked of poster boy appeal and she'd gone panting over to see if she could be an assistant or some such at the clinic. She was still waiting around on that score, but I don't know about any other scoring that might have gone on.

When my daddy visited, he chanced to meet Nichol at the Cascade Kitchen. Well, of course daddy thought the new vet was a better act than most men. He figured being a vet is close enough to a doctor and he's of the ilk that would like his daughter to marry such a man and make a family. Thrilled, my daddy isn't, that I'm a horseshoer living in sin with a cook and he will never see a grand-child.

I think it was a wise person who once said there's men who are studying up to be a horse's butt and those who are naturally gifted and kind of oversee others along to help them become hind ends of humanity. And I don't mean any disrespect to my daddy but maybe he was both kinds—a horse's butt and a teacher on how to be one.

I say *butt* because it isn't ladylike to say *ass*. What and all with me promising myself I'd Turn Over a New Leaf and I try not to talk like a sailor or a trucker or an otherwise trash-talker. I've also become regular as can be about things like birthday cards, Christmas cards, Mother's Day and Father's Day. Guy did a Valentine's Day card some months back and that was one I hadn't thought about. The chocolate mousse he made was incredible. It truly melted on the tongue and tasted of strong coffee at the same time. We ate it out back, where he's got a picnic table that gets the southern sun. I could picture us there as I rode in through the back field and past the bench again.

Guy didn't build that picnic spot, of course. It came with the place, like the woodshed and a dog house he calls the future poultry palace. He's not a man without plans, just a man without the kind of plans I'm used to.

That little poultry house hatched an idea in Guy's food-obsessed brain. He's got the sterling notion of getting some goslings. I like a Christmas goose as well as the next person, but Guy can't do something normal, no. He wanted to raise them up, then overfeed them corn mush for a couple weeks and then butcher them for their livers. I ask for mercy here, their livers. Just get your goose cooked and call it good, right? Why all the fuss of force-feeding and digging out some trendy organ?

And then he came to admit he's not going to be overfeeding or butchering anything, he's too sentimental.

Doesn't have tools, couldn't use them if he did. Can't kill a bird and he's a cook for a living. And he says he's stuck on me, a gal he doesn't really know, who's just barely making it as a horseshoer.

Red's fine for letting me open and close gates off his back. I rode into the pasture, then stowed the mecate reins in Ol' Blue's cab. I need horse-handling gear in my truck for just in case. Some clients can't seem to rustle up so much as a lead rope in a pinch.

No sign of Guy outside or in. So much for a slow morning together. I wondered where he skedaddled to.

His scooter was gone all right and there was a note for me on the kitchen counter, wishing me a nice "horseback" ride. Wherever he'd got off to, he wouldn't have taken my truck even if it was raining. It's mine. He understands Ol' Blue's my living. He doesn't have keys to my truck. Besides, he'd never drive it 'cause he can't drive a stick.

I know, I know, what kind of guy can't drive a stick shift?

* * *

"Ms. Dale?"

I was glad I hadn't gotten to the phone in time, 'cause I hate it when people call and don't have the manners to use the phone properly. It'd be like knocking on someone's door and asking the person inside for her name before telling who you are. Callers should say who they are, that's my view. And this man on the phone was having to say it to the air, because I wasn't moved to lift the phone from its cradle. Guess I'm not a big lifter-from-the-cradle type.

"Ms. Dale? Are you there? This is the sheriff's department."

Now, I doubt it was the actual sheriff's department. A government entity can hardly dial a phone. Maybe it was a dude who worked for the sheriff's department though, I'll give him that.

"Ms. Dale?" the deputy said again.

I made out the condolence card to Mr. Harper and drank two glasses of water. The sheriff's department didn't say anything else, just hung up.

Chapter 8

THE PHONE RANG AGAIN ALMOST RIGHT away. I grabbed it to shut up the ringing but right away wished I hadn't, in case it was the police again. I got a lot more comfortable when it turned out to be Owen Weatherby, who'd never been a client, but needed a shoer pronto. Said his roping horse had overreached and her shoe was hanging off. She was locked in her stall now and he wanted to use the horse tonight.

"We usually use Talbot, Dixon Talbot," Weatherby said.

Talbot's a shoer from way back in these parts. We'd about bumped chests in the co-op feed store once. He saw my cards posted on the bulletin board and felt called upon to comment on my inexperience to both the clerk and to some stranger buying chicken scratch. I'd let him know who I was. He let on he'd been shoeing since before I was born and I'd itched to ask when he was going to get any good at it. Anyways, Dixon Talbot hadn't been available on short notice, so the new girl got the Weatherby job. This is a good reason to not schedule all mornings too heavy— leaves time for emergency calls.

In twenty minutes, I pulled Ol' Blue into Weatherby's place, the Rocking B. I've heard he inherited it from his grand-daddy and he's nigh grand-daddy-aged himself. He's The Man for selling great old-style stock Quarter Horses in Butte County, and his old stud was the go-to around here for breeding until Patsy-Lynn started marketing Spartacus. Foundation types really don't usually make great cutters and reiners. There's a line in the arena sand between them and true old-style workers. As a breeder, Weatherby doesn't cross the line, just selects dams carefully and makes good matches for his stud.

Weatherby's not a real cattleman, though. His steers are just for working horses on. His big outdoor arena is all set up with pipe chutes and pens at both ends. Every cowhorse challenge in the west end of the county gets done at the Rocking B, has for eighty years.

Soon as I eyed the ground where I'd be working, I started hauling my gear. Anvil stand first, then anvil. Tool box. Swing out my beater forge and put on my shoeing chaps.

Owen Weatherby eyed me with a heaping helping of something like disdain. His lower lip was pooched out over a load of chewing tobacco. There'd be a lot of spitting in my morning. "Dixon Talbot generally does the shoeing here."

"Heard that," I said, because it was true and because I reckon Talbot's lamed a few around here, so who needed this conversation?

The clip-clop of hooves demanded my attention. A shoer like me listens to the stride before the horse is out of the barn and in view.

"She scheduled sometime soon?" I asked, as soon as his barn boy brought the mare up. I hoped her feet weren't overgrown because he was cheap. I hate that.

Weatherby cleared his throat hard, brought a hand over his mouth as he looked away, talking on about everything but the business at hand, embarrassing as it was. He talked about his old stallion, people wanting more substance and falling for pretty muscles instead of working stock studhorses. He talked about his great dog and his operation in general. Then he fessed up.

"Well, she's overdue. We had to reschedule a couple times. Guess that's part of why she was able to pull this shoe half off." He pointed to her right front where old clinches had yanked off part of her hoof wall when she'd pinned her front heel with a hind toe.

"It doesn't look pretty," I said, instead of going after him about her feet being over-long and how he should have known better. "I'll have this foot right to run in no time." I patted her neck and brought her hoof between my knees as I doubled over beside her belly.

The shoes on her other three feet were thin. Something should happen and I wondered if it might. The wind picked up, blowing in from somewhere chilly. The work helped warm me.

Before I was done driving the first nail on the repair hoof, it happened.

Owen Weatherby cleared his throat again. "You might as well give her a full shoeing."

"Yep." And I kept working.

But it was brisk, what with the wind and her being a little wet— mud in the pastures had helped unbalance her and let her rip that one shoe part way off in the first place. The sun hid behind clouds and we were in the shade of his barn's north side anyways.

Weatherby turned up his coat collar with gloved hands. I huffed warm breath hard onto my icy fingertips. I can't use full gloves while shoeing because I need to feel and hold nails. A horseshoe nail only works—makes the right curve as it's hammered—when the correct side of the nail is oriented to the correct side of the shoe. I've got to slide a finger along the side of the nail head. One side is flat, with smooth metal. The other side is shaped and has hash marks so shoers know where the angled side of the nail's point is. When I feel the hash marks, my finger knows where the bevel is and I put that side in, toward the horse's frog. That fine detail's why I can only wear fingerless gloves. Gotta get me some.

The barn phone rang and made the horse flinch. She yanked her foot to her belly and I swiveled my grip to her toe. Bending my wrist to avoid the wrung-off nail ends burring out, I guided her foot out a little so she didn't slice the inside of her other leg with ragged metal.

If there was a god of horse shoeing, the world would be a peaceful place during nailing. I'm not asking that horses never sway or jump or fuss at any time, just during nailing when it's dangerous for me and the horse. I've never let a horse get hurt and I'll hate the day when one I'm working on rips a nail through his belly or opposite leg. Or through me.

This is the moment when clients should pay attention to me and the horse. Pretty please? It takes me fifty-five minutes or more—sometimes much more—to shoe and all I want is careful attention just four times for six or eight nails per hoof, tops. A couple minutes per hoof. But no, deathly important phone calls and such.

"Yeah, Felix, sure. I got some I could loan you. I can be over in a little bit." Weatherby listened, muttering and mm-hmming. This fascinating conversation left him flipping the end of the lead rope in a little circle meant to occupy his hand that wasn't holding the phone. But it also boggled the Quarter Horse's tiny mind. Her eyes and ears were in alert mode as she stared.

"Got the shoer out right now," Weatherby said. "No, the new girl."

Been here a year, but I'll always be the New Girl to the folks who are living on their dead folks' land.

I got the mare's foot positioned on my hoof stand, rasped the nail burrs smooth, and set to doing the clinches.

"Yeah, yeah, it's a girl. Doing the footsie."

Footsie. 'Cause I'm a girl, the hoof's a footsie?

He snorted. "Yeah, good worker. Oh, I don't know, I'll ask."

That was my cue to look up but, for mercy's sake, I was busy. Didn't I look busy? The pause went on while I worked instead of making eye contact with my client.

Finally, Weatherby spoke directly to me. "You shoe reiners, right? Got sliding plates?"

I nodded, doing my final rasping on that foot. Weatherby went back to the phone. I was about done paring her other front hoof by the time he hung up and said there was a job waiting for me twenty miles away.

Huh. So all the sudden, arrogant horse owners realize they're going nowhere without a shoer and I'm hot property.

Work's what I need, so as soon as I had the last footsie done on Weatherby's mare, I told him I'd help his friend out. Weatherby even wrote down the number for me, which I took as a sign that this other fellow might become a repeat client. I mean, he could have just dialed it up and handed over the phone, but he put pen to paper and gave me a little yellow note. And he smiled.

"You want to carry some bute over to him for me? Since you're headed there anyway and I've promised it to him." Weatherby turned to get the horse drug without waiting for my response.

I'd have thought running bute to a buddy would be a good job for him or his barn-help. Being in the middle of clients passing phenylbutazone back and forth is not a good place for me. Bute is basically horse aspirin, but I didn't really know Weatherby or the other guy, and I didn't know if either was the sort who would short the other and try to blame me. It shouldn't be a big deal, but I just didn't know. I wanted to say "no" but he'd just gotten me another job and so, well, heckfire.

Weatherby brought out a big baggie with two kinds of bute—tablets and a few fat syringes of paste—from his feed room. He handed the baggie to me, saying, "The owner's name is Felix Schram. You'll be fine there."

Of course I'd be fine. I can take care of myself.

Chapter 9

FELIX SCHRAM'S BARN WAS A GOOD little drive away for me and Ol' Blue. This is where shoers take a beating, in their vehicles. Mileage, fuel.

Schram had nice fencing, plenty of land, and lots and lots of horses. Another Quarter Horse man. Well, Cowdry still raises more'n its share of beef and rodeo's a high school sport.

Schram's horses could silhouette for Red and my horse was a Texas-born boy. There are horses in Texas and those out of Texas. It's the same with men and maybe everything else. Some of these hardcore working horses will cut a cow from the herd just for the need to work, moving loose livestock when the horse is pastured with cattle. Worrying livestock like that is naughty, but it's also just plain admirable in spirit when a cowhorse or working dog like my Charley does it. It's beautiful.

Schram's shoeing candidate was handsome, an old hero who'd had everything roped off his back and was making a hand as a power reiner now, even though he was in his late teens. A god, a horse like this is. But his metal was just too thin all around. And his owner was the kind of good old boy with a gut hanging way past his belt buckle, tipping it over. You'd think a fellow would notice when he starts to grow a stomach like that, but Schram clearly hadn't caught sight of it or anything lower in some time, though he still seemed to think himself quite the he-man.

Good ol' boys got together at Schram's place or Weatherby's for roping and reining. They used their horses plenty, these he-men.

This horse had about burned his shoes through in a few weeks of arena work. We need to come up with kryptonite shoes or something for these reiners. This old boy of Schram's was apparently some kind of champ who liked nothing better than burying his hind end under his belly from a dead run, making sliding stops that drag half the arena.

From the box in the back of my truck bed, I brought out a stronger shoe with a wider web and offered it up. Schram hefted it, frowning over the extra iron.

"The Good Lord didn't intend horses to have all this weight on their feet."

"It's a heavier shoe," I allowed, not adding that the Maker might not have planned on horses carrying Schram's big belly around, or for the ropers to yank steers into the air.

"You really think this'll last him and not slow him down?"

"I do."

Schram nodded. "We'll give 'er a try."

Didn't take me too long, with a pro patient like that old horse of Schram's. My hammer made steel ring on my anvil. Shaping shoes for a gelding like this is a pleasure. I had Schram's horse dressed in the new sliders in jig time and went to loading my tools.

What is it about men that they find it sexy when a woman can power lift a hundred-and-twelve pound anvil up to her truck bed? I do wear my T-shirts tight, but it's because I spend my working day bent over. A loose shirt just hangs in your face, getting in the way. Shoers need a shirt snug in the belly. Maybe it was my hand-washing ritual, drying my palms on my back pockets that captured Schram's interest. Anyways, I felt his eyes, the way guys bore into a gal they're interested in, felt his stare the whole time I loaded my tools onto Ol'

Blue's tailgate. As I turned around with my appointment book, just in case shoeing here was going to be a repeat thing, he made his move.

Schram curved an arm out, making like he was going to settle a hand on my waist and let it slide down from there, no doubt. I butted my palm against his chest as he leaned in hard.

Grinning and wiggling his eyebrows, he pushed back and said, "You another one of those women who likes it rough?"

I brought up my right knee just high enough to let my right hand pull the hoof knife from its scabbard on the lower leg of my chaps. After all my shoeing time, the slightly rounded feel of its worn wooden handle is mighty natural in my palm. I tossed the knife up and caught it without looking after it made a three-sixty in the air.

"Here's a bargain," I said. "You don't put your hands on me and I don't carve your nose off like it was excess frog."

Schram looked at a woman standing on his property ready to do him an injury if he didn't keep his hands to himself, then he got both brain cells firing.

"Deal," he said.

* * *

Back on Vine Maple Lane after a good shoeing day, I scraped the soles of my Blundstones off on the bottom step and kicked the spur rests against the top step to get shed of the boots. Charley came over wagging and gave my boots a good sniff, reading the Cowdry horse news.

No horse pucky in the house, that's Guy's rule. Do I dare say he's a bit of a neat freak about horse manure? I like horses, everything about them, and that includes their scent. A whiff of horse is life at its best. Their sweat smells real and so do their turds. Still, it's Guy's house, so I pad around in my socks on days when my boot soles are full of grass that's been run through a horse.

Not long after I found Red and told my mama I'd be staying here in Oregon, she sent me these Australian boots. They have elastic sides and fit great, stay put on the foot, yet slip on and off easily. So, a bootjack was one more thing that I didn't have or need. Before the Blundstones, I'd needed a bootjack for my cowboy boots. I taught Guy how to be a human bootjack. Straddle my shin, hold the heel of one of my shitkick—I mean, one of my cowboy boots—grab onto my instep with both hands while I put my other foot against his butt and push. That's the human bootjack position and it's a crying shame that Guy and me are so flipping different that I had to actually show him how to do it. He was properly Texas-born like me, he should have known.

It means something, the differences between us. The standout fact is we're likely too different from each other to last.

Guy smiled and offered me his glass of tea. He's been in Cowdry three years, cooking and assistant-managing the greasy spoon in the middle of town called the Cascade Kitchen, with catering jobs on the side. Sometimes he opens the Cascade and works the early morning on through getting dinner ready, sometimes he does the lunch and dinner rushes then closes up. Sometimes he works a sixteen-hour shift. And all he wants in this world is to open his own upscale restaurant and elevate the local palate. Guy thinks our town's just close enough to Portland's farthest 'burbs to get occasional customers from there, the like I call the hoity-toities.

Those city people with their silly clothes and cellular more-than-phones stuck in their ears, they grate on me. Guy has a smart-phone, of course, and tried to talk me into getting one, but the reception at home and other remote places away from the cell towers is so bad, I can't hardly see how it's worth big dollars.

Guy plunked on the top step beside me and snapped his fingers as a tiny thought crossed his frontal lobe. "The police left a message for you today. I think they want to talk to you some more."

I'd forgotten about that call. I was doing poorly on my paying attention promise. I handed him a glare with a growl on top. "All the sudden you're Mr. Message, are you?"

He looked like I'd slapped him, which might have been a fine idea if I hadn't Turned Over that New Leaf and all.

"Why are you taking my head off?" He followed me inside.

Clearly, his head was still attached, miracle though it is that no one's handed it to him yet, so he was talking nonsense once again. Anyone would be tight with the idea that she might be suspected of killing someone. I'd been all distracted with work earlier, but now the reek of Patsy-Lynn's death and the police questions threatened to smother me.

A tiny ruckus, rustling sounds at the back door, broke my mood.

"I've bought some babies," Guy said.

Iced tea ran up my nose the wrong way and stung like the dickens. I don't recommend anyone wash their sinuses in strong iced tea. It'll make the eyeballs tear right up. I wiped my eyes and sniffled to get the gaggy tea out of my nose.

"Hey," Guy asked, "are you okay?"

It's best to step outside to spit, as spitting is hardly the most ladylike thing a gal can do. I pushed past Guy, burst myself out the back door to the fresh air of earth and rain and forest, but noticed the lack of house scent. The kitchen had smelled really good.

The ground was moving with little gray dumpling-looking geese babies. I about fell over and Guy was right on my heels.

These goslings were cuter than speckled pups. Soon they'd be broke to hang around and could wander the grass, grubbing for bugs and warning us of intruders. I could like geese around a place.

"I'll have to keep them out of the herbs," Guy said.

He's got all sorts of weeds growing around here. Some, like chives for potatoes, are mighty handy, but the purple flowers he grows for their little middle thingy that he puts in rice and chicken seem like so much work they're not worth the bother.

I pointed at the flower patch. "What are those again?"

"Crocus sativa." Guy beamed. He sort of turns on like that when he thinks I'm paying him a tiny bit of attention.

"No, I mean what are they, um, kitchen-wise."

"Well, I use them in paella and chi—"

"No, I mean what are they called, when you use them for cooking?"

Guy makes me crazy sometimes, he's so slow to get my meaning. "Saffron," he said.

That was all I was asking.

Still, Guy can figure out when he's making me wiggy or starting to. He sidled up to nuzzle. This late in the day, his jaw's sprouted enough stubble to Velcro my ponytail to his cheek. By now, Guy knows to arc his head away 'til he reaches the end of my mane and gets loose. I'd had to teach him that, too. Guess he'd never had a plain long-haired girl before me. Probably all styled, fluffy types, Bambis and Heathers and Tiffanys and such. I'm fair to certain Guy's never before been with a gal who hasn't got a high school diploma, but I'm not going to put too fine a point on it and ask.

He kissed me all gentle-like. Sometimes it seems like I could tell Guy about the parts of me he'd find so horrible. Thank all he saved me from my own blabbing mouth.

"I'm making you some comfort food, started it earlier today. Will you come back inside? Tagliatelle Bolognese."

It turned out to be noodles and they were pretty daggummed tasty.

Soon he had some crab-stuffed mushrooms coming out of the toaster oven. That's what had been making the house smell so good earlier, I realized. And why in the world hadn't I noticed before? I reminded myself again that I had promised me to pay more attention to everything. Everything. I'd have to remember to call the sheriff's office tomorrow.

"Smells good," I said, embarrassed over not noticing before.

He grinned and sort of gave a modest shrug. He has an Oh-Gosh-and-Golly attitude that could make most girls melt. He poured some white wine for himself, filled a wineglass with tap water for me, then explained, "It's just some gruyère I had left over from the salmon quiche the other night."

Yeah, he'd had a cheese crust baked onto this fish pie-cake type thing that looked like used food inside but was really fine eating. Guy knowing things like this doesn't bother me, though I admit it used to raise my eyebrows. Like, the sponge painting bit. Who knew? On some kind of whim, he'd painted his bedroom in this special way. First, he'd painted it purply-blue, then he slobbered a couple middling blue shades on in blotches and then a creamy, barely blue.

We went to his night-sky bedroom together again. On the top of the bed is a huge white down comforter that his folks sent last Christmas. It's like being in the heavens, covered in a cloud.

A cloud with a bunch of cat hair on it.

The call came in about three in the morning, which is not my finest hour.

Chapter 10

THE HORSE SHARED HER EMERGENCY WITH the owners, the vet, and me. And as far as she was concerned, we were all late.

The mare was right. She'd gotten her hoof caught under the edge of their barn's foundation and freaked before her family found her. Panic made her tear off a huge chunk of hoof. Top to bottom, the outside of her right front foot was messed up, bad. Bloody through her sole, it hurt my soul to see it. Imagine part of the lateral cartilage sheared from its rightful place, missing hoof wall that's supposed to hold its share of a half-ton body.

She sweated and grunted, eyes glazed, hind feet shoved under her body to try to get weight off her dying front foot. And she was an old family pet. The couple'd had her before their son, and that now-teenage boy was trying not to go to pieces in front of everybody.

The vet on scene was the new fellow, Nichol. His fancy Ford was angle-parked out front and I'd had to scooch Ol' Blue by like second-rate help.

Nichol leaned up from the horse, and barely turned his sexy-stubbled face to me.

"Get more ice," he barked, to no one in particular.

The owners' boy beat for the house to fetch.

57

"They want her saved, comfortable," he told me. "They're not asking her to be a riding horse."

I nodded and made for my tools, getting them into place quick as I could, but bumped into him as I turned around to set my anvil stand on the ground.

"Can you genuinely help her?" Nichol asked through his teeth, tense and sweaty, leaning in so his face was an inch from mine. Genuine worry showed in his eyes.

"I'll do my best."

Nichol shook his head. "If there's no real hope, I'll let her go now. I can convince them."

Should I say things I don't necessarily believe? Hope is such a flighty thing to me, a desperate thing. Past the vet, I could see the family, holding vigil, the boy jogging back with a salad bowl full of ice cubes. The kid's face was getting younger by the minute, tears dripping out the corners of his eyes, his nose leaking, too.

"I can help her," I said.

The first contact was going to be the worst, because the old girl's pain was the killing kind. Before I got there, before Nichol arrived, she'd grown weary. Now she swayed, wanting to go down, but we needed her to stay up. Still, this horse was a gentle soul, the sweet kind who loved her people, let me be one of them, and wanted help. I gave them my plan, not ordering people around like a vet who thinks he's a general, just letting them know, soft and firm, what to do.

They closed in on her, locking arms and coming together to steady the sedated mare when I got set to ask her to pick up her right front.

I used everything and used it fast. She wasn't too happy to let me bring that shredded hoof between my knees. I worked quick and careful and complete. I found the one place where she could bear a little touching and got that mare's weight off bloody tissues. While I shaped the special Z bar shoe at my forge, Nichol worked at the torn tissue, examining and debriding. Then I dressed her out and pulled enough clip so the shoe wouldn't slide, made it so she bore no weight on her injury. By the time the sun was up, she was standing almost comfortably.

She loved me for it, it was plain to see and hear. I tried not to gurgle back when she planted her flat forehead against my chest and murmured that stressed-horse sound we hate to hear.

Out of earshot of the owners, while we were packing up our gear into our trucks, Nichol made a big point of bringing up something that had apparently been bugging him.

"You refused to shoe for another client of mine."

I shook my head. "No, I need work."

"The Frichtlers, with the Walking Horses up on Stag Loop." He folded his arms across his chest.

"Oh, them. Yeah, I won't do what they're asking." Those poor horses. People want to shoe those gaited horses in an unnatural and painful way, leaving their gaits artificial and no doubt agonizing. I wanted no part of it.

"How's that?"

I shrugged. It didn't need any explaining, to my mind. Nichol raised his eyebrows, expecting an answer, and danged if I didn't spit it out. "I won't shoe Big Lick."

"Big words." He shook his head and tsk-tsked.

"I just won't do it."

Nichol lifted his big, hard-looking shoulders in a little shrug. "Sometimes in our professions, we are subject to certain traditions."

What was he, running for political office? I gave him a growl and said, "Yeah, well if I was a vet I wouldn't be docking tails and cropping ears just for fashion. I wouldn't be cutting cats' fingers off either."

Mr. I Got Tons of Fancy College Under My Belt and Make Pots of Money looked a tiny bit put in his place. Chagrined even. "Touché."

Why is it we're supposed to go all weak-kneed when they talk a little Frenchie?

And why didn't I half-hate this guy?

Then, proving his small talk runs the range, Nichol put on a somber face and said, "You heard about the Harper woman?"

Wariness fell over me as I nodded and wondered what exactly he'd heard, and whose version of events. That I was the last one there? That she killed herself?

Or did he know about the bloody rasp?

If Nichol knew I'd been questioned and was going to be questioned again, he didn't let on.

Aside from all that, Nichol's tag for her—the Harper woman—rubbed me the wrong way. Me and Patsy-Lynn hadn't been best friends, but it seemed disrespectful to call her the Harper woman, like, compared to the Harper outfit, the Harper spread, the Harper stud.

Her name was Patsy-Lynn.

"She was one of the first to hire me," Nichol said. "Other folks wouldn't give me much business in the beginning, but she did."

I pondered on that but a second. "Yeah, me too."

"Well, it's too bad she died." Nichol made a wry face and gave a sad little shrug to go with it. He put his hand lightly on my shoulder. "Nice work in there." He nodded at the mare, now hanging her head in exhaustion.

Nichol really was a lot nicer a guy than I'd thought at first bump.

And there's no doubt he was a big handsome fella and he sort of acted in a way, well, in a way that lets a gal know there could be something there, right there, if she's willing to do anything.

I wonder a lot about what I'm willing to do.

* * *

Back at Guy's stoop, I pulled my boot heels against the step and toddled inside. Being bone-tired first thing in the morning is a heck of a way to feel only mid-week, but my appointment book didn't have anything for the first half of the day, so I could nap.

It used to worry me when I wasn't full-booked, but it turns out a shoer needs some holes in her schedule to accommodate emergencies, referrals, thrown shoe fixes, and whatnot.

The specialty call-out for the old sweetie's emergency paid better than a couple trims, that's for sure. Maybe I was going to make my way at this shoeing thing after all.

I waved my check at Guy while I rubbed Charley's noggin. "That Nichol's really not such a bad fellow after all."

The house smelled of cinnamon rolls. Makes a girl waver on whether or not to try and start the day or go to bed. I yawned at Guy, who looked a little tight-jawed about my compliments to the new vet. What I meant was that we'd saved the old pet mare, not that Nichol was a mighty impressive fellow. But I was real tired and distracted.

Patsy-Lynn had gotten new help all around, a shoer, a different barn dude to muck stalls, a part-time day laborer man. But we all got a new vet when Doc Vass retired and Nichol came to town. And he seemed to know what he was doing. I liked him knowing I was good at my job.

Guy put a mug of java in my hands.

He nuzzled me, fairly laughing at my wooziness. "Perhaps you can have a day of rest this coming weekend."

Imagine him getting biblical. He's the heretic who says the trinity means green peppers, onions, and celery.

They're a godless bunch, cooks are.

* * *

And who, please, whaps on a door when Wednesday morning's barely getting going? Guy opened it right up and let in two men. A man in a suit and a uniformed deputy I'd never seen before, far as I knew.

The fellow in the suit turned to Guy. "Can I talk to Ms. Dale alone?"

"Think I'll go saw a plank of wood," Guy announced in this voice of unparalleled manliness on his way to the carport.

Mercy.

There I was, in Guy's house with the sheriff's plainclothes detective. Now he was all official and serious, packing a clipboard and a consent form and the like. He was wearing a different sport coat this time. Suit Fellow explained that he'd had the deputy try to schedule an appointment, and thought he'd take a chance stopping in. And he had a socker for me.

"Do you have any other injuries?"

I looked at my hands. "No, don't think so."

The uniformed deputy shifted on his feet and rubbed his stubble-free jaw. I could smell his aftershave.

Suit Fellow asked, "Would you be willing to let a female from our department check?"

"Check?" I thought of the three-digit check in my pocket, wages I'd earned on the emergency call.

"Yes, check. Verify that you don't have any injuries under your clothes."

Oh. "Can't say I would." The words were out before my mind had thought much about what he'd asked, so now I had all kinds of time to blush and sweat.

After all, I just wouldn't be willing to be given the once over. Scrutiny, I can't stand.

Suit Fellow gave a bare nod. "Well, I could go make application for a search warrant, but tell me this, would you be willing to give us a blood sample?"

"A blood sample?" Really slow, looking calm as a canoe on grass, I faced the lawman. Po-lice.

"They can do a blood draw at nine a.m. Is that convenient?" He gave me the address of a medical clinic where I was supposed to go give an official sample with a lab technician. Then he asked me to sign a piece of paper giving consent for a blood draw and looked all kinds of satisfied and pleased with himself.

I strode to the back threshold and stared into the carport where Guy had begun the project of constructing a gosling feeder. The saw chattered on the wood plank 'cause Guy wasn't drawing the cutting edge firm and clean across the wood. A pencil rolled over another plank, coming to rest by Guy's silly new tape measure. He looked confussed by his own making.

"They want to take some of my blood," I said. Not that I needed Guy's advice, it's just that I was chewing on this notion the police had. I had to chew to get all the flavor out.

"Well, we're cooperative." Guy said this with raised eyebrows as though waiting for me to agree.

"I have my moments," I admitted, twisting my ponytail around with one hand until it was tight as a stick. I turned back and addressed the detective in a voice quiet enough that Guy couldn't overhear. The uniformed deputy had moved to near the front door and probably couldn't hear me either.

"Why are you asking me for blood?"

"Your blood shouldn't be in the Harper garage," Suit Fellow said. "Should it?"

"No," I said, not looking right at the man. "It shouldn't."

Chapter 11

PSYCHO LIGHT GLINTED IN THE SPARE morning rays above the kitchen counters as the rack of copper and stainless steel pots and pans turned slightly on their hooks. When I'd been at Guy's place about three days and he saw me forge welding more supports on my anvil stand—I hadn't done too great a job when I'd first built it—he asked if I could make him a pot rack, as if I'd known what he was talking about. Once I'd wrested more words from his gullet, it turned out he'd wanted one of those metal thingies people have over their stoves or sinks to hang skillets and the like off of. I guess they cost a pretty penny.

"Save me hundreds, if you can make one," Guy'd said.

So the hooks are old horseshoes, but they're cleaned up real well and I used some spring steel I'd raided from a junkyard back before I'd headed for Oregon. Car steel's better stuff, more consistent, than the leftover rebar I'd gotten from a construction place when I'd started to set myself up in business and scouted scrap steel to make my kit. Guy's mighty proud of that rack, says it makes the kitchen.

I plunked down, watching the light dance off Guy's pots after the police left and Guy came inside.

"Do you know the Solquists?" Guy asked. "Have one or two horses? Neighbors of the Langstons?"

I shook my head without looking at him.

"What's up with you?" Guy asked.

"Did you ever know someone who died?"

He nodded. "My grandparents, my mom's folks, went while I was in high school, one right after the other."

I cleared my throat. "Did you ever know someone who killed herself?"

Guy shook his head. "Not sure I have, not sure I do."

"What do you mean?"

"Well, obviously, it seems like the police don't think Mrs. Harper killed herself after all."

"And did you know her?"

He drew his face back and pinked a little. "Well, her husband is kind of the reason I moved to Cowdry—"

"Mr. Harper? You moved to Cowdry because of him?"

"I was working in Portland, my first job out of cooking school, a nice restaurant called Clams, but I only got to cook when the head chef was sick or on leave. Otherwise, I just did prep. One of my cooking nights, Winston Harper came in, complimented the meal. We talked. He told me he lived in this small town, Cowdry, that didn't have any fine dining. I checked it out, liked it, started working at the Cascade. This little house was a foreclosure. It all worked out. And I've been waiting for my chance to—"

"Mr. Harper went all the way to Portland for dinner?"

"I think he was probably going to a show, overnighting at a hotel. It was a date."

"With Patsy-Lynn?"

Guy shook his head. "Before her."

"You never told me any of this before." I stood, pushed away, needed to think.

I mumbled about wanting to figure out what happened to Patsy-Lynn because I knew I hadn't tangled with her.

When I turned back, Sherlock Holmes was sitting at the table, wearing a Guy-skin suit. He pursed his lips and spoke real slow.

"Well, that wasn't Mrs. Harper's blood on your rasp." He unscrewed his bottle of vitamins and popped one in his mouth. It must have been a new bottle because it still had the little packet of silica gel on top of the pills. Knowing I forage for these little packets and put them in the bottom of my toolbox for rust relief, he pushed it across the table for me. Finally, Guy spoke his piece. "I mean, if they're asking for blood samples, then it's someone else's blood, not hers on the rasp."

"How'd you know there was blood on the rasp?"

He folded his arms across his chest. "Didn't you tell me?"

I didn't bother to shake my head because I don't waste motion. Wasted motion is what makes some shoers slow as Christmas. I'm quality work at good speed.

When he didn't get an answer from me, Guy let his gaze fall on Butte County's weekly paper on the table. *The Western* showed a story on Patsy-Lynn's death. I reached over and folded the newspaper back, then flinched at the front page below it in the newspaper stack. Guy also takes the *Trib* and the *Oregonian*. Their cover stories were miserable, stuff like a big car pile-up outside of Portland, the Middle East was not peaceful and—God help us all—an adoption thing had gone ugly to the point that a kid ended up chained in a basement. Let's take car wrecks and old blood feuds on the other side of the world any day of the week. I was not going to read this newspaper. Teeth clenched, I walked that paper over to Guy's recycle pile.

I will not cry. I will not cry in front of Guy, ever.

"What's wrong?" Guy asked.

Everything. Can't he see that? I wasn't about to spell out for him how horrible the world and people in it are but I did consider whether or not it'd help matters for me to haul off and run my knee through his unmentionables. And then I thought, what in the world is the matter with me? I mean, there's no helping what waffles through my messy brain, but am I just six kinds of awful or what?

Enough changed in my face for him to reach for me.

I pulled away. "Just leave me alone."

"Hey, why are you snapping at me?"

One place that's good to go when I catch myself being a knot-head is the ladies' room. I needed a bath, except Guy's little house is standing room only on that account. Getting civilized, being able to take a shower every day, was a real luxury to me after I got settled here. And no one sweats like a shoer. Soap and water sounded like a real solution. A shower'd help my mind, too. I tried to remember what Guy had been saying about Langston's neighbor, something about a missing horse and the pasturemate squealing and running ragged. Another something from Patsy-Lynn's last day tried to wriggle up in the back of my brain.

I took the overdue shower and puzzled about Patsy-Lynn, the police knowing I was the last one at her place, and I wondered what I should know about the other folks in this town. I shaved my legs while I stewed. Patsy-Lynn's barn-help and the help she fired for stealing stuff needed some consideration, too. That made me flinch and I nicked myself. And what about that fake cowboy walking on foot and the truck that nearly ran us both over? Another flinch and another nick. Even though I half wanted to run away, I also wanted to poke around a bit. How long would it take the *po-lice* to figure out whose blood was on that rasp? I winced as I cut myself a third time.

I dabbed at my legs. Most of the bloody spots quit oozing. A disposable razor can last six months before they bite too rough. When I'd settled here, I bought a ten pack of razors on sale for two dollars, so I was set for five years, but the way things were going, that seemed ambitious.

* * *

Since coming to Butte County, I'd never needed any kind of doctoring. The clinic that the detective sent me to hadn't intended its parking lot for a big truck like Ol' Blue. I jockeyed around, trying harder than I should have.

Suit Fellow was waiting in the lobby and waved me down the clinic's hallway to a medical tech guy's little office. I made myself stand calm, blowing like Red when he's talking himself down from flushing quail on a trail. As long as Horse Planet doesn't send stupid orders, Red can manage and so can I.

The lab-coated tech guy pulled out an alcohol swab, a needle, gauze, white tape, a glass tube, a piece of blue tape labeled *evidence*.

"This won't be bad. One little needle." The tech sounded like he was calming a young horse caught in wire. He picked up the syringe and fit on the needle. "Quick poke and a little blood."

But he didn't know all I'd done. They didn't know how I'd hated it.

Things were bad, but not at their worst, back when I'd sold my blood for money.

Really, it was my platelets, cause they're worth more. Two needles, two hours, free orange juice and cookies before and after, plus a movie to watch while I lay on a thin plastic mattress with both arms straight.

Once I got myself out of that time when I was scuzzy-needy, I swore I'd never sell my blood again, never again be poked by a needle.

No one knew about this. Not my mama, not my daddy, certainly not Guy.

Sweating as I looked at the tech's medical malice, I had to turn my eyes away.

I hate rubber tourniquets. I hate the sound they make and the stretch and pinch, the grippy feel when they pull just below the bicep. It's a bad feeling. Wanting to disappear now set me to thinking about how I'd been disappearing when I'd parceled out my platelets.

Maybe the only way out of this was to be cooperative, pretend to be, anyways.

Maybe I should strip for one of the sheriff's women employees after all.

Isopropyl alcohol is a nauseating scent.

I kept my eyes staring hard at the clinic wall. I didn't blink.

Suit Fellow tried to start a conversation about doings among horse folk—something about vials of drugs—but I mumbled, "I dunno," like a robot. When that thick nail of a needle drove into my inner elbow, when the little vacuum tubes sucked a shot of my body's blood, when the pinching tourniquet snapped off, I never flinched.

Their little murmurs of "thanks for your help on this matter" got nothing from me. I let the corners of my eyes air-dry as I walked away.

Behind the wheel in Ol' Blue, I stared at the windshield and thought about redemption. Too long without blinking makes the eyes dry, then wet, but I wasn't going to blink. So driving away, trying to be tough, I cried.

Chapter 12

THE MINUTE I GOT HOME FROM shoeing that evening, I parked myself in front of Guy until he got off the phone, then used one of my better attitudes to ask, "What was it you said this morning about the Langstons' neighbor and—"

"I've got a ton to do. Don't set anything down in the kitchen. Don't move anything." He smiled sideways, stuck a plate with a sandwich and some fried thingies in front of me, then turned back to scooping flour, dusting it from one place to another.

I ate the fancy sandwich and cheese thingies on the plate he'd offered.

Looking frazzled was unusual for Guy. He'd probably been tiffing with his boss, Dennis McDowell. Guy had been getting pretty touchy lately about that owner of the Cascade Kitchen and the man's so-called ineptitude with presentation, variety, and the like. Guy fears food not much better tasting than salted farts gets served on the diner's chipped plates when he's not around.

Plain enough, he wasn't going to haul his brain back to whatever he'd tried to tell me before about the Solquists and a missing horse.

Cooked cheese with brittle browned edges and a scent to match met my tongue. It did make a nice meal. "Good stuff."

"Croque monsieur and aigrettes de fromage," Guy said. "You got home just in time. You know what happens if they're not served right away."

"More big words?"

"Oh, please, Rainy. You're such an iconoclast. I think it's a bit of an affectation with you, playing hick. Your mom called while you were out and we talked for a while."

My spine stiffened and I fixed Guy with a hairy eyeball. "Huh?"

He was grinning now, looking all delighted with himself, which is often not a great thing. He gets delighted over things that don't really rate delightment. "Well, she called while you were gone, so we chatted a few minutes."

Oh, mercy. "And?"

"And now I know about the prep school."

I tried not to act like I was deciding whether to kill him first then my mama or the other way around. What is it with some people that they go talking to folk who are practically strangers and they want to gab about stuff that's nobody's business? Why'd I get birthed out of one and half take up with another? My mama could gab to a fence post and that's where she ought to confine her gabbing. And just how much of my past world did she commit to Guy? I graveled up my throat with a few heaves. I needed to get the chef clear.

"The thing is, is that prep school stuff, that's just not who I am."

"The thing is, I don't get to know, do I?" Guy had this reasonable tone going and looked wistful, like he wasn't arguing, though clearly that's what he was doing.

That, and butting in.

"No, you don't get to know. Leave the past where it is."

"Rainy, your mom said you did super well in school when you wanted to."

I'd wanted to make her happy enough or mad enough to let me go back to Texas and stay with my daddy again, so I could be with my horse. "Then you know I flunked out."

"That's not quite what she said."

Not looking at Guy, I said, "I bet. Just how far did you two take this little chat?"

"Well, not too far. But you always give me the impression you're almost estranged from your folks and I don't get that impression from them. Even as different from each other as your parents are, they're not—"

"They're not your business," I said.

He clammed up, more annoyed with me and pleased with himself than he had any right to be and I wished we'd never done the Talk To Each Other's Parents thing in the first place. Folding my arms across my chest, I winced, just a little.

Looked inside my elbow and remembered the morning. It had been Guy's big idea, it seemed to me, that I let the police stick a needle in my arm. It hurt a little, was going to bruise, but I wanted no part of a pity party.

With his back to me, Guy asked, "Are you going to Patsy-Lynn Harper's funeral reception?"

"Um," I stalled, thinking that I hadn't been invited. Then I reminded myself it wasn't a party and she was the one who hired me after all, plus gave me a referral or two. I owed her. Attending her funeral was probably the right thing to do, in keeping with my Turning Over a New Leaf creed of sending occasional cards and trying to be a skosh nicer person.

"The funeral's tomorrow, at two," Guy said.

I shook my head, not needing to check my appointment book. "I've got a shoeing and two trims at the Rodriguez place scheduled for one o'clock. I shouldn't reschedule them."

Guy hit the play button on the answering machine. A message from my client Anita Rodriguez announced that they were going to Patsy-Lynn's funeral the next day, so wouldn't be home for our shoeing appointment and wouldn't expect me.

"I've got to finish fixing some hors d'ouvres trays," Guy said.

Quite a spread he'd started, must have picked up a catering gig. "Party?"

"The funeral reception for Patsy-Lynn Harper."

I thought out loud. "So, you're going as a Harper employee."

"You would be, too. You're a Harper employee since you shod horses for the Flying Cross."

True enough, I reckoned. I folded my arms across my chest, felt the bruise inside my elbow, and looked at its purple center and green edges.

* * *

The bruise was less tender when I came home the next day at lunchtime. Guy was spruced up, black pants and a white button-down cook's shirt, hair combed. Catering clothes.

"I'll go to the funeral," I said, shedding my dirty clothes and moving for the ladies' room.

From behind, Guy kissed the back of my neck and whispered that he'd see me at the reception.

I whipped around. "You're not going to Patsy-Lynn's funeral?"

"I can't. I'll be at the Harper house, setting up the reception food."

* * *

Sorry to say, I remember the funeral none too well. It was at a local church and there were a lot of cowboys, and there was talk of the Maker and a final reward. There were flowers.

Back at the Flying Cross, parking was a problem, even with all their driveway footage. Double lane to the big new barn, another that went to the triple garage at the fancy house, and a single lane going past the house were all crowded with trucks in single file. Down the driveway that stretched to the way-back of the ranch, I pulled Ol' Blue in behind another truck with a topper and could just glimpse an old cottage farther on. That was my kind of place, not the big fancy new house that I hiked back to now over a quarter mile of gravel.

This was the first time I'd ever driven over to the Harpers' without a shoeing scheduled, certainly the first time I'd worn my denim skirt to their spread.

Well, *his* spread, not their spread, since there was no *them* anymore. I bit my lip and tried not to think about the last time I'd been there, just Monday. Instead I looked at the fancy new barn, the well-kept, beautiful grounds with rolling green pastures and strong horses.

In his paddock, Spartacus shook his head then made a studly charge at his fence, pinning his ears at all the traffic, guffing that throaty stallion growl. I saw the gleaming hind leg scrape Patsy-Lynn had doctored with ointment, saw the edges of the shoes I'd put on him when he whirled away, bucking.

Blast, that stud was getting huge. I'd noticed when I shod him the other day, but man, had he always been so built? I thought about how old he was. Seems like he should have been done filling out, I think he's the better part of five, maybe even up to seven years old, but it did seem like he was getting beefier still. Late bloomer, I suppose.

The droopy cedar trees seemed in keeping with everyone's dark clothes and mood. A lot of town folks I'd seen at the funeral were milling in and out of the reception, which sprawled across the Harpers' humongous meant-for-show home.

Speaking of late bloomers, I was startled as I met Harper Junior inside the grand living room of that real estate-intensive ranch house. I'd met him briefly once about a year ago in one of my first visits to the Flying Cross. He was bigger than I remembered, blond and tan and overgrown, with pimples on his face that made it hard to guess his age, but he was probably not much older than me. I'm guessing he'd pop buttons on a size 48 shirt. His eyes were so close together, he could probably look through a keyhole with both eyes at the same time.

And there shaking his hand was a man I recognized as Patsy-Lynn's barn-help, all cleaned up in dress jeans and a crisp long-sleeved white shirt. His fingernails were scraped clean, which made me realize they were usually dirty, like mine.

Barn-Help shifted from one foot to the other, then noticed my blank look and said, "Ted." I dipped my chin in response to his introduction, or reminder, since he or Patsy-Lynn had probably told me his name before. He slunk off into the crowd. A decent-looking fellow, Ted, when shaved and showered.

No one can help the looks their born with. It's what we do that matters. What Harper Junior did was put a sympathetic hand on his dad's shoulder every time he was near. He shook hands with countless townfolk coming to pay their respects and he nodded with every condolence expressed. Like a good son.

Someone asked him when he'd gotten into town and how long he'd be around.

"Just a couple days. Drove and drove to get here after the bad news," Junior said. He and the cowboy asking went on with talk of the late breeding season and last year's foal crop.

In the cavernous living room, quiet chat kept on about the horse world, as can't be resisted when this many people with a hand in the business are together. I stood around feeling stupid and out of place as was apparently my lot to do at a dead client's funeral.

Guy was busy, moving here and there, keeping the tables on the side of the room discreetly inviting with pastries and finger food. When I caught his eye, and he smiled and scurried away. Business people and cleaned-up clients chatted all somber-like, so the gathering didn't have the atmosphere a catered get-together of so many of Cowdry's movers and shakers should have. And I was by far the worst dressed female there. I must have looked pretty Amish next to the slinky black number Cherry Edelman flounced by in. I own one skirt, this denim wrap-around thing I made at the end of eighth grade in home-ec class—proudly the last such class in the state and maybe the country, the school said—in Texas.

That year.

I had to put my mind somewhere else.

How soon could I leave?

Through a big archway was another sprawling living room and lots of funeral-goers standing around in their Sunday best, making quiet murmurs, either about ordinary things like weather and critters and the government or else they were making nice little comments about Patsy-Lynn. In death, my client seemed more real and human, cheated from her life. Now I wondered if she'd had children. How she met Harper. How she got her start in horses. I wished I could say something nice, but I didn't trust my voice.

"She was something else," someone said.

"Mm-hmm," a couple other people murmured to agree.

"It's such a shame," one woman whispered to another. "I'm sure she didn't mean to do it. It must have been an accident."

So, those ladies were going with the She Accidentally Killed Herself story.

"No, I heard there was money taken," whispered another. "That's on the hush-hush, but there's word going around that it was a *robbery*." She said it like a dirty word and I guess it was, being's this is Cowdry.

The women went on with their theories. Not knowing where I fit, I turned away. Owen Weatherby and other men sat in stuffed leather loungers and talked sheepdog breeding. The walls here were covered in framed pictures, all of a young guy in football gear. Junior, I suppose. I wandered.

In the bathroom, I studied out the window and gave myself a good stern talking to. I reminded myself of my mission to Turn Over a New Leaf, be courteous and kind. To be adult and responsible. There'd been a time when I couldn't wait to be grown up, thought my problems would be over. Then I got myself into real problems and found out pretty quick that teenage angst wouldn't be too big a deal if angst was the worst of it.

The room's little window gave a long view, down the back of Harpers' land. The orchard carried no deadwood. I thought of the day laborer Patsy-Lynn had hired to prune, the one she said made off with her new hedge trimmer.

Pretty, looking out that window. The sliding sun was painting the east slopes with pinkish-orange alpenglow. Straight west, a partly logged hill glinted like it was kissing the sun right back in gratitude. I remembered Patsy-Lynn once saying something about an old metal barn and cottage at the back of the ranch, near the federal and state forest lands bordering the Flying Cross. I guess it was the original homestead before Harper had the fancy house built. The big house had come along with wife number one—Junior's mama—and she died when he was young.

Probably this grand house was to Patsy-Lynn's liking, too. It was pretty fancy with wood floors and dark paneling. No doubt she did some upgrades here like she had in the barn.

Me, I'd have been happy with the shack and old tin barn out yonder.

Harper and Patsy-Lynn hadn't been together long when I came to Cowdry but she sure seemed to like it here.

I left the bathroom and followed kitchen sounds. Metal pot lid clangs and a whooshing oven door told me the kitchen was just around the corner. A catered funeral would have been Patsy-Lynn's choosing, but hanging out with Guy's hors d'ouvres—"whore's ovaries" is how my daddy pronounced that phrase to my mama's everlasting horror—was not what I felt up for.

The whole house was highfalutin, with big wide hallways, fancy floors, and molding along the upper edges where the ceiling and walls meet. There was a statue of the head and shoulders of someone who looked like Colonel Sanders. The dining room had those wood strips around the wall about hip high. There's a name for that kind of strip. I used to know the name, back when I lived with my mama.

But Mama's place was never like this, spacious and grand at the same time, with the extra tall ceilings and crystal pieces displayed in a fancy cabinet just to show off.

Low murmurs came from another room and I guess I thought the reception was all through the house when I pulled on the doorknob.

It was weird, a tiny part of my brain said, that a slip was hanging on the door's other side. The red silk thing fluttered like a giant tissue as I opened the door.

I don't own a slip, don't see the point of them.

But now I saw that a slip lets you hang in there for another round in strip poker. Cherry Edelman was obviously a poor poker player.

She giggled out a little shriek from the bed inside the room and pulled a pillow over her personals.

"Sorr—" I started.

Man, that man was like a big, overblown statue. And I could tell, 'cause he was bare-ass—he was nekkid from the waist down. Harper Junior's butt muscles had muscles. He'd kept his dress shirt on, but his tie was now on Cherry. Maybe he worked out so much to compensate for his complexion, which looked like an acned teen's. His build made the big veterinarian seem like a ninety-pound weenie-boy. All I can say about guys with pecs like that is they'd better not ever stop pumping iron, else in a month's time they'll need a bra like Cherry's lifter model draped over a lamp, whorehouse red with lacy edges. Thong undies to match dangled over one of her spike-heeled black shoes, abandoned on the rug.

All this took a split second to absorb. Backpedaling a lot faster than I'd toddled into the room, I was pink and breathing hard in the hallway. It's a serious hallway, wide with a wood floor and a thick rug that pads the way and a serious reason is why we were all there, all of us except Junior and Cherry.

Apparently, they'd needed to do laundry and were getting it all done at once.

Chapter 13

CHERRY HUSTLED OUT OF THE BEDROOM I'd half-walked into even as I stood in the hallway to that wing of the Harper house with my jaw still hanging down. Their exertions were not my beeswax. To me, beeswax is for lubing my pritchel and filling hoof wall nicks.

She was giggling. "Oh, Rainy, it was nothing." Then she said as an aside, "And unfortunately, I *do* mean nothing."

I was dumbstruck.

"And certainly none of your business. M'kay?" Cherry darkened up a little and looked like she'd like to wallop me but we both knew who'd win that catfight, if it came to it. A contest Cherry could beat me at is being on her back, feet in the air. In my mid-twenties now and I've been with exactly three different guys. And that's at least two too many, given the quality of choices I've made in the past. So Cherry could stand there annoyed, wanting to whack me, but she wouldn't dare push it. One of us works hard for a living.

Cherry looked away. I was just ready to congratulate myself on my scowl when I realized what a turd I was being, half-thinking about brawling at a funeral reception.

I never get it right. Not ever.

Cherry took her time returning to the main gathering. She peeked into the open arch at the far end of the hall and glanced over like she was waiting for me to go away. I did.

Guy set a tray of saucy chicken bits on a long side table by the statue of Mr. KFC. People started picking up the tidbits right away. I followed as Guy evaporated back to the kitchen.

"Very appropriate selection there," I told him.

He raised an eyebrow. "How so?"

I hinted. "Catch that little statue of Colonel Sanders around the corner?"

He gave me a big look and went back to work, messing with some white sauce he dripped over pieces of fruit. "You would be referring to the bust of Brahms?"

Mercy.

I toddled down another hall, hoping not to find more people celebrating a funeral reception with a quick roll in the hay. That last door was open, showing a master bedroom. A dead woman's jewelry tree sat on the bureau. I turned away. At the other end of the hall, I paused a good bit on my side of a metal door. There were a few voices, words I couldn't make out, but at least nothing sounding like anyone pouncing on anyone else's bones. The heaviness of the door should have clued me, but sometimes I think a two-by-four across the skull is needed for me to gather any wisdom.

The thing of it was, suddenly I was standing in the garage where Patsy-Lynn Harper died. And I wasn't alone. A voice rumbled, startling me to my toenails.

"Found your way here pretty well, Rainy Dale."

It was Paulden, the deputy who'd stopped me on the highway the evening Guy and I were coming back from the co-op. He was out of uniform, in black jeans and a dark sport coat, a bolo tie dressing up his shirt. Lots of guys were dressed that way in this house today. It's standard Sunday go-to-meeting clothes for country folk. My brain was still coming up with a response when he asked, "When was the last time you were in this room?"

How I hate it when my voice cracks, gets me gulping my answer. "Never. I've never been in this garage before."

"Hmm," said he, not the most articulate of men, though I may risk redundancy on the observation.

Someone from the corner waved Paulden off. It was Suit Fellow, wearing what could have been the same stained blue sport coat as the first time I'd seen him.

I faced Paulden. "That day, you said that I was the last person to see Patsy-Lynn alive."

Suit Fellow snorted. "I sure hope not. I hope you were the second to last."

"Huh?" I turned and tried to take in both of them at once.

Suit Fellow got elaborate, what and all with apparently talking to an idiot. "The last person who saw her was the one who watched her die or left her dying. And that wasn't you, was it?"

"No, sir." I wanted Patsy-Lynn's last hours to be as nice as possible. I wanted to be as nice as possible. "Maybe she started her car and the garage door got stuck and she got woozy from the fumes and passed out. She could have done it without actually meaning to kill herself, couldn't she?"

"Her injuries are not consistent with that version of events. And there is unexplained disruption of the scene."

Deputy Paulden moseyed back out to the reception as Suit Fellow settled into this chat, closing the door gently behind him.

I pointed at the door, beyond which muted funeral conversation droned. "Isn't the thing"—I hesitated, not liking that I had some schooling on this point—"that a killed woman is usually killed by the man in her life?"

Suit Fellow raised his eyebrows halfway to his receding hairline. "It is indeed. Ms. Harper had a husband, and an adult son. But at the time in question, one was in a meeting locally with a reputable person, and the other was hundreds of miles away, which is easy enough to verify with credit card receipts and surveillance footage from gas stations."

Without waiting for me to catch up, he shifted and faced the direction of the garage bay doors. We couldn't see out because the doors were closed, but we both knew the main gate lay beyond, fifty yards or so away. "The road out to the Flying Cross is a little lonely, don't you think?"

"I guess." I shrugged, just a little, to let him know that he wasn't Einstein with an observation like that. Then I startled and blurted, "Patsy-Lynn was on the phone when I got here."

He frowned. "And?"

"And she seemed pretty upset. No idea who it was though. She hung up when I walked in the barn. And she wanted me to stay after I did the shoeing. To have coffee or a soda. That was a first."

"And you're just remembering this now? Anything else you remember from that day?"

The strange thing was, I did. I could see the truck coming at me and the dude walking down the road.

"There was a guy afoot on Oldham road. A fake cowboy."

"A fake cowboy?"

My head bobbed. "Feathers hanging off the band of a dark leather cowboy hat. Like from a department store."

When I couldn't come up with anything more on the dude, Suit Fellow said, "Tell me more about the truck. Old? Late model? Say anything you can remember about it. The driver. What was the driver wearing? Any bumper stickers, parking stickers, a hat in the dash, anything. Better still, do you remember make and model?"

"I don't know what it was." Horses' legs are what I notice. I remember gaits and the horn quality, angles and shape of hooves. I'd little idea what anybody wore on any particular day, couldn't say much about their vehicles. Confidence and kindness with horses and dogs sticks with me, as does meanness.

The detective waved a hand, caught my eye, and asked, "Do you know what it wasn't?"

I gaped at him. He was serious. A different way to ask and answer the same question. A good idea. I about steamed my brains with the effort, smoke nearly coming out my ears.

"Well, it wasn't a diesel. I'd know that sound. It was big. It wasn't white or yellow or one of those pastel, freaky new colors." That would have revolted me and I'd have noticed it.

"Brown, green, black, dark blue?"

"Yeah, dark. And a dually," I said this last word suddenly. Though certainty on color wasn't coming, that truck was wide, way wide.

I could sort of see it in my mind's eye, making me hug the right shoulder of the road with Ol' Blue. Driving toward me as my mind moved on. I'd been thinking about my last appointment of the day, shoeing Abby Langston's little mare, Liberty. Something was going on with that kid.

Suit Fellow said, "Think about that fake cowboy of yours and who was behind the wheel of that truck."

I pursed my lips and shook my head, holding my temples. "There's just nothing there." I wanted to explain to him how I could see that recollection, even hear it. My brain recalled the sound of the vehicle coming toward me, the engine winding up then down for clutch action, that whole bit. I could hear it in my mind. But I hadn't studied on the driver, not at all. There'd been no reason for me to look at the man behind the wheel.

Blurting like a backwards hiccup, I said, "I don't think there was a passenger in the truck. And I think it was a man who was driving."

"Rainy," he said, "have you come across a fellow named Manuel Smith at some of the ranches? Does odds and ends work?"

"I don't know that name. Patsy-Lynn did mention a day laborer who might have made off with her hedge trimmer."

"What else can you tell me about that?"

"Not a thing."

He grunted. "You encounter a lot of different horse people in your job, go to a lot of peoples' property. If you see or hear anything a little odd, maybe money changing hands—"

"Was there money missing from this place the afternoon she died?"

He exhaled a long time, then added, "Or if you see people with drugs—"

I shook my head. "I've never seen anything like that around here."

"Has anything else occurred to you that seemed odd, out of place, or worth mentioning to us about the last day you were here? Think about that afternoon."

I could see it, feel it. My left hand curved the same way I'd held Spartacus's toe, getting the first nails driven. I could see the glimpse of Patsy-Lynn twisting her mouth when I'd slapped Spartacus, I could see the blur of her end of the lead rope as she twirled it in the air for no good reason. I remembered that I might have liked that soda she offered, if I'd had the time and inclination, which of course I hadn't. Besides, she was too clingy, a time-sucker, artificially upping our relationship.

She'd never before fetched me a soda, just once waved me over to the fridge to get one myself. She wasn't someone who waited on others.

Could there have been something in her fridge she didn't want me to see?

Suit Fellow said, "Why are you frowning? Remember something?"

I shook my head, not feeling too good, wanting to free myself of fog. "I was just trying to think back. I had another appointment and had to scoot as soon as I'd finished."

"That was at the Langston residence."

Whether he said this to prod my memory or to impress me with his figuring out where else I'd been, I don't know. Maybe both, but I don't like someone else knowing my business. Still, he said it friendly enough and for a guy who'd at our first meeting seemed a hair shy of slapping handcuffs on me.

* * *

Knowing better than to leave before I'd said something to Harper I found the widower in one of his big living rooms, no one else too close by, so it was time. What do you say to a man the day he buries his wife? And mercy, did he know the sheriff's investigator had quizzed me on the events of her death? Did he know they'd asked me for a blood sample? Did he know her death was being looked at with suspicion?

Did Harper suspect me?

Maybe I should suspect him. Patsy-Lynn had been about to order fancy wood paneling for her tack and feed room. Was Mr. Harper unhappy with the way his wife went through spending money? New paint, new fridge, rubber cushions in the barn aisle, fancy tack room paneling on the way. Were all the nice touches in the house on account of Patsy-Lynn, too? In front of us were more framed pictures of him and Patsy-Lynn, plus old ones of Harper Junior, which the widower stared at the most. I saw Patsy-Lynn was nicer looking without all that make-up. Winston Finch Harper was a much older man than I'd remembered. Maybe losing his wife had aged him some years this last week. His thin gray hair was combed back with some of that guy grease they use, but he'd bothered it since then. Long strands were messed about. Did his eyes always have that watery cast? I couldn't decide. I'd never been around him much. He'd had horses before he married Patsy-Lynn but was more a businessman who played at gentleman farmer.

"Um, sorry about Patsy-Lynn," I said.

"Thank you." He nodded, but with such a vacant expression, I wasn't sure if he knew who I was.

"I'm Rainy Dale, your horseshoer, um, I mean her horseshoer, I mean . . ." I studied my shoes. They're sandals, because I don't have high heels and I couldn't wear my work boots with my skirt, although maybe dressing worse wouldn't be as big a disaster as me opening my yap.

Mr. Harper smiled, just a little, but kindly. "You are still the shoer here, Miss Dale. You'll help us take care of her horses?"

Her horses.

She'd always called them her babies. I nodded and felt like bawling.

"Sure I'll help. We'll take good care of . . . her babies."

He blinked and looked away. "You know, she wanted children."

Of course, I hadn't known that. I really hadn't known poor, dead Patsy-Lynn at all. And it hit me, *one* reason why I felt so dag-gummed guilty. I itched with the feeling that she'd wanted to be my friend, especially that day I shod Spartacus. She was clingy and I'd blown her off. Hey, I had another job to do and I can't stay and jaw any old time one of my clients wants to. But still.

I looked up at Mr. Harper, hoping he wouldn't see I was half scared he might think that I'd had something to do with his wife dying and half scared that I might have. My voice cut in and out like it was wired wrong. "You have beautiful horses, a beautiful home."

What a stupid thing to say to a guy who's just lost his wife. *You have beautiful horses.* What was I thinking? If I was a blame-fixer, I'd say my inability to comfort was earned from my folks, but maybe I ought to own up to the fact that I'm a turd. Hate it, but there it is.

Guy set out a tray of broiled steak bits on skewers that smelled fantastic, got picked up right away by others while I denied myself. And Guy vanished back to the kitchen. Harper Senior turned to shake hands with some folks who came up to say how awful sorry they were for his loss. "Thank you."

Sorry for his loss. Those would have been a nice few words for me to choose. I turned away, almost bumping into more men in suits, including Abby Langston's bald, sweet-faced, potbellied daddy, Keith, who shook Mr. Harper's hand. I slipped away and ended up facing Felix Schram and some other cattlemen standing in a little group.

"Miss Rainy," Schram said by way of greeting, with a friendly nod, elbowing the cowpoke next to him. "Watch out for this one when she's got her hoof knife in hand. She don't want no help with lifting her anvil."

You another one of those women who likes it rough? Schram's coarse words when I was shoeing his horse came back to me like a bad dream. Could he and Patsy-Lynn have . . .

I swallowed and kept moving, just to give Schram the ignoring he deserved. I wondered about the shoer Schram and Weatherby usually used. Dixon Talbot. I hadn't seen him here at the reception. And I puzzled on the name the detective had dropped.

Chapter 14

"MANUEL SMITH." I SAID THE NAME out loud as I reached Ol' Blue, way down the Harper driveway.

"What about him?"

I turned. It was Patsy-Lynn's barn-help fellow, whose name had loped out of my brain, fixing to leave the funeral reception. I should have said his name aloud to help me remember.

He chewed a fingernail, then shoved his hands in his pockets and snuck a peek over his shoulder. We were alone.

"One of the sheriff's men asked me about him," I said as I climbed into Ol' Blue.

"Perfect. That's just perfect." He turned away, huffed, then leaned toward my open truck door. "What'd you say?"

"Nothing. I don't know him." Closing my driver's door felt better. Barn-help—

Ned? No, Ted—kicked the ground, then stared at me as I jacked Ol' Blue around.

Ted was at the Flying Cross after I shod Spartacus and drove to the Langstons' that day. Maybe he was the last one to see Patsy-Lynn.

That evening, I couldn't wait to tell Guy about the weird encounters. I started at the top.

Guy heard me out, nodding and shaking his head at intervals as I added in what the sheriff's detective said in the garage. "Manuel Smith."

"Yeah, like I told the detective and Ted, I don't know the fellow."

"He lied about being at the Cascade, too."

"Manuel Smith lied about being at the Cascade Kitchen?"

"No, the other guy, Ted Alvorson. Deputies came to the restaurant asking if he'd been there late Monday afternoon."

"The barn-help? Patsy-Lynn's barn-help said he was at the Cascade?"

Guy nodded, holding his chin.

My mind spun as I thought about the sheriff's men checking everybody's stories. "He was acting weird as I was leaving the reception. He said he was at the Cascade when she died? But you never saw him there?"

Guy made a face. "Ted came in for pie Tuesday late afternoon. Not Monday, as far as the server working remembered."

* * *

Later that night Guy took a knee, pinked up, straightened his expression like he was trying for something serious, then applied his Earnest and Hopeful face.

"Well, here it is," he said. "Will you be my wife?"

When my jaw hitched itself back up and I could manage a few words, I told the truth. "You're out of your gourd. Guy, we just can't."

"Can't?" He didn't seem to like the word's flavor. "We can't?"

My ponytail beat my face as I shook my head.

I had no words here, but I was percolating a response.

He folded his arms across his chest. "At least tell me why not."

Sometimes I really, really wish my brain would spend a moment considering words before they went falling out my mouth. Anything's better than blurting what I'd never considered admitting. "Because I've been married."

Naturally, Guy's jaw dropped a couple yards, more or less. He did a fish out of water impression for a half minute.

I gave him the tail end of the story. "And I said to myself afterwards, I said, 'Rainy, let's not be doing that again.' That's what I agreed on with myself."

Guy looked shocked.

I was careful in explaining, sparse on details, how it had been a bad idea.

He leaned forward, holding my hands, resting his chin on our knuckles. Guy was a prince as I told him I'd been a know-it-all emancipated sixteen-year-old, took up with a guy I had a quick crush on, got married, and realized by seventeen it was a dumb idea to hitch my wagon to a drunk. I spent a year being loyal, like a beat dog that stays by its rough master's side. Getting myself unmarried was the best idea ever.

I'd never felt comfortable enough with that bit of my life to chat about it and I'm maybe not exactly the Cry About It kind of girl to boot, so I left out the part about what happened in the years before I married that basically left me in the boots I was wearing and nothing else.

Oh, I couldn't have done much worse in picking a guy to marry. Eddie was the sort of trailer trash that embarrasses poor, uneducated folks who live in trailers. I should have seen it coming, that life, when we registered for gifts at Walmart.

The details didn't need to be shared, but I remembered.

We'd been married less than six months when he belted me across the room the first time, but there'd been plenty of signs— mean moods, boozing, and throwing our unbreakable plastic plates, which, by the way, broke.

The last time he clocked me, I figured out that my so-called husband was an idiot second only to any boneheaded woman who'd stay with him. I got up off the floor but he was coming at me with the lamp.

He needed a weapon? Well, I didn't. I kicked him right and proper and didn't waste any more time in that room. Later, he'd tried to tell me that there were reasons, that he wasn't himself, that he wanted to explain. Like he was going to pull some brilliant reason out of his skull.

That was the last Eddie got to see of me.

A few words from Suit Fellow echoed in my skull.

The last person who saw her was the one who watched her die or left her dying.

When a change of subject is needed, chewing the fat on a possible murder investigation makes a ripe distraction, I believe. And so I said, "Guy, someone killed Patsy-Lynn, had a hand in her death anyways. It was probably someone close to her. And that someone could well have been at the funeral and reception."

Or not there, because how stressful would it be to attend the funeral of someone you killed? Maybe the killer was the one who didn't come pay respects.

My frown got company as Guy furrowed up his face, too.

"Her husband is closest to her, I would think," he said. "But he didn't hurt her."

"What makes you say so?" According to the police, his only alibi was that he'd been with a so-called "reputable person" when Patsy-Lynn died.

"For one thing, he just doesn't seem like a killer."

I stifled a snort. "Professional killer-spotter, are you?"

"I do okay." He shrugged with all the humility he could muster, letting my mood go. Got to hand it to the man, Guy's kinder to my dark parts than I merit. Lightening things up by joking about marriage a minute ago, for instance.

"Someone hurt her. Maybe she hit that someone back with my old rasp. A Texas Ranger told me that most women who get murdered get killed by their own men. That's the way it is. Ex-wives get killed by ex-husbands, too. They get OJ'd. Once a man starts smacking a woman . . ." I swallowed and shrugged. "I wonder if Patsy-Lynn had an ex and if he was the one driving in as I was leaving when I finished shoeing Spartacus."

Guy had on his earnest face.

My jaw set. "I'm just saying that when a guy hits a girl, he can take it all the way one day."

Guy was staring at me way hard now. "Have you been hit, Rainy?"

I shook my head to indicate I didn't want to talk. What I haven't told Guy bulks up the space between us. There's so much more unspoken than said. And it has to stay that way.

I didn't want to believe Winston Harper hurt his wife. He seemed real bereaved. I'd thought he was a decent hubby to Patsy-Lynn. I have a warm spot for anyone who treats his wife kindly. I'd have felt that way even if he hadn't said I'd still be his shoer. To my way of thinking, any no-account who treats women the way that so-called husband of mine treated me doesn't deserve even a below average sample such as myself. I did Eddie a favor when I rid him of me. But when I quit being Mrs. Eddie Odendorfer, my eating money came from what I got out of selling my beater car. The thing was, without the car, I didn't have a place to live.

Those shelter days were some skanky living. Temporary but double tough.

I never did see that ex of mine again. And I never saw that boy—the one before Eddie—again either.

The happiest day I've known was my tenth birthday—back to living with my daddy, Los Angeles behind me for a while—when I watched Red get born. I always did best with horses and I knew, in my teens, I'd become untethered and needed to fix my life to them. A body needs a stake to start as a trainer, besides which, I didn't want to be buying or selling horses for a living. I'm no horse trader. I wanted to be a horse keeper, but Red was long gone by my mid-teens. Working as barn-help and an exercise girl at the track came easy, but it was a life below minimum wage. Worse, plenty of fellows in parts of the horse industry are equal to long-lost kin of my ex. So, while I liked working and living around horses, I didn't always like the company I kept.

And of course, I didn't like my own company, hadn't since my very early teens, but that's another story and one I don't tell.

There was one trade I could go to school for, something horse people always need. I could work my tail off and earn my own way. I could find Red and get him back. Realizing it would be the best salve for my second-worst sore, I got back in touch with my folks and borrowed bus fare to New York and tuition for the months of horseshoeing school. Now I know in my bones that shoeing is how I'll live my life as long as I'm healthy. And even now—with a dead client and a sort-of boyfriend who'd kneeled like a fool in front of me—it still seemed like a sound plan. Guy said, "With such a bad experience, I think I can understand why you never told me about your marriage."

"It didn't count anyways." Nothing much counts when you don't stick with it.

He pressed for more about the ex in general and Eddie's little hobby of belting his wifey in particular, but I said, "It's just ugly stuff from way back."

"Funny how people can get themselves in bad situations and have trouble getting out," Guy said, rubbing his jaw.

I started to sweat of course, like I always do when my mind runs a replay on how things came to be, then I rolled my eyes at the notion that Guy thought I was going all misty over the wasted time with the ex. If he only knew how my life going in the crapper had begun, he'd know my ex was something I maybe had coming to me.

Really, there's no *if* about it, because Guy'll never know.

Why Guy wants to know what's made me how I am, I don't get, but his poking into the past gave me the creepy-crawlies something awful. And I already had a raging case of the creeps, what with Patsy-Lynn's death hanging over me.

"Rainy, please. Can't you tell me what happened?"

Guy's no quitter, I'll give him that. And I blurted, "I was fat."

He chuckled and snorted a couple breaths. "That's hard to imagine."

"Then you don't have a very good imagination."

"Look, lighten up, will you? And I'll have you know that I led my class in spinning sugar during our pastry section and the instructors called me not only imaginative, but inventive."

I ask for mercy here. The man really does spin cooked sugar. I've seen him do it. These foodies get way too into desserts. And how is it that the fancy food people don't pack on the pounds like normal people?

My mind was a hundred and seventeen places, so I was thrown again when Guy said, "Hello? Rainy? There's got to be more to the story. Just who in the world said you were fat?"

Actually what my first boyfriend said was that I was built like a brick shithouse. Oops. Well, I mean, excuse me for excusing myself, 'cause he's the one who said it after all.

And for that, fuck him.

Oops, really, really oops.

Guy kept blabbing, shaking his head. "Maybe whoever said it saw you bent over under some horse and thought you were three feet tall and two feet wide 'cause you were doubled over."

I was stiff as bar stock. Guy wiggled around in consternation, trying to catch my eye, but no one can catch what I won't give.

"Hey, Rain. I was, you know, joking."

I woke up. "Then you don't know how to joke proper, 'cause neither one of us is laughing."

"We could build a life here, together," he said.

It was my turn for head shaking. "Guy, you make as much sense as iron shoes on a chicken."

His eyeballs took a lap around their sockets. "There's a line not too many guys hear when they're rejected."

"I didn't reject you." He was getting my hackles up. I might have wanted to tell him more, but just couldn't.

"See, lots of times, when a man proposes, the woman says yes. Men love that."

"Do they?" I snapped, all testy.

Guy was mild. "They do."

The phone jangled, making me jump. Little Abby Langston was breathless on the line over Liberty losing a shoe.

"I've looked everywhere. And our field's not that muddy."

"Okay, okay, settle down. I'll squeeze you in tomorrow afternoon, soon as you're out of school."

Charley and I excused ourselves and marched off to the garage for the night.

* * *

My work week was supposed to end with a morning of trimming, lunch, then a full afternoon. The six trims were all at one outfit, way back the opposite side of the highway from the chunk of Forest Service land that crowns the area. These folks want barefoot horses but the gravel road riding they do is tough on hooves. Still, they're careful and really pay attention to their ponies' feet, I've got to give them that. It made a lighter morning's work and would leave me tooling along the backcountry taking me by the Frichtler farm that could have been paying me big bucks for four horses if I could lower my standards enough to do the kind of shoeing they wanted, but I wouldn't do it.

Just the thought of those big lick horses—sore from the chains and wedges and chemical irritants so-called trainers use to force the horses' stride into that huge unnatural lick—makes me wince. Those poor critters move at a running walk because they're afraid of their own painful feet. I want no part of it, that's all. Big lick horses didn't ask to be made to move like freaks and they could do honest work if people wouldn't interfere with them. I turned my head away as I drove past the Frichtlers' herd of Tennessee Walkers and didn't think about anything 'til I got home for lunch.

* * *

"Dead."

Patsy-Lynn's face popped into my mind. "Who's dead now?" I asked Guy, seeing he was distracted by something in the utility room so bad it kept him from having an iced tea on the ready for me. Since he was home for lunch, he'd no doubt be working late.

"The washing machine."

I had a shrug for that news. "Well, you do all those towels and aprons all the dag-blamed time." Really, my jeans and shirts get beyond filthy, stinking of burnt hoof and horse pucky. How bad can kitchen stuff ever be?

Guy pulled a face. I just didn't see a problem. There's an old peanut butter jar full of quarters on the bathroom counter where we dump loose change. It's next to the water glass that holds our toothbrushes.

"Got to get a new washer," he said. "And a dryer too, this time."

There's no dryer in the utility room even though there's a hookup for one, so we've always used a clothesline out back or the one strung across the inside of the garage, my room. The wind works well enough and I've told Guy as much, though honestly, I've waited a week in winter for jeans to dry even in the garage.

"We can wash stuff at the coin-op place in town," I said.

Laundry World's next to the grocery store, so it's not like a person has to sit in the laundromat and pick her nose or other orifices while waiting for clean clothes. But Guy looked put upon, so I had to ask, "What's the big deal with using the public place?"

"I have a theory about laundromats. Would you like to hear my theory?"

I nodded and lied. "Love to."

"I think laundromat time is deducted from your life. Like every cigarette is supposed to be five minutes off—"

"You don't smoke," I pointed out. I like an accurate, complete theory.

Guy swung his hands around impatient-like. "Well, yes, I know I don't smoke. Perhaps you miss the point—"

"The pointy part being?"

"The pointy part being that time spent in a laundromat is just the most infernal drag I've ever suffered and I think getting a new washing machine plus a dryer in the utility room here would be just great."

I figure I told the truth next. "Guy, you haven't suffered much."

"Well, no. I've been pretty fortunate, haven't had any of what could be called suffering. Have you?" He wrinkled his forehead like we were having A Moment.

We weren't. I turned my pink self away. "I'm not saying I have. I'm just saying you haven't."

I'll never go down that self-pity road. I've done worse to another than's ever been done to me.

Guy was still working up some genius plan. "Well, new washer and a dryer, even on sale, would still cost a bit. What do you think?"

"Why in the world do you want my opinion?"

"This is a decision we could make together. Come on. What would you do with, oh, a thousand dollars? That's probably the least we'd pay for a new washer and a dryer."

"Huh?"

He gave me one of my very own looks. It was the I Ain't About to Repeat What I Know You Heard, So Don't You Huh Me look. And he was pretty good at it, probably because he'd been blessed with plenty of opportunities to study on it.

I said, "If I had a thousand bucks to blow, I'd buy a good shoe rack, up my inventory, maybe get a better forge." Mine's an old two-burner that's not as quick and consistent as I'd like.

"So buy it." Guy shrugged.

"You're hilarious. Where would I get a thousand dollars? B'sides, all the stuff I said is just too much money to think about. More'n this grand you're talking."

"Downscaling your dreams?"

I'd sure done some of that and I gave one nod with my chin. "Seems appropriate."

Guy sighed and handed me back a wry smile, also a look he's copied from me. "All right then. A few hundred to splurge with. What would you do?"

A splurge? That wasn't too difficult. "I'd get a Pocket Anvil."

"A pocket anvil?" His eyebrows headed for his hairline.

I nodded.

"And they're a few hundred bucks?"

"Yep." But worth it, I thought.

"Well, fine. Go buy one."

A snort is what he deserved and what I gave him. "Still hilarious. Where would I get that kind of change?"

"The cookie jar springs to mind." Guy's tone was still mild. "We've got a chunk of change stashed in there."

Guy's cookie jar is a chubby-cheeked, fat-bellied ceramic teddy bear, painted in rosy browns and yellows. His head comes off and the whole inside of his body can hold a good half-gallon of cookies. His other job's to hold down the inside corner of Guy's kitchen counter. Not being a cookie kind of gal—Milk Duds are my thing—I can honestly say I'd never had my hand inside the cookie jar before.

Cash money is what Guy pulled out of the bear now. He kept stacking the money, fifties, twenties, hundreds. He had thousands of dollars stashed away. The first thought that popped into my mind was that Suit Fellow didn't know about this and it needed to stay that way.

Chapter 15

IT WAS LIKE GUY WAS DARING me to ask, the way he grinned over the piles of cash on the kitchen counter. The teddy bear cookie jar stared, too. Double dog dare.

I don't take dares any more. I took myself outside, got in Ol' Blue, and drove off without lunch.

My afternoon held two resets at one barn, a bunch of yearlings to trim at a small time breeder, then one of my on-again, off-again clients who shops shoers too much.

Truly, as the days get longer, so do my working hours. In wintertime, I'm limited in the late afternoon on account of not all my clients having a decent setup for after-dark shoeing. Besides, horses' feet grow less in the winter. But there was enough spring sun left for me to tack on one thrown shoe after my usual working hours.

Abby was orbiting when I got to the Langston place, more upset than a thrown shoe should warrant. Apparently, a horse had gone missing from the neighbor's pasture early in the week. It bothers a lot of horses when their neighbors move. They like a set herd. Over-the-fence pasturemates count just like a horse they live with proper. Now an old gelding was alone in the neighboring field.

With his pasturemate suddenly gone, he trotted a fuss and Liberty had been doing fancy footwork too, running around, joining the protest of a mare being suddenly gone from the neighbor's outfit. The little mare whinnied and stared, missing her horse-friend.

"We're gonna walk this field and find that shoe," I told Abby.

And we did, while I fussed in my head about her mare being pregnant. But I didn't want more experience of Abby shushing me. At the back border, I raised my eyebrows at the girl and stretched the bottom string of the double twist wire, letting it ping back like an over-plucked guitar string.

Abby wrung her hands, knowing my meaning. "But this isn't even our fence. You think I'd have wire, if it was up to me?"

I grinned then, because she's so flipping cute, so Little Kid, and eager to be a grown-up. Take time, I wanted to tell her. But I know better than to act condescending. I wrenched my face straight and nodded severely.

"Guess not. This is the neighbor's fence, huh?" I jerked my thumb toward the house beyond the pasture that backed up to the Langstons'.

"The Solquists," Abby said, her voice pitching high, near whining. "It's been days and days now. They were out real late and didn't notice Misty missing until the next morning." Tears burbled down Abby's face. Pretty distraught, given it wasn't her horse, but then kids can be that way, wrap themselves around an axle for something to do.

There wasn't much for me to say but "Huh."

A vague recollection of Guy saying something about a horse gone missing simmered. Bad fences are the usual cause of gone horses. This fence wasn't great, but it hadn't been laid down. The staples were rusty on the old cedar posts, but there. The metal T posts, driven in to bolster the works, were straight. The wire was taut enough except for the low strand of one segment and that's where I found the pulled shoe.

"I don't know how I missed it," Abby said. "I did look."

Probably she missed it having her mind elsewhere, I figured.

Abby fretted something fierce while I put Liberty's front left tire back on, so to speak. The kid was awful worked up about her mare being so shrill and excitable even though I told her just to lock Liberty up in the stall 'til she settled down, and to get plenty of miles rode. If Abby didn't want to talk to me about what was eating her and how her mare came to be bred, then I couldn't force her confidence.

She looked ready to bust. "Is that deal with my dad and Mr. Kittredge still going on?"

At first, I wondered who this Mr. Kittredge of hers was, then I realized she was talking about Guy. My Guy. "What deal's that?"

"I don't know. The deal they were working on."

Darned if the girl wasn't full of secrets. I frowned and looked away. Guy makes a big act sometimes about supposedly telling me everything and being Mr. Up Front. And now little Abby wouldn't look at me, back to freaking out about the fence and the neighbor horse that wasn't there. Liberty shivered, fit to scream, too. I pointed my clinchers at the kid to get her attention.

"What do you know?"

Shrugs are a blasted means of communication in my coloring book. I'd have liked to rattle the teeth out of the kid for the little shoulder toss.

"I heard 'em talking about it the other day, just before Mr. Harper left."

"Left here?"

A nod.

"And Guy was here with them?"

Another nod.

Driving away, it irked me that the kid was so unforthcoming. What was Guy doing at the Langstons' place? I took Ol' Blue slowly by the dirt road next down from Langstons', where the Solquists lived, and pulled over across from the driveway to their farm. I felt sticky about Abby and her secrets.

Heckfire, according to her, Guy was hiding something from me, too.

And I still just plain felt bad about Patsy-Lynn. That might have been my real problem. It was certainly the last black thought making me stare out Ol' Blue's window.

Abandoned there on the road shoulder was something worth a good forty dollars, and I could slide it in the back on top of my tools. A full sheet of plywood. It looked to be in decent shape and who couldn't use such a thing? I dismounted Ol' Blue and grabbed the goods, then grunted with the weight, realizing it was three-quarter inch stuff. And marine grade, a really good find. Beaming, I canted my new sheet of plywood around my forge to get it in the truck bed.

Something about road shopping just makes me happy.

I was near starved by the time I got home. I do love having a physical occupation that leaves me raring for a dinner plate by the day's end.

And I got home to Guy pinching pastry crust.

He looked pleased. "I'm making veggie quiche."

Oh, dandy. Is it just me or has real food gone completely out of fashion? I failed to stifle a moan. "I could murder for a hamburger."

Guy looked at me real quick. I felt clammy for no reason. "Just a figure of speech. I thought you were working at the Cascade tonight."

"I get a night off once in a while."

Come to find out, over green pie for dinner, that Guy's goosey about the word *murder* because the police had been by and had a chat with my landlord, cook, and sort of boyfriend. I sure hoped Guy wasn't counting the contents of the cookie jar when they dropped in. And he didn't have much more to say about that, getting all distracted by what he *did* want to blabber about. Namely, my growing up years.

Unable to help himself, since I let slip about my previous marriage, Guy flooded me with questions.

Sighing, I told Guy what he straight asked about. I don't know why I shared more stuff, but I was glad my mama hadn't when they spoke the other day. While neither of my schools was virgin village, I reckon I learned more stuff that I didn't need to know in California. They never taught me how to gentle a horse in Los Angeles, and they tried to tell me all about coffee and condoms. Besides, California folk talk funny. People there had issues and wanted empowerment and complained about enablers. Classes were facilitated, not taught. It was everywhere, their speak, their chic clothes, their food. One sort-of-friend's mom wore a weighted vest to go mall-walking and called it spinning when she rode an exercise bicycle. We got a trophy when we lost at lacrosse. They called tortillas *wraps*.

How a good-ol'-boy, cold-blooded, ultra-conservative ranch-hand-turned-truck-driver like Gerry Dale and a hot-blooded hyper-liberal gal like Dara Kuhnt got together is beyond anyone's figuring, except that Mama was mighty glad to get a new last name.

Can't imagine anyone was surprised when they couldn't make the marriage stick after a few years' try. Then they started passing me back and forth across the Southwest.

They probably both breathed a burp of relief when I emancipated, then again when I got back in touch after those late teen years on my own. After my shoeing internships, settling myself up here in Oregon was the first I'd truly stood on my own back legs. I'm still getting the feel of it. And sometimes it seems like I'm cheating, not enough on my own, since I'm living in Guy's house and he does all the cooking and whatnot.

Bacon inside green pie fills it out nicely. For dessert, Guy browned an R into flavored sugar over a custard. Most evenings, by the time I give Red and Charley some time, maybe forge-weld some hooks out of old horseshoes and generally putter with my tools, I'm beat. Tonight, I needed to get something off my chest first.

"What deal you got cooking with Keith Langston and Winston Harper?"

Guy waved his hands even as his face went to pulling his eye-brows back down from his scalp. "Uh, it's a surprise. Not ready yet."

"I don't like surprises."

He tried a smile. "What else are you thinking about?"

"Ugly stuff."

He sort of frowned. "There's ugly stuff on your mind?"

Him wanting to talk set me in the other direction even though a little spark of a thought, something I wanted to say, tried for birth.

But he was too chatty, asking again what was running around in my head.

"Just for the sake of it," I said, "explain what good reason is there to gab about ugly stuff? If there's no fixing it, why talk about it?"

"Well, if it's hard on you, it creates stress. It drains your energy."

"Sounds sort of like your laundromat time theory."

Guy nodded, like he was all pleased with my learning. "Very much like that."

"I have a theory of my own," I said, "on jabbering about things that are ugly."

He beckoned with both arms, begging for it. "By all means, let's hear your theory."

"Well," I explained, "it's like a butt pimple."

He molted to a shade of pale I'd never seen before. I waited for him to get some color back. It was his turn to talk anyways. In a minute, he was pink again. "A butt pimple," he said, savoring the words.

"Yeah. A butt pimple is annoying and unattractive, but, like ugly stuff in the past, is not something other people need to know about."

Guy didn't have any snappy retorts for this good answer I'd served up. All he did was repeat three words in wonder.

"A butt pimple."

Charley followed as I marched myself outside. My good dog tried to lick the mood off my face. Last year when I found him, he'd looked pretty well used up, but with me caring for him—how I'd wanted to care for someone—he started looking loved.

At first, I'd taken my new old dog in Ol' Blue as I made my shoeing calls. As Charley got settled at Guy's place, I let him hang around the house while I was away working. But he's still ready to keep me company anytime. Since he was with me when I got Red back, Charley thinks he's been in my life the longest. My dog and horse are the only ones I talk to with complete trust. My good dog knows how to keep a secret and, while he does have his quiet side, he's not a pouter. So I tried not to be a pouter, tried to shake the black cloud that'd been dogging me. Shoeing's tough stuff most days. But starting up as a shoer is tougher. My first shoer's toolbox was a five-gallon bucket. Before I had enough good tools, I blocked horseshoe nails with my nipper's edge and I hammer clinched. I didn't have chaps, pull-offs, or crease nail pullers when I started either. Not even a rasp handle did I have in the beginning. And no spares of anything. If I'd ever broken, say the handle on my driving hammer, I was done shoeing for the day. Now I have full tools plus spares, and I've spent the bucks for touches like a clinch blocker and the magnet I wear on my right wrist to hold nails. Still, I do look forward to the days when I feel like I've truly come into my own, and have the bonuses like a hotter forge, a substantial shoe inventory, and a Pocket Anvil.

Tonight, it was time to better my outfit with an improved tool-box. Getting to putter at home, I enjoy. Guy wanted to work on his goose pen anyways, in his version of carpentry. Mostly, he used his arm to measure and his fingernail to mark where he wanted to cut or nail something, so I didn't hold out much hope for the little geese getting improved quarters.

A new toolbox would be a great use for the three-quarter inch plywood sheet I'd collected from the road by the Solquists' place. My mistake in my first box was the plywood was too light, I'd nailed where I should have used screws, and I'd never glassed it where extra strength was needed. This time I'd cover my box with fiberglass cloth and epoxy. Later, maybe I'd add casters. Tonight I'd get the new toolbox roughed out unless I had to drive Guy to get stitches, which was a maybe, given the way he was using the hand saw as a measuring stick now.

See, the measuring thing is lost on Guy. He just doesn't get it and sort of wings everything like he's throwing spices into a soup pot. His fancy new tape measure was going to end up being a paperweight, I bet.

"You left it in the kitchen," I said.

He headed in, happily muttering about how I'd read his mind.

When he came back outside, he was packing the measuring tape plus a notepad and said, "Oh, you had a pile of calls earlier. Owen Weatherby called twice but didn't leave a message or phone number, just said to tell you he'd called. He's one of your clients, right?"

"Kind of." My nod got chased off by a frown as my right hand found the base of my ponytail. I took to twisting it hard enough to make a stick of hair. Weatherby, Weatherby, I pondered.

A sick feeling iced my skull as I remembered a forgotten chore. If Owen Weatherby had been testing me, I'd failed.

Chapter 16

O H, GUY WAS FULL OF MESSAGES. A regular secretary.

"A man called and asked for you but he hung up when I said you were out. And someone called a few times but hung up when the voice mail picked up. Why do people do that? If they wait long enough for the machine to come on, then why not leave a message? Also, a Mr. Merrick wants to reschedule his next shoeing because his wife's got a doctor's appointment that day. And someone named Linda Cless called and said one of her horses threw a shoe. She said you'd know which hoof and, yes, she found the shoe."

That youngster of Linda's has some kind of shoe bulimia thing going on, hurfing up his front right shoe a couple weeks after I put it on. Bobby's full of vinegar and every time he gets to getting rowdy, there's a good chance Linda will be out in her pasture looking for a front shoe and I'll be squeezing her into my schedule to tack it back on him. We joke about screwing them to him or else fixing the problem with a two-by-four applied between his ears. But really, even though I lose time on that account, her big silly Bobby-horse makes me smile. He's just a happy, playful boy and he will grow up.

No, I don't charge for putting a thrown shoe back on and yeah, I know lots of shoers do. I'm not trying to steal business from other shoers, no matter what Dixon Talbot mouths around town. It's just that when I was a little kid living with my daddy and our shoer came out for a thrown shoe, he never charged for the favor, so I grew up thinking that's the way things ought to be: thrown shoes get tacked back on for free.

After rescheduling with Merrick and finding a time to squeeze in Linda's youngster, I flipped to the back of my appointment book to get Weatherby's number. I thought about him calling but only leaving his name, like I was supposed to know the message.

Damn. Oops, and darn it.

Before returning Weatherby's call, I checked Ol' Blue's glove box, more upset with myself by the minute. No reason why the bute wouldn't still be waiting there, but I sweated at the thought that I'd lost Weatherby's drugs.

Turns out, I hadn't and I was blamed glad the baggie of white tablets and syringes of paste was still there.

The detective's questions about drugs came back to me.

Yep, Suit Fellow had definitely said something about money and drugs.

Did horse drugs count? Phenylbutazone, common bute as paste in syringes or tablets or white powder, is what us horse people use for our critters' pain. Maybe vets get it where it can be injected in veins or muscles, but it's basically our horse aspirin. And I was holding some for Owen Weatherby that I'd been sent to carry over to Felix Schram.

If Weatherby or Schram had been considering using me as a regular shoer, they'd no doubt now be figuring I wasn't responsible. I wanted to run Ol' Blue over to Schram's right away and give him the bute Weatherby'd promised to deliver through me.

I wanted to have done it days ago, when I was supposed to have done it.

What I didn't want was what I had to do, suck it up and get Weatherby on the phone.

It wasn't a good call.

"It's Rainy. I'm realizing I forgot to give that bute to Felix Schram for you. Do you want I should do that right now?"

"Nah. Bring it back to me." Weatherby's phone voice was slow.

My throat was tight as I yessirred him.

Then he told me, "Can you come by my place now? Everyone's here."

That sounded like one of Weatherby's roping, tale-telling, Friday night potlucks. I'd never been invited and didn't exactly feel I was welcomed into his inner fold now. More like, I'd been summoned to a public dressing down and would have to try to be a good sport. My stomach made knots, while my mind wondered on what the conversation between Schram and Weatherby had been like and if they truly got to bad-mouthing me.

Pretty likely, I thought.

Did Schram let on he'd been grabby and I'd prepared to carve him up?

Pretty unlikely.

Did Weatherby and Schram talk about the quality of my shoeing, mentioned I'd been fast and good, or just that I forgot to give Schram the bute? Twirling my ponytail, I was bugged by the idea that I'd done an awful lot of forgetting, which is truly ironic as there's some stuff I'd love to forget but can't.

I'd likely blown my chances for Weatherby and Schram to employ me again. Probably other shoers rope and ride with those guys anyhoo. Dixon Talbot might and he wouldn't be best pleased to see me at the Rocking B outfit with my shoeing rig.

The thought of Talbot gave me pause. Lately, the business cards I put at the feed co-op, hardware store, and grocery store bulletin boards where everyone puts up business cards and notices for lawn service and litters of pups and the like . . . well, my cards are disappearing. And I'm not getting as many calls from new clients as all those missing cards would seem to suggest.

Probably someone takes my cards and files them in the garbage.

Who that someone might be, well, I had an idea. Only makes sense that it's a shoer who doesn't want to see me getting any more business. For what shouldn't have been the first time, I wondered who'd shod for the Harpers before I came to town.

* * *

"We-elll, what're ya doin'?" Guy has this goofy Texas drawl that's more for show and he only breaks it out when he thinks he's being charming. Sometimes it's a thing to smile at and sometimes it gets under my skin no end.

It's far more likely to dig me like a chigger when I have to hustle.

"Making chili for this thing at Weatherby's right away." My stash of supermarket brand cans of bean bombs rolled on the counter, a couple going sideways.

Guy caught one before it hit the floor and wrinkled his nose, obviously unimpressed with the quality of my offering for the potluck. "You know, Rainy," Guy said, "you can ask for help."

Mercy's sake, no I can't. Guy shouldn't need this explained. I've been under his roof coming a year now, didn't he have me the least little bit figured?

"Well, fine." Guy got out his super fancy Euro can opener, set it right on the counter next to my cans of chili, and left the kitchen.

He acts like I can't even make a bowl of Cap'n Crunch, but it's not true. Sometimes I pour Apple Jacks instead, for a little variety. And even if I do spill the milk now and then, the point is, I can make my way around a kitchen all right, maybe not like Guy but to suit my purposes. Besides, let him try to shoe a horse and then just wait for a vet and ambulance to be needed.

Even if I'm not in danger of winning a cooking contest, I can run a hand-operated can opener as well as the next person. I cranked six cans open and found a big plastic bowl to dump it all into, then checked the directions. If it's two minutes for one can, would it take twelve minutes for a half dozen? I twisted my hair around, considering, then settled on eight minutes of microwaving on high for starters.

While that was in the works, I planned how to deal with Weatherby when I saw him, trying to imagine the right amount of respect without being too whipped about forgetting to give Schram the bute. I wished again that Weatherby'd never asked me to carry it in the first place. I'm no one's errand girl.

The beans started bursting before the microwave timer dinged.

It looked like a quick little old murder had happened in the microwave. No one should have to see this kind of gore, bean bits everywhere, the sides and top of the little plastic oven all red.

Guy came in looking a smidge alarmed and actually spooked when he followed my stare for a look-see in the microwave.

"I'll clean it up," I said. Of course, I'd clean up my own mess. I just didn't itch to hear Guy go on about how I'd made a mess of things.

I know I've made messes. I know.

He took a deep breath, but no sad sigh came out. Instead, Guy said, "I have some beans ready to go, actually, for a cassoulet I was going to try."

"Huh? This is chili, not a casserole."

Then he did sigh, a painful-sounding sad blow of air. "Cassoulet. I was going to do a non-traditional cassoulet, red beans instead of white. It normally takes quite a bit of lead time to do beans in a dish like chili, but I have hydrated beans in the fridge and I have browned stew meat because I was going to make—"

"Something fancy?" I didn't want to hear his three-dollar name for whatever concoction he'd planned. Guy suffered my insult in silence, so I became the width of a size 5 nail nicer and asked, "Wouldn't chili be a little lowbrow for you?"

"I would be happy to make you a wonderful batch to take to your . . . evening engagement. I won't even sweat the presentation."

We've gone around a few times on what he calls *presentation*, which means adding bits of weeds on the side and dripping sauces in lines and zigzags over the plate or bowl. He says presentation makes the meal. I say a fork does.

"Wonderful? It doesn't have to be wonderful." I waved my hands. How could I make him see it was just a bunch of ropers getting together and special food was lost on them?

"It will have chocolate in it." Guy sounded smug. He knows I love chocolate. Love it and have myself on a rationing program.

"Chocolate, no. That's just too high-bred. I don't want to stand out with some fancy pants miss of a dish when all anyone wants is a mouthful of beans and beef."

He waved me away. "Just trust me."

* * *

The Rocking B was packed, a couple dozen rigs, most visitors ready or saddling up for roping, bugs flicking by the big arena lights. The outfit used to be owned by Weatherby's folks and some partner, but I guess the other man sold out years ago and Owen and his family have put everything they do into breeding cowhorses ever since. Mostly ropers, some cutters. His stud has covered a lot of mares, but Weatherby's not been greedy about it, hadn't overbred. Doc is a real built horse, solid and all that without throwing problem babies and he's made a real good reputation for the Rocking B.

The ranch had a regular little old hootenanny going on, set to last late. Folks from near everywhere were standing around jaw jacking, some mounted up and swinging loops, plenty of wives and kids there, too. Across the lawn, a boom box blared a ballad about trucks and dogs and whiskey. Several couples were shaking their legs.

Not wanting the bute tablets to turn to powder in my pocket, I left the baggie in Ol' Blue's glovebox for now and went up to the tables of food with Guy's chili crock.

"There's beer here. Whiskey, too," one good old boy said between swigs on a brown bottle as he leaned toward me.

What an offer. And so beautifully presented. Yeah, he was quite the ladies' man.

"I don't partake." I turned away only to run smack into another skinny guy in jeans and snap front shirt, his boot heels cowboy cut.

"How about it, Miss?" The cowpoke with a well-plastered grin looked set to dance. "Do you only swing with the one who brung ya?"

"I brung my own self," I told him and turned away before he could get to thinking that my being alone meant I was up for grabs. Thoughts of Guy's surprised—maybe hurt—expression when I headed out here without him rose. I pushed the memory away.

Past the long table of grub were the ice chests of beer and soda. I cracked open a can of diet pop. Since my other hand needed something to do, I got a paper plate, blended into the line that formed up, and got a couple biscuits with gravy.

When did food, real honest food like country gravy, get so bad? Worse than used spit, this was. And the biscuits? These things were like bran muffins without the pesky flavor.

If I didn't like it, then this food was bad. Might have killed Guy. But everyone was going at the chow like a bunch of, well, a bunch of scrawny cowboys and pudgy starved people. A lot of those belt buckles were tipped over from the bulge bearing down. Either that or they were thin enough to live in southern California without being an eyesore. Still, I liked these folk. Cattlemen are a good kind of people to bide time with.

But I was antsy, on account of the reason I was there.

Weatherby strolled over just as the announcer at the ring called ten minutes to the first steer going in the chute. Someone at the far end of the tables started going on about how good some pot of chili was and someone else scurried up to the boss and said his heeler just half tore off a front shoe.

"Dale will fix it," Weatherby said, then turned away to spit tobacco juice.

When I get referred to by my last name, am I one of them? I was trying to decide if he was giving me an order or paying me a compliment.

Turns out, I was the only shoer there. Anyways, the cowpoke, Andy Somebody-or-other, just looked at Weatherby, wanting his horse's messed up shoe on so that he could rope. Andy was lanky and agitated and didn't believe what his host was saying.

"You're really a shoer?" he asked me with eyebrows hauled up to his hatband.

"Yep." I headed for my truck, asking where the horse was, so I could get positioned to work, and was soon down to business getting his horse's shoe back on. Things went quick and uncomplicated until the stinker pulled hard and I went to the ground hanging onto him.

I have a rule about horses pulling. They shouldn't. And I didn't want this gelding to win the foot from me. So I took a good dusting, then got his foot back on my stand and finished. If Andy was appreciative, he forgot to say, what and all with this apparently being his first time watching a sheila shoer.

"You a lesbo?"

Hard to know what to say to someone who's so beneath-bullshot stupid. In the end, I came up with, "You ever been wrong before or is this your first time?"

He twisted away a bit and slanted his hips as he shifted his weight. I figured he was trying to hide some wood. But what is it with guys and lesbians? He was getting a stiffie just thinking about girls going at it. For mercy's sake, he had trouble settling into the saddle as his partner—not a wink-wink type partner, but the header to his heeling—called that they were next up. I'd fixed his horse just in time.

Emergency shoeing done, I went and found Weatherby again for the other repair.

He didn't make me bring up the waiting subject, just said for me to put the bute in his trailer. So I set the baggie inside the trailer's tack room where Weatherby couldn't miss it and went back to watch the roping.

The spectators were talking about all things, the way it happens when a bunch of cowboys and cowmen get together. There was the muttering about the newspapers scaring the public about mad cow disease. We all know it's not in the muscle or milk anyways, so let's calm down, huh? The upshot of the media hysteria in the cattle-raising counties of Oregon—Butte, Baker, Douglas, Grant, and Union—is that it's led to mad cowboy disease.

When they'd chewed up that subject, they gossiped about who'd been up to Hermiston lately to buy horses and who was going to whip who at roping tonight. And someone with careful English, his hat's retainer string making a slash across his neck, mentioned that really good chili again.

"Don't be farting in the truck on the way home," a man I knew from somewhere said. He grinned at me. Oh, yeah, Patsy-Lynn's barn-help, Ted, who got kind of creepy and weird as I was leaving the funeral. I turned away, then noticed that cowpoke Andy doing the same. I turned back and studied Ted and the smaller man with the careful language and manners and hat retainer string making a black line across his throat who'd mentioned the chili. Manuel Smith? Ted looked like he'd let something slip. Andy didn't like them, shot them dark looks and kept his distance. Some of the other ropers ignored it all. Trying to figure out what I'd missed, I realized the Smith fellow was Ted's . . . boyfriend. I thought about lies told, someone saying he'd been at the Cascade Kitchen when Guy or someone else at the diner said it wasn't true. And I knew Ted had been with Patsy-Lynn when I left the Flying Cross.

A loud whoop from the arena drew everyone's attention that way and we scattered to watch. The team up had just nailed a steer in double-quick time, were going to win the night's jackpot unless a roping miracle happened. Harper Junior racked a boot on the nearest panel of the arena fence and griped about the live-foal guarantee coming back to bite him on a few breedings last year. I guess they'd hoped to push Spartacus pretty hard as a super stud. Weatherby cleared his throat hard at that and stepped away. My jaw twisted as I considered the two men, their two studs. Weatherby's stallion had never had fertility problems, but Spartacus was apparently having trouble delivering the goods in the baby-making department. It's easy to see why people given to muscular stallions would have been sold on Patsy-Lynn's baby. Her husband's baby, Junior, looked too sun-blond and tan for Oregon. I spend about as much time outdoors as can be spent, but I don't get that much sunshine.

Junior grinned when that Andy character told some folks I was a horseshoer.

"She's our shoer," Junior said good and loud, nodding at me. "Flying Cross."

I loved the endorsement, loved it. Now there was a guy who had no heartache with the idea of a woman shoer. Good for him.

Weatherby's dog was called to cut and bring up another steer. I moved over to watch the boy work. Everyone knows about this dog. Story is Weatherby traded acres and acres of pasture for him, got him from the neighbor who raises sheep and sheepdogs.

Biddable, keen Swiftsure was a machine. I can't even imagine what it's like to have that much concentration and work ethic. The dog was dying to move cattle for Weatherby. Some of the guys behind me, naturally, fell to admiring the dog while some of them started bellyaching about sheep ranchers. I don't care if ranchers raise woolies or things that go moo, but for some folks, cows versus sheep is their politics.

"Smelly bastards," one fellow commented. No one else said anything to that bit of wisdom but someone started the old joke, "You know what sheepmen say?"

I knew. We all knew, those of us who cut our teeth with cattlemen.

"Sheep are liars." I turned my ponytail to their hooting.

Done with working his dog, Weatherby waved me over and I braced myself for a trip to the woodshed, so to speak.

"Schram told me that he was maybe out of line when you were at his outfit. I sent you over there thinking he'd behave. He will now."

I opened my mouth and shut it when nothing came out, on account of not wanting flies to land in there.

Weatherby cast a hard look over at Schram, who was a-horse-back. Schram gave me a howdy with a face that meant he'd gotten himself a little old trip to the woodshed with Weatherby. I was feeling better and better.

Schram wasn't using the reining horse I'd shod for him, of course, as the sliding plates I'd put on his reiner wouldn't let a horse stop a steer. A jug-headed, raw-boned nag was under him now. Schram shook out a loop readying to head his steer while he studied me from across the fence panel.

"You're all dirty," he called, being as he was Mr. Good Grasp of the Obvious.

Well, his horse was ugly and would still be so in the morning. I, on the other foot, could take a shower and wash my clothes. Besides, there was something a little dirty in his tone. Made me think about him asking if I was another woman who liked it rough.

Right then, I wished for a crystal ball.

I wanted to know what secrets Patsy-Lynn had taken with her to her grave. Had she been keeping company with a man other than her husband? With Felix Schram? A wild thought about Abby's daddy and Patsy-Lynn bubbled up. Surely Keith Langston got company somewhere, sometime. I didn't want to consider such nonsense, but random rudeness just popped into my brain as I stood too near Felix Schram. His coarseness gave me more than pause.

Turns out, not all of these country people truly are my cup of coffee. Being a hick might not be the qualification I should be look-ing for in a person. Guy's never made me feel second-rate, never, but he sure had some explaining to do. There was no explaining a guy like Schram. An unaccustomed feeling settled over me, which I dared identify as me trying to figure things out before they got ugly, instead of after. That was new. And good. High time for me to squint at some things that deserved studying. If Guy had a secret—and he'd pretty much admitted to it—I needed to know what it was.

If the sheriff's people thought I or Guy had something to do with Patsy-Lynn's passing, I should figure out who did have a hand in her death. There were plenty of potential suspects. Some right here at the party.

Harper Junior cornered me and said good and loud, meant for all nearby ropers to catch, "You still going with Martha Stewart?"

I heard the snorts, felt the looks, heard the whispers Andy made to some of the other guys. Someone repeated the fiction that Guy was a poof. Early would have been a good time to leave, but I got distracted with joy when Weatherby asked if I wanted to run Charley sometime. Right away, I'd forgot what I'd told myself about paying better attention to everything.

Most folks were gone by the time I got Martha's empty chili crock off the food tables, but heading home, I remembered to wonder why Mr. Harper's son might have a case of the apples against Guy.

Chapter 17

CHARLEY'S DAY IS NOT COMPLETE WITHOUT giving a good barking to someone. On the job, he bayed into the darkness, little growls shaking his chest. He kept it up as I opened the garage's side door to the night and one of the sheriff's men.

Deputy Paulden held up a rounding hammer—the kind us shoers use to shape horseshoes. But this one in the deputy's hand was in a clear plastic bag sealed with blue tape, labeled EVIDENCE.

Made me think of a bloodied rasp in a similar bag.

"Miss Dale. This was used to break into a veterinary office in town tonight. Thousands of dollars in damage."

Guy came out of the house, a robe around his boxers. My mouth wasn't working, what and all with my brain not coming up with a whole notion. When I did manage a thought, the deputy asked it as his next question.

"You missing any tools, Miss Dale?"

A vision of my truck broken into and my tools stolen made me sweat. I whipped my head around, craning to look at Ol' Blue. I hadn't been home long. Ol' Blue should be fine. I made for my boots.

The deputy nodded, like he'd maybe already had a look-see at the other side of the carport before knocking.

"Let's go take a gander, shall we?" Deputy Paulden grinned grim.

We went out into the night, to Ol' Blue resting and rusting beyond the carport.

"Which vet's office was broken into?" I asked. Cowdry has two, one with several vets in it, a place for dogs and cats and lizards and ferrets and hedgehogs and birds and whatever else people decided to have for keeping company. And then there's old Doc Vass's place that Nichol took over. My breath frosted in the cooling night air.

"Doctor Nichol's practice," Paulden said. "Back window smashed out, lots of cabinets vandalized. And this hammer, a horseshoeing tool I'm told, was at the scene."

He drew out the story while watching me. I knew my face was screwed up and my lips about turned inside out. Then he asked, "What do you make of that? Looks like some horseshoer has it in for the vet."

"Huh." There aren't all that many full-time shoers around Cowdry, but there are four times as many part-timers who do a few backyard horses. I looked up at the deputy.

It was like he was playing with me, taunting. "Could be you or could be someone else."

"It's someone else," I said, hoping he'd believe me, hoping Nichol would, too. Had the deputy and Nichol already discussed which shoers were likely suspects?

Paulden nodded. "Could be someone making it look like you. How do you feel about that?"

How'd he think I felt? I wondered hard on the hammer and someone beating up Nichol's office with it. Just about any iron-hanger with a few one-horse accounts has a rounding hammer. I got ready for some growling as Paulden kept up his questions.

"Can you prove this isn't your hammer?"

I couldn't. It was just a stupid rounding hammer, a Diamond. My first was a no-brand from foreign parts and my new one's a pricey Jim Poor. Besides, I only have the two and both were in my truck, right where I left them. Furious, I used both hands to twist my ponytail.

Finally, my jaw unclenched enough to speak. "No, I can't."

The deputy said, "Of course not. Can't prove a negative, can you?"

"I can't prove much of anything," I snapped. Then I saw only one of us was fit to spit.

Deputy Paulden smiled and gave me a nod that said I should talk a bit.

"I've never even been in that office," I said. "Even back before it was Nichol's, Doc Vass came to me, farm called, when I had him out to do my horse's teeth."

The deputy smiled again. "Then this'll be easy as pie. Your fingerprints won't be in there. Let's get a complete set printed at the office."

I tried to tell Paulden that they'd already swiped prints from me, but no, he wanted proper prints, whatever that was. And I thought about protesting that anyone vandalizing Nichol's office should have been smart enough to wear gloves, so my prints not being in there wouldn't really clear me, but suggesting how to be a skilled criminal didn't seem like a good kind of argument to make.

"Come to the office tomorrow. We've got part-time office hours Saturdays now." He handed me a business card with a case number written on it. I was to give the number to the person at the counter when I went in to get fingerprinted.

Remembering how Guy had told the police we were cooperative, back when they wanted my blood, I thought about the suggestion at hand. Guy would say that I had spare fingerprints, so giving up a set wouldn't hurt.

The deputy seemed of the same mind, but looked at me sideways. "Have you given up your full fingerprints before?"

"Nope." And it seems like a gal can't get 'em back once she gives them away. A bit like virginity, fingerprints.

* * *

Just on principle, I took my time in the morning before making my second trip of the week to the sheriff's office. Being innocent doesn't keep a person from feeling kind of guilty. I knew I hadn't broken into Nichol's place, but I fretted that other people might not. Much as I wondered who might have busted up the vet's office and left a shoer's hammer at the scene, it wasn't something I could solve any more than I could figure out what happened to poor Patsy-Lynn.

There was another mystery I was better suited to work on— Abby's neighbor's missing horse. This puzzle swirled in my mind, ignored by everybody but the Solquists, who owned the horse, and Abby, who seemed to have enough to fret over without spiraling herself over the neighbor's horse.

Puzzling on the missing mare more and more, I considered the surrounding land. There was an awful lot of backcountry in the northwest corner of the county. I needed a map. The Solquists' mare could have made miles, but usually horses stick close to home. They don't just walk to the next county if they're settled in a place with good care. The Solquists were solid horse people, from what I heard. Their mare had a decent home.

Stealing a horse should still be a hanging offense.

This time in the sheriff's little lobby, I paid more attention. It was time to turn my brain faucet all the way open anyways. My mind's done more than enough trickling.

A giant map of the whole county decorated the sheriff's front office wall. When the old gal at the front counter said the finger-print-taker wasn't ready for me, I spent time studying the map's perspective on this corner of the world where I'd tried to make a bit of a life for the past year. I wondered how long I'd last.

Hiding places can become living places, can't they? It's all about the body in question and the lay of the land.

Butte County's a rectangle, simple and true in shape, possessing plenty of valleys and peaks to give the eye something to catch on. It seemed like Red and I rode a good deal of this ground, but now

I realized just how big the place was. We hadn't covered a tenth of
the backcountry even though I know every trail for about twenty
miles to the north, south, and west of Vine Maple and even east of
the highway. A few of the back roads I know because of traveling
to clients. Just a couple of my accounts—Harper and Delmonts on
opposite sides of the highway being the bigger ones, but Langston
and a few other one-horse accounts, too—are further off where the
highway curves west. The huge chunk of state and federal forestry
lands south of that curve goes from Old Man Harper's place to
forever, it looks like. Little-traveled valleys lay tucked between
Black Ridge and Stakes Ridge, then acreage stretched for miles of
ranchland and backcountry.

I reckoned the Solquists must have checked the open country
both sides of the highway for their missing horse. Unlikely as it was
for the mare to wander south of the highway on her own, if one
thing leads to another, a horse can get in too deep to get herself
home.

"I do not steal and I am sorry for the lady."

The man's voice startled me from the map and my mind. His pro-
nunciation was precise, his hair black. The hatband on his leather
cowboy hat dangled feathers down the back of his neck. The girl
walking him out looked at me. "You want to come this way?"

I pulled my fingernail from my mouth and blinked at her. The
clerk toed the heavy side door open, one hand on her cocked
hip. She had a tan uniform that showed she was with the sheriff's
department, but a gunless grunt, not a deputy. She was about my
size, my age—might have been a shade younger—and also used a
ponytail instead of a hairstyle.

"That's the dude," I muttered as we went down an inner hallway in the sheriff's station. "He was coming to the Flying Cross last
time I shod there and then I saw him at Weatherby's place, like,
maybe riding with the barn-help fellow, Ted."

"Brilliant." She motioned me to follow her to a crowded little
room. All cupboards and a big sink, it was like a laundry room

without the washer and dryer. Clean pieces of paperboard, all pre-printed with blank squares for each print, sat on the countertop.

I snapped my fingers without meaning to. "He's the dude who was walking to the Flying Cross the day Patsy-Lynn died."

"The day she was killed," the clerk corrected me. "And yeah, he was. Would have been sweet if you'd said that to Deputy Paulden and Detective Gerber on day one."

Jeepers, I didn't think of it then. I tried to put my fingertips on the black ink pad she opened.

"Let me do it," she said. "You just relax. Don't push down."

Having someone else move your hand around is skeezy, that's all there is to it.

Definitely involved more than a simple set of my fingerprints. After she used my fingertips to fill in all ten squares on the paper, then added prints of all four of my fingers held together in some bigger squares, she said she'd take my palms.

"They didn't make me do all this when I was here before," I said.

"There's such a thing as probable cause and consent." She snapped rubber bands over heavy paper rolled onto a fat cardboard tube. Again, she told me to relax and let her do it. I tried to discon-nect from my hands while she rolled my palms across the paper.

"Great," she said, "these are good clean prints. Sometimes peo-ple have trouble cooperating and smudge them. You did fine." And she went on about the specific points on my prints and how bigger departments all had scanners, but here in Butte County they still hand-rolled palms.

Dandy, I thought, one of those show-offy know-it-alls and a blabbermouth to boot, just dying to say every piece of police lingo she could. I had to hear about ridge endings and dots and bifur-cations. A person would have thought she was talking about the forest lands on the lobby map. She made it real clear that she knew a lot of things about partial prints and whorls and loops.

To me, loops are for roping and whorls are the cowlicks in a horse's coat where the hair grows every which way. I'd helped vets mark whorls on passports for horses to be shipped internationally, but my know-how of fingerprints and other police stuff was nowhere. I wished someone would ask a horse question, better still a hoof query.

"There's a horse missing," I said, "and—"

The clerk snorted, like Red when I refuse him extra hay. "The sheriff's department can't throw everything into it every time someone has a missing animal."

Getting into it with this gal would be a waste of time. I was made of questions, with no good answers. My hands were dirty and I wanted to know more about the break-in at Nichol's place. This fingerprint tech, or whatever she was, didn't actually seem to be investigating me or anyone else. She was a flunky, like the barn-help who fetched horses, especially at the racetracks and big training barns when I'd done my shoeing internships. Flunkies and gofers fetch like Labradors, but they don't run the dog show.

The flunky thanked me for being cooperative, noting I was one of the ones, like the Kittredge dude, who had given blood, too. She set out gritty borax soap for me to wash my hands of the blackness.

"Guy Kittredge was asked to give a blood sample?" I rubbed my chin, thinking.

"And maybe wash your face, too."

I rubbed borax on my face like some kind of beauty queen. "The detective only asked me for blood when he came to the house. He didn't ask Guy."

"Right," she said, dismissing me.

A loop spun in my mind, wanting to prove negatives, like: I didn't bother the vet's office, I didn't hurt Patsy-Lynn. And for that matter, Guy didn't hurt her either. But all of us newcomers seemed to be painted with the same broad brush of suspicion by the townfolk in this place that was founded on farming and ranching over a hundred years ago.

As Deputy Paulden said, a negative can't be proved.

Something clear, like a missing horse, that's an easier problem for me to tackle, but not as important as a woman dying. My
fingerprints not being at the vet's office wouldn't prove I hadn't
bothered Nichol's business, but a lot of people could say I was at
Weatherby's that evening, having chili same as everyone else.

I hauled myself to the other end of town, to the vet's office,
where there were things to say.

* * *

Nichol glanced over his receptionist's frizzy head and waved me
back right away to a treatment room. It was one of those little
rooms with a door on each end, the other door going to the office's
surgery and main work area.

Beyond the door, Nichol muttered to someone about a just-
spayed dog. He let the door to the surgery area stay open when
he came back in, affording me a view of shattered cabinets, a pile
of broken stuff swept into a corner, a clipboard and prescription
bottles lined up on the counter. Disinfectant wafted. They were
still doing clean up and inventory from the break-in. Nichol stood,
looking fixed to wait for my words.

"I'm sorry someone broke into your office and all. And by the
way, it wasn't me. That's what I came here to say."

He raised his eyebrows and then mine with "Yeah, I know it
wasn't you."

"I thought you might have figured it was, on account of the
rounding hammer." Horse vets tend to know shoer's tools. It wasn't
like talking to Guy, who couldn't tell a rounding hammer from a
driving hammer, didn't know the difference between my clinchers
and my crease nail pullers.

"The deputies said you were out at the Rocking B, some shindig
going on there."

Nichol hadn't been at Weatherby's hootenanny, I realized.

So it was possible, I had to admit, that Nichol could have vandalized his own place just to make someone else look guilty. Which worked for about a minute in my case.

Then, instead of continuing down this stupid road of thinking Nichol had tried to frame me for vandalizing his office, I named the people who'd been at the Rocking B, people who had definitely not been bothering his office that night. Weatherby, Schram, all those cowpokes and semi-regulars.

"Mr. Harper wasn't there," I continued, "but his son was."

I thought again about Patsy-Lynn. I mean, things were peaceful here in Cowdry before she died in her garage. It seemed like there was a crime wave of sorts, given a death and a major vandalism and—

"Rainy."

I focused. Nichol looked to be waiting for me to make another comment. He knew I knew he hadn't been at Weatherby's potluck. Come to think of it, Nichol had been missing at the funeral and reception, too. Really he was as much a newbie in town as me. I considered this and sort of liked it. Maybe I am doing all right. Sometimes I feel ready to panic, like no one can understand how it is, me trying to make it on my own, with my head and hands to support myself. A vet, with a big money education behind him and a big money future ahead, he can't understand the boots I'm wearing. And lots of folks, me included, would have rather stuck with Doc Vass.

Other folks weren't at Weatherby's the other night. I wondered if the detective was already making a list. I could think of one who'd probably had a spare rounding hammer.

Chapter 18

A BIG BLACK RIG LURKED IN the grocery store parking lot beyond the veterinarian's office. As I walked back to Ol' Blue, I realized the lurking truck was Dixon Talbot's shoeing rig. With six wheels and a professional shoer's box in the back, his rig's a sight more truck than mine. I listened, satisfying a sudden powerful urge to know if Talbot's truck carried an automatic tranny or a stick shift. Wind up, clutch, wind up.

Stick.

Talbot drove off as I reached Ol' Blue, never looking my way. Instead I was treated to a profile of his clipped cut and size extra-large Adam's apple. I can't be the only one who thinks of skinny turkeys when seeing the side of his throat. If Dixon Talbot was tall, he'd be one of those super thin lanky types, but he's not much higher than me. His make-up-for-shortness white cowboy hat was on the dashboard. Maybe it's too big to wear in the truck. He cleared the traffic light late, his truck roaring. I'd get shed of that attitude, myself. If we needed to have words, let's have 'em.

I flipped my key in Ol' Blue's ignition to warm the glow plugs, waited, then fired up to follow Talbot down the main street. If

I could flag him over, we'd parlay, provided he'd give me the daggummed time of day. But I got caught at the red light by the almost-dead second strip mall at the bottom end of town.

Here on the south end of Cowdry, things are a little more run-down than the north end. A few blocks past the sheriff's office, this other strip mall is half empty. It used to have a pizza parlor, a used bookstore, and some sort of cheapie trinket store, but they all gave up the ghost. There's still a tiny library, a tanning salon, and a drug store there, but one thing this little town could use in a big way is that pizza parlor. Lordy, I do love the stuff. The pizza place that used to be here shut down not long after I moved to Cowdry. The place deserved a sad, longing look from me and I obliged.

Guy's scooter, in front of the shut-down pizza joint, caught my eye. I let go thoughts of chasing down Talbot's truck. Instead, I parked Ol' Blue next to the plastic motorcycle-wannabe.

The front door of this not-open business was open and Guy was inside, sitting in a booth with Abby Langston's daddy. Neither of them were quick enough to look up at me and I caught the tail end of Langston's words.

". . . You'd sure think he would have offered every assistance."

Guy was frowning, and muttered back. "If Harper won't give a blood sample voluntarily, well, I mean, he must have something to hide. But no, that doesn't make sense, of course he can't have had anything to do with . . ." Guy saw me and got up with open arms to try and hug me.

Langston said hey to me as he rose, allowing as to how he and Guy about had things wrapped up so he should excuse himself.

My mind was trying to catch up, but it was tailing so far behind I was never going to make it, not today, not tomorrow. Guy got to blabbing, but I wasn't listening because some of my brain cells were chewing on what I overheard. About busted a fan belt inside my skull, the thinking gears whirred so hard.

Keith Langston rubbed his temples as he made for the door. "I've got to check on my kid. She's about dropped her basket, lately. Says she's sick. I think she's playing hooky, but she's old enough to stay home by herself."

"Thanks again, good talking to you," Guy hollered, loud enough for me to know I was being corrected for my missing manners.

"Bye," I called, getting a wave from Langston in response. Soon as he was gone, I demanded of Guy, "What's all this? What were you guys jawing about?"

Guy nodded like Talking Time had come due. "Well, we both gave statements, blood samples, fingerprints, everything the police asked for, but Keith heard a rumor that Harper wouldn't give blood, just fingerprints. And the investigator didn't think he could get a warrant for—"

"Huh? Winston Harper? Warrant?"

"Harper was with us too, you see."

Guy had left out a few things and that, coming from Mr. Let's Talk About Everything, was pretty rich. I took a seat in the booth across from him. "He was with you . . . when?"

"When Patsy-Lynn Harper died that afternoon. When you were with Keith Langston's daughter, shoeing her horse. We're each other's, well, witness, alibi."

Alibi is a word that provokes consideration. I pushed myself back in the booth, farther from Guy. "Why would they be wanting blood samples from all of you? If you were together, you don't need to be eliminated from the Harper garage."

Guy shrugged. "I didn't ask. Maybe they were just covering all the bases."

But they couldn't cover all the bases if one of the three wouldn't give a blood sample. Could Langston or Harper have been driving that truck to the Flying Cross as I was leaving that afternoon? I remembered the clerk taking my fingerprints, talking about police things like consent and probable cause. There was quite a bit more going on than I understood. The sheriff's man got a blood sample from Keith Langston? It occurred to me again that Langston was a man without a woman . . . unless he had a woman on the side. Could Abby's daddy have had something secret with Patsy-Lynn? The Langstons did live pretty much right across the highway from the Harpers.

People have secrets, that's for sure.

"Rainy?"

"Explain all this." I bellowed to help Guy understand that he was the one being a bonehead. "What are you doing here, in this place?"

"Well. We're going to have a restaurant, trying to, anyway. Surprise." He paused, leaning back and fairly gushing in a grin. "What do you think about calling it *Rainy's?*"

My name means my shoeing business, which is all mine. It's me. I'm the one who makes the appointments and keeps them, shapes the shoes. I nip and rasp and nail. I clinch. I eyed Guy. "You're giving me a size 5 headache."

"And size 5s are the really big horseshoes, right?"

I nodded. It had taken Guy a while to learn to tell a triple aught pony shoe from a burly draft horse's size 3, 4, or even 5 footwear. He thought a size 5 nail would go in a size 5 shoe, too. It flips him that for much of my work, I use size 5 nails in shoes that are size 0, 1, or 2.

"I'll get you some aspirin." Guy hopped up. Lickety-split, he rounded up a glass of water and two white tablets.

I took the bitter pills. "What were you and Langston talking about when I walked in here?"

"The restaurant, of course." Guy beamed.

"No. You weren't." I looked at him stiff and square to let him know he'd best come clean.

His eyeballs took a couple circuits around their sockets, then an Oh Yeah look showed up. "The blood samples. And I mentioned you were going to the police station."

"You mentioned that, did you?"

Guy did a frown with the nod. "Why? Does it bother you that I mentioned it?"

I took one hand off my head long enough to wave a demand for him to keep trying to explain himself, encouraging him with, "Keep going."

"Well, fine. Keith and I both thought it was remarkable that Winston Harper wouldn't give a blood sample. After all, he certainly wasn't at home when his wife died."

"You never told me that you knew Harper couldn't have been the one headed to the Flying Cross as I left. You were all Mr. Gee Whillickers when I was chewing on this stuff before."

His eyeballs took another lap. "Rainy, I had this surprise cooking, so I didn't tell you about my business with Keith Langston and Winston Harper. This is a big deal."

"Isn't you giving a blood sample for a murder investigation a big deal?"

"I have a dream." Guy made a tiny speech that no doubt had the good Dr. King spinning. "Thanks for your enthusiasm and support."

"When did you give the deputies blood? The night they first questioned me?"

"Later in the week, like you. They asked a lot of people."

That made no sense to me. And why didn't they ask me right away? "And they asked these business associates of yours? The ones you never mentioned to me?"

Guy shrugged, going all the way with pretending I wasn't mad at him. "Not Keith at first. I guess they've asked Winston Harper a couple times."

"But, really, what's Langston got to do with anything here?"

Guy looked around the ghost restaurant. "He's helping with financing, setting up the business end, helped get Harper to come on as a backer."

"So, you're trying to get money out of Winston Harper."

Guy looked offended, sitting up straighter and squinting at me with his jaw set.

I felt defensive, too. "I mean, he's my client. He is now. And you never said."

"Well, Keith and I think your client ought to give the sheriff's office a tube of blood. We cooperated. So did you. And you gave fingerprints, although that was regarding the vet's office, right?" Guy beamed. "Your alibi for when that happened is that you were at that chili-feed cow-catching-thing."

Reconsidering that crowd at Weatherby's—I needed to have a think about Ted and his boyfriend—I was a little impressed with how Guy had obviously already thought about the Harper stuff and the vandalism at the vet's office. "You know who wasn't at the hootenanny?" I hadn't intended to speak out loud, I was just thinking too hard.

"What is a hootenanny?"

He knew high well my meaning, so his words needed ignoring. I held out a few fingers to commence counting. "Dixon Talbot wasn't there. Winston Harper wasn't, but his son was. Lots of regular horse people were there, like Felix Schram. Weatherby was there, of course, being it's his place."

"Who else?"

"Keith Langston wasn't there." I said, counting off a third right finger.

"Well, fine, but why would he be?" Guy said.

"The sheriff should know about this," I said. "He wasn't there either."

Cowdry's as far as it can get from the county seat, which is why the deputies' office over here is just a few rooms in a strip mall. Maybe because Magoutsen isn't kicking around here day and night, he makes an easy target for some good old boys to smirk and call him Mr. Magoo. People who ride on glass horses and all that sticks and stones stuff would seem to say a person shouldn't be teased for his name, certainly not the sheriff. Teasing's awful and really finds my fire. It should be outlawed in early adolescence, that's for sure and for certain.

Rainy fainy fatty. Fatty, fatty, fainy Rainy.

They'd needed new material in the worst of ways, those skinny, trendy witches and their preppie boyfriends. Their kind of bullying was, well, it wasn't physical, but I'd have rather it was. After I'd get miserable enough to get my mama to send me back to Texas, when daddy'd go on the road again it was even worse to think about coming back to the school in Los Angeles. I dreaded facing those bully-girls and their talk.

Then one day they let me come to a party. They said they were my friends and they gave me beer.

They introduced me to Jesse.

And things went downhill from there, but I didn't know it at first. Blamed near wrecked my life over it all. In a lunge, I shoved away from Guy and his old pizza joint table then and there. I needed air. Made for the door, telling Guy to give me some space.

But outside, all over again, I felt put upon because Ol' Blue's longhorn hood ornament was gone.

Chapter 19

FOR CRYING OUT LOUD, WHO'D BOTHER my truck? I marched right back into the old pizza place. Plastic booths, some patched with duct tape, chipped tables, stained carpet. All stuff I hadn't paid attention to when I first spied Keith Langston and Guy inside. Outside, the strip mall effect dimmed the beauty that is Oregon, part buttes and prairies, mixed with mountains and evergreen forests. Crowding out that natural world with flickering fluorescent lights so a body wouldn't even know what's being missed seemed like a terrible idea.

Did Guy really think he was going to turn this dump into an upscale eatery?

"Rainy? Is that you? Are you okay?" Guy entered the beater dining area from the commercial kitchen.

"My truck was ripped off."

"Your tools?" He looked appropriately concerned, setting aside his dream for my dirt. I knew he'd been none too thrilled with my refusal to chat about his Big Dream. I'd been adjusting to that idea, among others. The back of my brain nagged me to try thinking on some things, but wasn't exactly fetching a pencil and making a list.

"The hood ornament. Someone ripped it off. I saw Dixon Talbot on my way here." No need to say I was following him instead of the other way around.

"Oh, he's a horseshoer, right?"

I nodded. "Drives a black truck. Not too keen on me, being as I did quick fixes for a couple of his clients this week." I wondered if he hated me enough to try to frame me.

"I saw a big dark pickup truck drive by while you and I were talking," Guy said, frowning. "Someone really, like, vandalized your truck?"

"Like that." My back had been to the window when I came inside on Guy and Keith Langston. I twisted my ponytail now and gave it a tug.

"Well that's the kind of thing that doesn't usually happen around here."

"I'd say." And I'd say more unless I kept my lips from flapping, but here goes. "I don't get the deal with the police looking at you and Keith Langston. It doesn't make sense. Where were you meeting that afternoon she died?"

Guy squirmed. "We were here. All three of us."

"There's more to it."

He studied the sorry carpet. "I guess Harper's son told the police Patsy-Lynn wasn't big on his dad investing in this. And he said there was money missing from their house."

It was all a little fuzzy. A vandalized shoer's truck notwithstanding, Cowdry doesn't see much evil. And the police thought Guy might have killed her to get backing on an eatery? I had news for them and him. "I'm another alibi. I could clear you of being the one who was driving up to the Harpers' that day. How does that grab you?"

Looking like I'd landed my anvil in his back, Guy gaped like a guppy for a while then said, "That's a little weird, Rainy. It's well established where I was that afternoon."

"But people make mistakes. And people lie. Maybe the po-lice thought your, um, alibi wasn't as good as you thought."

"My alibi is fine. And I can't believe anyone really thought for a second that I had something to do with the poor woman's death."

"There was cash missing from the Harper place, and you had all that money in the cookie jar."

"Rainy!" Guy fair gasped. "That was all your rent money!"

I gave him the shrug that Abby'd schooled me on so well. This earned me an annoyed look and a little old tirade.

"You thought you had a way to clear me—not that I need it— yet you kept quiet? It doesn't grab me really well. How does that grab you?" Guy said this with a little spunk.

"Shabby," I admitted.

"We're so much alike, you and me," he said.

This ought to be good. We were alike in no way. Anticipation built up as I fixed to see how Guy's new We're So Alike game was going to go.

"I don't get it," I said when he didn't elaborate, not bothering to make the long list of things I didn't get.

"I know you understand what it's like." Guy was on a roll. "We both went to trade school and are self-employed—I mean, I'm self-employed in my catering business and I will be with the restaurant once I get my own place. We're making it with both our heads and our hands. We create. We serve others. I see a lot of similarities in our jobs. And they're not just jobs, they're callings for both of us. Don't you see that?"

Guy bustled back to that commercial kitchen, waving his arms like he was directing traffic. "I've got to show you something. Would you come here?"

In the kitchen, Guy set out a plate of dark brown ravioli with smooth white gravy on top and some green leaves on the side. "Dessert. Chocolate ravioli with cream sauce and mascarpone filling. Mint garnish."

Took a taste to be polite. Got four on the spoon and packed them into my ravioli-hole. These chocolate ravioli? They were way better than Milk Duds. Quick as can be, I belonged to the clean plate club.

Guy grinned. "Do you want more?"

What I wanted was to be nice. So I really tried to make nice talk about his dream, this restaurant that will not be named Rainy's.

* * *

There was a horse show that weekend, so in the afternoon, I went and found a spot to hang out with my forge fired up, waiting for work. I got to do three quick shoe fixes and hoped I might get future clients out of the deal. It was one of those mixed events, good for getting to know a wider range of horse folk. There were a few English style classes, kids' gymkhana, western pleasure and roping, plus a practice endurance ride had headed out early in the morning, with the last of their forty-milers not due back 'til late afternoon.

By then the calf-ropers were sponging off their sweaty horses as the team ropers started their final jackpot round. Sheriff Magoutsen moseyed my way, giving a nod.

I wagged my noggin right back at Mr. Magoo, then thought cuss words over that teasing tag being in my brain. Luckily, I didn't open my mouth, but I wondered if Deputy Paulden had told him I wasn't the one who busted up the veterinarian's office with a rounding hammer.

"I didn't," I said.

"You didn't what?"

Since I'm an idiot, I babbled on, telling him about not vandalizing the vet's office, thinking all the while that if someone had wanted to make it look like I had done it, leaving shoer's tools was smart.

But it didn't make sense that Dixon Talbot would break into Nichol's office to get me in trouble, since he's a shoer too.

Unless he had a great alibi.

A false one.

"Rainy, didn't you go over to that last deal over at the Rocking B?"

I nodded, thinking hard enough to steam my brain. If I hadn't accidentally hung on to the bute Weatherby wanted me to hand over to Schram, then I probably wouldn't have even been asked to the Rocking B hootenanny. Dixon Talbot hadn't been there, so he might not have known I was at Weatherby's that night. Most evenings, I'm just home. Maybe Talbot had a fake alibi all ready, then went and beat up Nichol's office and planted the hammer. I realized the sheriff was watching me and I didn't want him to think he'd missed out on a swell party. "It was a great hootenanny provided you'd never been to one before."

He chuckled a nod and I swear—if I was the type to swear—watched me sideways as we both watched the next steer make fools of two horses and two grown men. Then it occurred to me Magoutsen knew clear as glass I'd been at Weatherby's. He knew exactly who'd been there and who was missing.

A new distraction kept him from torturing me. We both looked up to watch a group of endurance riders come in to practice vet-checking their horses. It was the first I'd noticed that Nichol was working beyond the main arena. He and a woman vet started checking pulses, listening to the sweaty horses' chests and bellies with stethoscopes, pinching their skin and lifting their tails. Riders moved their mounts into shade. Crew started sponging over the blowing horses' great blood vessels, along the horses' necks and high up inside the legs. The riders grinned and joked with each other as they readied for another ten or twenty miles.

Some of them were talking about how well conditioned the leaders—a couple riding with their teenager—were.

"Drew and his family, they've been trotting the Forest Service roads this side of the Buckeye ranch, doing a lot of interval work the last couple months," one fellow nodded, sponging his dancing, steaming horse. "They said they heard a lone horse out there."

"I heard it, too," a young gal with soggy braids sticking out of her helmet said, all serious-like. "A horse was calling somewhere in Dry Valley but we never did meet up with another rider. Must have been trailered to the first spur road, other side of Stakes Ridge. Off Black Ridge. Don't know anyone who rides there."

I was studying the horses' feet, the hard-worn toes of the front shoes, breaking over their hooves nice and quick. Nice feet, nice shoeing. One of them interfered a bit though. The gelding had mild scars on the insides of his legs where he'd struck himself with his own hooves. I wondered who their shoer was, but couldn't ask 'cause that kind of question can seem like I'm bidding for the job, a no-no among shoers.

Okayed by the vets to keep going, the riders pulled out at a hardy trot. I figured it wouldn't turn into a race with these folks until the last mile. Until then, they rode like friends.

Sheriff Magoutsen walked on over to Nichol and they talked together, then Magoutsen came back and said something to me while I was thinking about how the backcountry riders use their horses like horses. By the time I paid the sheriff any mind, I reckon he'd already tried me one or two times. I gave him my Sorry face and he tried again.

"This is a nice clean group of horse folk, don't you think?"

"Yessir."

"And this is your adopted state?"

Gripping my elbows to keep myself from jumping out of my skin was about all I could do. I couldn't talk.

He could. "You're still new in Oregon. You like it here in Cowdry? Getting a good client base, aren't you?"

I nodded.

He did too and said, "It's good to see young people settling here. You meet a lot of different horse owners."

Nodding was something I could still manage.

"Rainy, you'll let us know if you see or hear something that doesn't sit right?"

Breathing out while talking low, I could handle now. "Yessir. I'll do that."

But I wasn't doing it. I'd have to make myself come clean.

Sheriff Magoutsen eyed across the grounds at all the horses and riders and trailers and other rigs. Buckets and dust and dogs, people talking, some hurrying, some not.

Confession time. "At Patsy-Lynn Harper's funeral, one of your men . . ."

"Yes?" Magoutsen was a watcher.

"He asked me about drugs."

"Go ahead," the sheriff said.

"The truth is, I was asked to carry some bute from one client to another."

"Bute."

"Yessir."

"You're sure it was bute?"

That question had never occurred to me. "Pretty sure. It was syringes of paste and tablets, he had both kinds. Do you want me to tell you all about that?"

The sheriff smiled and put a hand on my shoulder. "If I do, I'll let you know."

As I left for the day, I considered what Sheriff Magoutsen said, then thought more about the rider saying a horse was hollering in the first valley—that'd be Dry Valley—and distracting the long riders.

All of the sudden I knew what had been bothering me, one thing, anyways.

I'm a detective of horseshoeing, that's what I am.

Just how often did horse theft happen these days, in these parts? Was I the only one who perked up about the idea of a horse hollering in the backcountry? On the way home I detoured from the show grounds with fresh eyes, soon rattling Ol' Blue over the cattle guard at the head of the Solquists' driveway.

Suppose the missing mare hadn't wandered off, but really was stolen?

To tow a trailer right up to the Solquist house, even if they were gone for the night, wouldn't work well here 'cause what if the thief was spotted by a next-door neighbor, or a fence-line neighbor like the Langstons? Plus, the Solquists' driveway was straight, no turn-around room for a trailer. Backing a rig took time, especially in the dark of night.

The question on the table was how to steal the Solquists' horse. I'd no idea who or why, but it seemed I could figure out how if I gave the situation a good looking-at and plenty of thought. Was she shod? Could she be ridden away?

The Missus came out of the house then, gave me and Ol' Blue a looking-at and a nod. "You shoe for the Langstons, right?"

"That's right. Rainy Dale." I wondered who shod for her, why her gelding was overdue and if the missing mare was in the same shape.

"Can I help you with something?"

Made me feel a little silly, the idea I was a horseshoeing detective, at the lady's house just because I had that kind of time on my hands and loose ideas in my mind. "I heard about your mare gone missing. I guess curiosity made me come take a look-see."

Mrs. Solquist sighed. "Our daughter's away in college and heart-broken to hear that Misty's been stolen. It just doesn't make any sense. Our gelding's a bigger, better horse. We called the police but there's not much they can do, apparently. We're putting flyers up at the co-op and different trailheads, and we put it on out to the auctions. Why would someone want to take our little mare?"

We were agreed that it was a shame and I left still scratching my skull about the how of it, never mind the who and the why. The only other clue I'd noticed was that the Solquists didn't have a dog, at least not one who came out to woof at me. Leading the horse away might have been the quietest and quickest thing to do. If I'd wanted to liberate Liberty's neighbor, it would have been easiest to just lead her by the house, drive away with her in a trailer that I left on the highway.

But, no, there was a problem with that plan, the cattle guard, a grate over a ditch that hooved animals refuse to walk across, which is how cattle guards make sort-of gates that a vehicle can drive right over.

My mind circled this puzzle all the way home, then it hit me. There's exactly one good way to get a horse over a cattle guard, but it's heavy and awkward—a four-foot by eight-foot piece of plywood. I'd found the evidence days ago, but I'd chopped it up to make my new shoeing tool box.

* * *

I don't know what kind of trinket store he found it in, but Guy had a little tiny paperweight-sized anvil. It was kind of cute, if a girl was given to liking cute things, which of course I'm not.

"What's this?" I asked, wishing I could ask things that mattered.

He was beaming. "A pocket anvil."

I made gentle and explained. "A Pocket Anvil is sort of like a rebar bender. It's also called a Shoe Shaper. It's a way to shape horseshoes without having to haul out the anvil stand and anvil and bang around making plenty of noise."

"Ah," he said.

I'm pretty sure I lost him at "rebar" but there's no telling. We were saved from this alien conversation of no-understanding by the bell.

Chapter 20

THE EMERGENCY CALL WAS FROM NICHOL, an acute laminitis—
inflammation of the sensitive laminae under the hoof wall.
Chronic laminitis, a shoer treats, but in acute cases, especially if
they're extra gnarly, horses need both of us, vet and shoer. He was
calling from the Flying Cross.

Before I got Ol' Blue properly stopped, I heard the screaming.

Spartacus's thick neck arched with rage and his little Quarter
Horse nostrils flared like he'd gone Thoroughbred. Nichol was
talking quiet-like to him from the safe side of the rails, a syringe
in one hand. Beside him, Ted, the barn-help dude, wearing what
looked like the same blue-checkered shirt and jeans he wore the
last time I did shoeing for Patsy-Lynn, held a halter and a thick
lead rope with a stud chain.

"How was Spartacus landing before? Was he a level traveler?"
Nichol asked.

"He was straight and clean," I said. "Just a little flare on the
right hind that was getting better with time."

Ted opened the gate. I slid in a slow glide meant to not further
upset the agitated horse, glad I could hear the guys coming in right
behind me.

The studhorse started to wheel in the paddock, making like he was going to try to scoop out our spleens and use them to decorate the walls of the big barn. He's a cresty-necked hunk of horse with enough power to kill, but he decided kicking put too much weight on his front end. Spartacus tucked his hind legs back under himself, way under, and reconsidered any activity that involved slamming or even weighting his front feet. Those front hooves hurt and he wanted off of them.

Nichol had to be careful about sedating because to deal with those hooves we needed Spartacus to still have a pain response, but we also needed him to quit trying to kill us. It took me and Nichol and Ted together, using a stud chain over Spartacus's nose, a twitch, and two syringes, before we got the digital X-rays shot.

"Have you read radiographs?" Nichol asked me.

"X-rays, yeah," I said. And I whistled at the pictures, looked back at Spartacus's left front, and groaned. I was needed here. A partial resection of his toe, that's what was called for. A very careful trim using the films as a guide, and a special-built shoe that would let him put more weight on his frog. His right front hoof was foundering too, but not as bad.

By the time we were done, I had blood on my chaps.

Anytime a shoer gets blood, someone screwed up. In this case, Nichol and Ted didn't pay one hundred-plus percent attention when Spartacus didn't cooperate, leaving me vulnerable.

Back in shoeing school, they joked about blood, shoer's or horse's, meaning experience. This was an experience Spartacus would have been happier to live without. Unlike the last emergency horse Nichol and I had worked on together, there was no thanks from this big stallion. Not the grateful sort, him. Spartacus pinned his ears and swished his tail. Drugged as he was with sedatives and painkillers, the stud tried to strike with a hind leg, showing the scrape Patsy-Lynn had thought was from kicking out a fence board a week or so back. The minor injury was still red and ugly. Again, the hurting horse remembered he didn't want extra weight on his front end. He snaked his head and neck, teeth bared at the man turning him loose.

Ted avoided the assault and scurried back to safety out of the paddock.

"I haven't been around this stud all that much," Nichol said, "but this sure is an ugly side of him to see."

Spartacus grabbed his water bucket and flung it, spooking when water splashed and the bucket tumbled.

I said, "That horse has gone loony is about the size of it."

Nichol furrowed up his face toward me. "Have you been around him much?"

"Shoeing him about a year. He's usually a bit of a baby, one of those who rocks and sways and can hardly handle being corrected for it."

Nichol's eyebrows hiked up. The stud before us would have hurt somebody for sport at this point. True, Spartacus never used to be such a nasty cuss, but pain is something that changes everyone.

"No shoeing or significant hoof problems at all?"

While Nichol frowned at Spartacus ahead of us, I shook my head and stepped back to speak low to Ted.

"Hey, I'm curious. You hear anything about any of Patsy-Lynn's tools going missing?"

"You mean the leaf blower or hedge trimmer or whatever? She and Junior thought Manny swiped them."

"Manny?"

"The Mexican she had doing some work here. Repainted this whole place for her, too. Doesn't have a car. What, was he going to walk away carrying her trimmer?"

I'd have thought Ted would have been happy to have someone other than himself suspected of wrongdoing at the Flying Cross, then I remembered that Ted might have a reason to protect Manuel Smith.

Nichol turned to us. "Feed changes? Too much spring grass?"

I nodded as Ted shook his head. Laminitis in the springtime is almost always caused by the excess sugars and starches in the rich new grass causing a colic, then the disturbed gut leaks toxins, which cause a laminitic episode. While Nichol grilled Ted on feed changes that Ted denied, I slipped down the barn aisle toward the tack room.

When I heard the banging in the end stall, I remembered how Patsy-Lynn had hurried past this stall. Heart thumping, I opened the upper door. A lovely chestnut, like my Red, thrust her head out, ears pinned.

"I don't blame you," I told the angry redhead. Horses weren't meant to live in cells. She was no doubt here to be serviced by Spartacus and I could only hope her owners would come for her soon and she had a pasture at home.

Patsy-Lynn never did get her new paneling up, but it was a lovely tack room. The scent of leather met me. I looked past the bins of clean brushes, the well-oiled tack on hooks and racks, the shelves of medical supplies and fence repair gear. I looked for a little tool collection that some horse people keep. And I found it.

There was no nailing hammer or rounding hammer, but there were a couple of rasps—of which one was new and one was very used, probably an old one I'd given to Patsy-Lynn, and a set of pull-offs. Common as straw, standard stuff to take off a loose shoe in a pinch. Sometimes horse owners buy quickie shoeing kits that come with cheapie tools, including driving and rounding hammers, even though no one needs a rounding hammer unless they're going to shape shoes on an anvil. I tried to think about other clients who once had a rounding hammer they didn't need.

That day I shod for Schram, I hadn't looked in his tack room. Back then, I hadn't had my suspicion meter turned on, but now I wondered exactly when Felix women-like-it-rough Schram came and left the Rocking B get-together, and if he'd been to the vet's office with a rounding hammer that same night.

But I couldn't think long on Felix Schram and his tools 'cause I was looking at a baggie of vials in the Harpers' tack room. They must have fallen down from the medical shelf above. The vials' labels were peeled away. I took the baggie over to the light at the doorway to get a better look, thinking that they should be in the fridge if'n they were vaccines.

"You bet!" Junior's booming voice echoed down the barn aisle with bootsteps on the way.

I about scraped my spooked self off the ceiling and panicked to get out of the tack room, shoving the baggie into my jeans pocket on my way out.

The three men were at the aisle's edge, talking breeding. Junior wanted to go artificial insemination with Spartacus next season. Getting down to business, so to speak.

"Absolutely. You bet," he told Nichol again.

With enough bookings and a hefty stud fee, a stallion can naturally cover enough mares to make a small mint, but with artificial insemination there's no limit except demand, so at a couple thousand bucks a pop, AI can generate big bucks. But Spartacus . . . well, there's money in breeding studs once they've got a reputation of producing good progeny, but he hadn't been around too long and wasn't proven.

Nichol walked out to the truck with his gear and Ted moseyed off to a wheelbarrow, pushing it down the barn aisle, but stopped when Junior blocked his way.

"We're not having Brokeback at the Flying Cross. No visitors, got it? Keep your boyfriend visits off the ranch." Then Junior turned and tossed a horseshoe at me. "One of the new horses lost a hind shoe. Again."

I caught the rusted shoe left-handed. My right hand was still in my pocket, sweating about getting the baggie back into the tack room.

The rusty shoe was nearly circular in shape, but it wasn't level. It had a twist to it and nails curved out from the medial side. I didn't know whose shoe I was holding, but I did know it wasn't likely to be from any horse's hind foot—it was just too round. Hind feet don't have that shape; they're pointier in the toe and not as wide through the quarters.

"If we're going to have problems with your shoes staying on, we're going to be getting another shoer." Junior lunged toward me. I jumped back, my face turned away. All that old fear boiled up. I thought I was about to be hit, but Junior just snatched the shoe back.

Down the aisle, Ted met my gaze and raised his eyebrows.

I tried to think about what I knew, what was real and what mattered. Horse feet. Patsy-Lynn only had the riding horses shod up front, left the hind feet bare.

Junior scowled at me, looming large like the human hulk he was. He shook a finger in my face to commence a lecture, but the hand became a fist and his jaw clenched, too. Any sane woman, any smart person, would have backed up. I worked to stifle a gulp. Couldn't do it. Junior was just a hair from exploding.

His voice rang off the metal barn roof. "Are we clear?"

Actually, we were a pretty long ways from clear. What I wanted to say was that neither of us was perfect, but at least I didn't shtup the local hottie at my stepmama's funeral reception. But I didn't have the ornery in me to share that with him. Really, it was self-preservation keeping my mouth shut. This wasn't my first time standing in front of a man who was looking for an excuse to thump on me, but this time was going to hurt bad. I'd be getting coloring books for presents if Junior smacked me in the head a couple times. I hated being scared of him.

"Everything all right?" Nichol called, striding toward us.

My relief came out in a sigh, but I hated how rescued I felt.

Junior snarled that we could both bill his old man for our work and it would be my last check. He punched a finger at my face. "You're fired."

What would have happened if Nichol hadn't been there? Six years old and spanked, that's how I felt as Junior stormed off. Seventeen years old and smacked for not having the right dinner ready.

But that wasn't me anymore. I'm me now. Now.

Farriers get fired. Someone else comes in with a different idea or a lower price or the owner isn't a big enough person to accept that he's a moron who ought to take better care of his horses and property and—

And the thing is, I've never been fired. A year here now and my client list only builds. I've even let a couple clients go, the third-tier type folks that don't keep appointments, don't pay up, that kind of hog hale. But Harpers had been a good account, at least five mares, the stud, and other peoples' mares who rotated in and out, plus sometimes a riding horse or two. Though I'd always worked for Patsy-Lynn, hardly seen hide nor hair of her husband or stepson. Junior didn't even live in Cowdry most of the time, was the way I understood it. I thought the horses had been mainly her deal. Guess they were Mister and Junior's deal now. But Junior was stacking up to be a bully-boy who needed nothing so much as a speedy de-boying with my hoof knife.

So now I got to see how Nichol would treat me after Harper Junior bawled me out. We were both needing to get our gear back into our rigs, but I didn't want to do it under anyone smirking at me.

Nichol glanced toward the barn and seemed to change his mind on something. Instead, he said, "Do you do anything with camel-ids?"

Usually, I'd like to know if someone wants to give me a test but if it's this easy to ace, I don't mind grabbing a quick A. I shrugged Abby-style. "I do a few."

It wasn't true, what they'd said in shoeing school, that real horseshoers were struck down by lightning right away if a llama's cloven hoof touches their chaps.

"Those critters sure have caught on," Nichol added. I reckon this was by way of showing he was just having a conversation, not checking to see if I knew a three-dollar word, *camelid*.

I grinned. "Yep, the fiber freaks across the highway have a huge herd." Those alpaca and llama people sell bales of wool—they call it fiber—every year, and their critters need their toes done regular enough, though not quite as often as a well-used riding horse. Often enough to keep a shoer's horse-friend in hay though.

Nichol's conversation was a relief after my lecture from Junior.

"There's been a conference this weekend down at the college," Nichol said as he stuck his head and hands in his vehicle, loading up a couple medical kits and a cooler where he kept drugs. "I'm going down in the morning to catch the last of it. Do you want to come along?"

"And what's this conference on?" I asked, turning away just as casually to load up my stuff.

"Headlining with land management, special section on BSE." He tapped one finger against his temple. "Just more tools for the old toolbox."

When did the yuppie-types start saying *toolbox* when they meant knowledge? And hadn't I already taken a quiz from him? I know what Bovine Spongiform Encephalopathy is and I don't reckon it'd be cured this weekend.

"Not my field," I pointed out.

"Well, there's a section on non-equine hoof care and an equine lameness segment in the afternoon."

"Really?" I perked right up. I hadn't heard about a clinic and I do keep my ear to the ground for that kind of thing. There's a reason why I'm not like a lot of newer shoers who basically repeat their first several years over and over. I've put so much mental and physical effort into this job choice of mine, I'm a sponge. Sponge-form, no longer bovine-shaped, and no encephalopathy. Though I'd been well on my way to being a bovine-shaped, corn-fed, breeder-type in school, that changed. Look at me now, a good shoer, slim and strong, and always eager to improve my work through clinics, experience, and working with anyone who could teach me something. I had clients aplenty, though I could no longer count the ranch of the one who'd been maybe murdered.

Handy enough, my brain found the next gear and the clutch disengaged, so when Nichol pulled his head out of his fancy rig, I asked about the lameness conference. He said, chatty-like, "Oh, according to the program there's a session for horse owners, so shoeing instructors will be there. And the shoers have some kind of session, too."

Among the owners who think they're going to be their own shoer, a few are worth the time of day, but most are not motivated enough to help their horses and shouldn't be messing around with anything more complicated than their own toenails.

"I could pick you up bright and early," Nichol said. "I'm coming back tomorrow night."

Getting out of town for a day had some real appeal. I followed the notion and told Nichol I was in; he could come get me.

* * *

Shedding my boots outside Guy's house at least kept Spooky from puking on them, but there was no stopping that fine, flying hair he put everywhere. Charley was happy to see me. He wasn't the only one.

"I waited up for you," Guy said. "Hungry?"

"Yep. Are you still going to be able to start a new restaurant if Mr. Harper doesn't back you?"

"I think he'll back it. He's still interested." Guy piled broken crab legs into the blender with some water and made an unholy racket grinding them up for his garden.

My thinking scattered in about five directions at once. "Was Patsy-Lynn maybe not wanting her hubby to spend money on your restaurant?"

"Look, even if she wasn't thrilled, her disapproval wouldn't necessarily have been a deal-breaker. Winston Harper said he likes community investment opportunities."

"What's the deal clincher, then?"

Guy sighed, like we were a long way from understanding and I guess we were. "There're some things to work out." Pretty soon, he put a slice of weird pie at the ready. I pulled up a chair at the dinette and shoveled some in my weird-pie-hole.

"Good stuff," I allowed, 'cause manners say I have to say that. "What is it?"

"Seafood frittata." Guy looked a trifle annoyed that I'd had to ask. He pushed over some silica gel packets that apparently came in the last batch of spices he'd bought.

I bet Nichol was sitting down to steak and potatoes for a late plateful. And I don't know where the thought came from, but I bet Nichol would be perfectly willing to save little packets of silica gel for me. He probably gets them all the time in stuff that's shipped to his vet office.

"Come to bed with me tonight?" Guy smiled up, earnest and sweet as a person can be.

I couldn't take much more of that.

When I didn't respond he tried an extra enticement. "I'll vacuum the pillows."

"No, I'm shoving off early, conference thing in Corvallis. Going to ride down with Nichol." I turned away and heard Guy coming after me as I cleared the kitchen, headed for the side door to the garage, Charley at my side.

"The vet? You're going down to Corvallis with him?" Guy followed me to the garage. Which is my space, I pay for it. I turned to give him a good growl, but he stopped at the doorway, like he'd remembered some manners. "Look, Rainy, I'd just like to kind of nail down our relationship here a little. Are we still together?"

I looked at Guy and thought, well, I thought a whole lot of things. I know a bit about nailing things and clinching them, after all, that's me. But I know nothing about nailing down a relationship. Nothing.

"Ask me a shoeing detective question," I suggested.

"What, like about that hammer the deputy brought over here?"

Guy tries too hard sometimes. Anyone should know that all I'd really wanted was for him to shut up, but he kept flailing away at the quicksand of my mood.

He rubbed his jaw. "That hammer that was at the vet's place. You know, like the one you use, to nail on horseshoes."

I was ice. "That was a rounding hammer, used to shape shoes, not a nailing hammer." And I gave him a pre-growl look.

Guy bit back with "Please, don't do that."

"Do what?"

"Look at me like I'm an idiot. There's nothing wrong with not knowing the difference between a nailing hammer and a rounding hammer."

I growled and gave him the You're An Idiot look again. This sure wasn't a night when Guy would launch into singing "If I Had a Hammer" in his usual good mood. I sighed. The emergency call had broken my evening routine. I still needed to take care of Red, but I gave Guy this scrap. "I'm going to Corvallis on a professional thing."

What would have happened if Guy had been at the Flying Cross instead of Nichol when Junior all but belted me?

"I've got to feed Red."

Outside, I scowled at Ol' Blue, resting my hands over the little hole in my hood's center. Who'd bothered my truck? And why? Dixon Talbot? Just because? And did he break into Nichol's office? Then Guy was beside me, cupping a palm over my fists.

"I can fix that." Guy's voice was gentle as though he was talking to an injured foal. Since he can't fix much outside a kitchen, and that doesn't include the plumbing and electrical matters found in such a room, I held my breath to keep ugly from coming out.

Guy said, "Give me fifteen minutes."

I suppose I owed him that much.

By the time I got back from feeding Red and telling him again how sorry I was for his getting sold back in the day, blinking away the awfulness of how I didn't fix things that mattered more, Guy was done, capping a bottle of stinky contact cement.

The little anvil he'd thought was a Pocket Anvil now rode the front center of Ol' Blue. My work truck again had a hood ornament, a real horseshoer's hood ornament, way better than miniature Texas longhorns.

Wasn't it silly that I teared up?

Chapter 21

A Ford Expedition with a leather interior makes for a mighty comfy few hours' road trip, yes indeedy. Nichol picked me up early enough for the morning to be cold, and pointed out the seat-heating button.

We both eyed Red dozing in the side pasture when we drove out, and Nichol asked, "Been getting in much riding?"

"Not enough." I always say that. What would be enough?

We had the same vocabulary about horse feet, could talk physiology, anatomy, gaits, and therapeutic shoeing. It was nice talking horse with Nichol.

Despite Guy's sweetness and good intentions, we just aren't alike enough, I reckon. No matter how he tries to present the deal, no matter how much I try to teach him just to say *riding* instead of *horseback riding*, or learn him the difference between my tools, or how to tell a bay horse from a brown. And forget him understanding the difference between overo and tobiano patterns on pintos and Paints. But Nichol? He knew these things.

"When I first met you," Nichol said, "I thought you had a bit of an attitude. If I came across as arrogant or disrespectful toward you, then I apologize."

If? As if. But since we were getting cozy and reminiscing, should I tell him I'd thought he was a total prick? I mean, turd. He was a turd. Capital T and a big, juicy one at that. Something not to kick on a hot day as he'll stick all over your shi—

"Rainy?"

"Yeah, hey." I studied him. He looked sincere, and my gaze fell from his face to what he held out. His right hand. I took it, shook it.

He watched me. Too long. Watch the road, I almost said. Someone's got to and I'd always vote for the driver to give it a run, especially once we neared I-5. It's a greenbelt of a freeway, but hardly hints at the grand forests beyond the concrete corridor. Turns out, Nichol chews cinnamon gum while he drives and his manners have him offer it to his passenger. We visited about the school we were headed to, and Nichol was properly impressed to hear I'd attended Ivy League shoeing school. He'd graduated vet school right there in Corvallis.

The forecast rain didn't show up. Before we made it to the campus, the windshield was coated in road boogers and bugs.

The main conference was mostly about pasture management, leading into laminitis issues for horses and grass production for raising beef cattle. Then they talked mad cow and watershed protection and specified risk material and advanced meat recovery and confined animal feeding operations. Blah blah blah, heard it all before. Nichol mentioned to every little group at every little break that he was just really pleased to be there. Guess he's trying to win points wherever he goes. He pumped hands and looked at me, like I was supposed to say the same thing.

I nodded. "Yep, real pleased. You bet your bippy."

There were a lot of vet types in this crowd, plus cattlemen and gentleman farmers. A lot of posturing. Jeans and clean shirts, bolo ties for those dressed-up. During the late morning break, a couple of bible-less guys in suits walked across the campus.

"Do you know who they are?" Nichol asked me, sounding like he well knew and was Answer Man if only I'd beg of him some wisdom.

"Feds?" I can be Idea Woman, if pressed.

He gawked at me and laughed, his face lit up.

"Feds?" Nichol shook his head, still laughing. "Have you ever heard of the World Anti-Doping Agency?"

"Nope." I kept myself from asking him about it. I didn't want any questions directed my way, 'cause I remembered what was in the pocket of my other jeans, the ones I'd kicked under my cot when I'd turned in for the night after Spartacus's emergency.

Toward the end of the first afternoon session, Nichol sat up front with a final Q & A panel that talked safe grass to avoid laminitis and everything else under the sun. I made my way to the gathering of horse owners and horseshoers who were having a chitchat and hands-on bit in an outdoor area across the way. Talk of preventing laminitis with this group turned into a basic owners' shoeing class, how to remove a twisted shoe, even how to tack a shoe back on in an emergency. Those demos always grow into owners' general questions and complaints about their past experiences with different shoers.

The lead instructor looked to be about a hundred and seventy years old. He had a couple of young bucks apprenticing under him, swinging hammers, getting some anvil time in hopes of taking their intern test soon.

The geezer brought to mind Willie Nelson, but with less fashion sense. He caught my watching things, realized I was one of them and nodded me over. Then one of the young knuckleheads got altogether flustered when he asked the old man for a hand pulling some clips on a shoe and I got waved up to take a turn.

"But you're just a girl," the punk said. There was more gear to be set up. I moved to the empty anvil stand and went for the last anvil. It looked to be about a hundred-twenty-five pounder. I gripped it against my body, set it on the stand, and we had no more of that just-a-girl business.

The young knucklehead was a cold shoer and could no more hand-make a horseshoe from bar stock than he was going to have any success pulling those clips. With one more nod from grandpa,

I jumped in, held the hot shoe with the tongs at something more like a forty-five-degree angle to the anvil's face. I struck steady, even blows with the rounding hammer to force a bubble of metal. The young fellow got the idea as the clip was forming, and I let him finish before we lost the heat in the shoe.

The silly man wore his jeans so tight his religion was near evident. Given that he would have numb feet if he crouched under a horse in skintight jeans, I figured he didn't really have much of a habit of shoeing. Plus, he wore Lee jeans. I'm a Wrangler person, myself, and as I've said, I wear them loose enough to crouch—and to stuff my pockets full of drugs.

The old man was another can of beans from the young fellows. He was good and sure with his nippers and rasp and had an eye that put away need for trim gauges and hoof levels. I don't use them either, mind. I use the horse's foot as my guide. But the young guys just starting out like 'em. Experience doesn't like gadgets. Pastern angles flowed right into the hoof when the old-timer was done and he had all the old cowboy ways that made me remember being a six-year-old, watching the ranch shoer while I played at shoeing, a rasp in my chubby little hands.

The old shoer where Daddy had been working kept fresh nails in one pants cuff and wrung-off points in the other, which is exactly how this grizzled guy did it here for the crowd. The young buck would likely never, never reach the old man's level of proficiency. I would try.

For a teacher, the old man wasn't much for talking. He grinned some questions over to me. One owner wanted us shoers' thoughts on a vet putting a horse with a mild lameness on enough bute to make a rideable mount.

"Some vets would," I allowed. I saw Nichol easing into the back of the crowd, his piece of talking over and done with.

"What would you do?" someone else in the audience asked me.

"I think pain is what tells us to try something else. Maybe a horse who's hurting needs to rest but if we mask that pain, he doesn't know to settle down."

The old shoer liked my advice, but also clearly enjoyed that I was willing to buck a vet's recommendation. This wasn't lost on Nichol as we headed back to Cowdry.

"Vets masking pain to make a horse rideable? You boned me," he said, grinning like the fool I expect he was raised to be.

Boned him? In his dreams.

We talked horses and horse feet and trucks and everything. We talked about Patsy-Lynn. We gabbed the whole ride home, and the talking helped me think. I shared what the sheriff's Suit Fellow told me at the funeral reception, that Patsy-Lynn's death wasn't accidental.

Nichol thought out loud. "The police think there was a fight inside the garage?"

My sigh was a quarter-miler, but Nichol had the Expedition going well over seventy. "At first," I said, "I thought it was an accident. When I realized they thought—"

But I couldn't say it, that in the beginning, the police seemed to think I'd had something to do with it.

Finally, I said, "Well, I think folks want it over, cleared up and done with. The sheriff's men seem to be looking at just about everybody in town, asking everyone—her husband and the banker and Guy included—to give interviews or fingerprints or blood samples. And apparently, the old man refused to provide a blood sample."

"That's not good," Nichol said. "Damning. Pretty typical, I think, for a woman murdered in her own home to actually not be the victim of a stranger but rather her, oh, family."

"Her husband. You can say it. I know." I fixed my gaze straight down the interstate.

Nichol rubbed his jaw and we drove in an uneasy silence.

Finally, Nichol wanted to know, "Did they ask you for a blood sample?"

I nodded, but got distracted from asking him the same question when he fired again right away.

"Did they ask you anything unusual?" Cinnamon scent filtered toward me.

"Such as?"

"Something that only you would know?"

"They wanted to know about a truck that was heading up Oldham lane as I was leaving that afternoon."

"Someone was going to the Flying Cross just as you left the day she died?" Nichol's voice held wonder.

"Oh, good for you," I said, to let him know he wasn't breaking new legal theory here.

"Harper Junior?" Nichol suggested.

"Nah, he was on the road. The detective said something about surveillance cameras and receipts to back that up."

"Makes sense that they could get all that, but have they yet?"

My mind was back in the Harper garage, the day of the funeral, deputies asking me about the truck I'd passed when I left the Flying Cross the day Patsy-Lynn died.

In my mind, I was driving Ol' Blue on Oldham lane right after I last shod for Patsy-Lynn. The dude on foot with the leather cowboy hat had his back to me once I passed him. Before that, the big, dark American truck—

I remembered the dually truck going around the man on foot, coming at me.

"What are you thinking?" Nichol asked.

I squinted, unable to remember the driver, but still annoyed with the way he took his share of lane out of the middle of the road, making me scoot my rig to the shoulder. I could hear it well, the way the engine—a gasoline engine—revved, spun down as the clutch went in, and revved again in the next gear.

Nichol was looking at me and I stared back 'til he kept his eyes on the road better.

In a few miles he let out a breath and said, "It sounds like the sheriff's department is interested in this guy you're living with."

"I'm not really living with him. I rent there." Man, I felt like a traitor.

Nichol wasn't going to let it lie. "How carefully did you vet your landlord? What do you know about him?"

"I know that the person driving that truck up to the Harper's the afternoon Patsy-Lynn died wasn't Guy. And the dude walking up at the same time, that had to be Manny. Manny Smith. Manuel. Patsy-Lynn thought he stole from her. Ted, Patsy-Lynn's barn-help, didn't seem to think so."

"Ted was at the Flying Cross with her when you left?"

I nodded. "And I have the impression that Ted and Manny are more than a little friendly."

My nod kept up with Nichol's next observation.

"I imagine the police are looking at Ted pretty hard."

Chapter 22

M Y MONDAY STARTED EARLY. FIRST THING, I pulled the jeans out from under my garage cot and studied on the vials in the baggie I'd swiped from Patsy-Lynn's tack room. The drug labels were partly missing. Only the letters *sterone enantitate* remained.

Before climbing into my clothes, I threw my wool blanket on the cold concrete garage floor and crunched a half-thousand each push-ups and sit-ups. A shoer needs core strength, it's not all in the arms and thighs. When I was fourteen, my stomach looked like a humongous beach ball. Now it's ribs and abs.

Guy was gone. Must be an early day at the Cascade if he beat me out of the house. He'd made himself scarce when I got back last evening, still pouting about me going to Corvallis with Nichol.

I pulled a dining chair over to Guy's kitchen computer. His internet connection was slow as Christmas, but I had to get this drug thing figured out and dealt with, sure enough. I typed in the part of the drug name left on the vial's ripped labels. Didn't like the answer that came up, but didn't have time to keep clicking because someone whipped a diesel rig up and honked outside. I pushed the baggie in my pocket and went to the door, saw Dixon Talbot in the driver's seat, and was not at all interested in inviting him in. I tugged on my Blundstones and went to kick the day in the teeth.

"Called you the other night," Talbot said. "Guess you were at Weatherby's. Talked to your little houseboy."

Well, here's an idea to grab hold of, I thought, feeling a surly coming on. Guy's taller than you by a long shot, don't call him *little*. And the Friday night I was at Weatherby's? Talbot knew where I was and I knew where he wasn't. "Called the house here, huh? How'd you get my number?" The landline was listed under Guy's name in the phonebook.

"From one of your . . ." He looked away and shrugged. "One of your cards."

I eyed him and took a step back, considering the whole picture. Could it have been Talbot's rig coming to the Flying Cross when I left Patsy-Lynn? I walked right to his driver's window and peeked.

Definitely stick shift. Talbot raised his eyebrows, calm enough. Maybe he'd thought I was looking to see if he had a bunch of my business cards on the truck seat.

Talbot launched into the next bone he had to pick. "You were sniffing around the Solquist place."

I parted my lips and paused, needing time before my mouth faucet leaked. "I was, uh . . ." I thought some more, fast as I could. "I was curious about their missing horse. I didn't even know you were their shoer."

Was he? Had he been the Harpers' former shoer, too?

When Patsy-Lynn hired me, I hadn't given any thought to who was her shoer before me. I should have. But isn't a year a long time to wait if you're going to chew someone out for stealing your client? And getting fired isn't exactly a motive for murder either.

Talbot shook his head. "You just don't go sniffing around horse owners like that."

This noise from a man who was probably trying to ruin me. I wondered if he'd deny tearing down my business cards, too. Was that why he was so tetchy about me being around the Solquists' little piece of land? I was about to point out a few things when he took to accusing me some more.

"You undercut us."

"Huh?"

Talbot pointed a finger at me, not quite like we were fixing to battle, but near enough. "You came into town, shoeing at a low rate. You undercut us established shoers."

"I, I . . ." I had. Strictly speaking, I had started on the cheap side, but I'd been new to the area and still fairly new to shoeing and . . . "I didn't mean to."

He barked a laugh making that giant Adam's apple bounce. "How do you not mean to do something like that?"

"I really didn't mean to undercut. I started where I did because it seemed like the right thing to do. I mean, gosh."

"Gosh?" he mimicked, as if not cursing somehow made me laughable. Fact is, I can out-mouth a rude trucker, but I like to believe I've moved beyond that.

"Last week," Talbot said, "I happened to give Winston Harper's boy a lift. He told me he might be looking for a new shoer. Know what I said?"

I shook my head, on account of my crystal ball being broke and all.

"I said shopping shoers wasn't good for owners, horses, or shoers. I shoe for the Frichtlers now, but I knew when I took the account that they were already shopping around, I wasn't taking food off another shoer's table."

"I never took anything from your table. I never took anything. I'm just trying to make it. And I was never trying to work for the Solquists. I didn't even know who shod for them. Is it you?"

Talbot glared and still wouldn't give me an answer. "You know I shod for Weatherby and Schram."

Schram sort of followed after I'd done the short-notice call-out for Weatherby, not my fault.

"I was new when I came to Cowdry," I explained, trying to get Talbot back to his other complaint. "That's why I started a little on the low end when I came here."

I made it sound like an apology and I did feel humble about it now. Really, I hadn't meant to step on anyone's toes, but looking back from where we stood, Dixon Talbot was right. I should not have underpriced my work. I'd been wrong. "I'm sorry."

Couldn't this go both ways? Was he sorry for throwing away my business cards? For ripping off my hood ornament? Why couldn't I ask him? And what really mattered here? I cleared my throat and stood tall. "Did you bust up the vet's office with a rounding hammer? Leave it there?"

Talbot's snort was so hard and sudden, spit flew. "That's ridiculous. My rounding hammer cost over two hundred dollars. My tools are my livelihood."

"Me, too." I should have asked Deputy Paulden to let me study the hammer left at the vet's office. I could have figured out if it was a cheapie, like the kind that comes in a lay kit, or the real deal, like a working shoer would own. The nippers that come in those forty-dollar kits aren't worth using as a doorstop. My nippers alone cost well over a hundred bucks.

"I got no beef with that guy who replaced Doc Vass," Talbot said as he got back in his truck. He spun out.

Squeezing time between clients to go and ask Nichol the real question became my priority. I tended to Charley and Red and got gone.

* * *

Looking sharp with my glued-on anvil hood ornament, I parked Ol'Blue at the barn of my first client, one of those book-smarty-pants types who reads lots of little things, but does hardly a handful. I'd shod for him last fall and thought his hoofpick needed to get out of the tack room. He'd not called me out to work on his

horse again 'til last week. I suspected he'd pulled the shoes for winter and not had a proper barefoot trim put on. His horse's feet
were struggling, grown out of what I reckon were his first shoes
of the year and maybe his first hoof picking, too. The earth side
of those feet had black goo and a rude stench. I trimmed away all
the necrotic hoof, made gentle mention of cleaning up the horse's
bedroom, and heard some unnecessary advice.

"Paring the frog down too much can make a horse thrushy."

Someone had been reading his junior 4-H pamphlets. Not
enough, obviously, but he'd read the part that would make the
thrush my fault. His horse lived in mud and manure up to its eyeballs. Sloppy conditions, that's the main cause of soft, smelly feet.

And sloppy thinking's been the cause of every bit of trouble I
ever had, so I'd better locate a noodle wrench and tighten up my
noodle. I tried to get this owner thinking about cleaning up his
horse's house, then turned my mind back to cleaning up my world
as I took the client's check—he didn't want to schedule the next
appointment—and moved out. There were things to consider.

Spartacus's laminitis came on so suddenly, putting him in such
pain when his front feet started dying right out from under him.
Sure, it can happen for no great reason, but generally a body can
point a finger at something like overfeeding. I thought about stuff
that other people knew, little things. A lot of folks knew a bit
about what's going on in Cowdry, I decided, including me. At my
next shoeing appointment, I was quiet and fast and got paid by
check.

Instead of an early lunch, I went to the bank and made a deposit,
mostly so I could pause at Abby's daddy's office door to ask things
that were none of my business.

Keith Langston didn't seem to find it too awful strange, my
questions about this restaurant proposal of Guy's and how that
notion got on with the Harpers.

"I think his son has some heartache with the idea," Langston
said. "Maybe feels his father's spreading himself too thin, so we'll

see what Harper wants to do now." He confirmed that he and Guy and Harper had been meeting on the restaurant deal at the old pizza place the day Patsy-Lynn died, and they were fixing to meet again.

"Is Abby still sick?" I asked.

"So she says." Clearly, Keith Langston didn't believe his little girl.

* * *

On my way to the vet's office, I passed the blooming apple trees at the edge of town. Our winters aren't cold enough—the tree planters from fifty years ago came to find out—to force much fruit from an apple tree. All over left-central Oregon are well-intentioned trees that don't bear well, aren't productive. It's sort of sad and sweet at the same time. Plants, both natural and introduced, along with history, tell the tale of a land. The landscaping trees in front of Nichol's brick office were English hawthorns standing tall against native sword and deer ferns.

The frizzy-headed gal at the vet's front counter, she was a transplant, introduced, I bet, from California. Too sun-streaked and tan. I thought back on that clerk at the sheriff's office. With her dark eyes and plain hair, she might be at least part homegrown.

"Do you need to make an appointment to see the veterinarian?" Frizzy asked, seeing I had no critter with me. But Nichol came out, walking a woman and her poodle to the door, and he waved me back to the treatment room.

I thought of Nichol as an introduced plant too, then I realized it's Guy who's all interested in plants and horticulture. Seems Guy's interest had rubbed off on me. I wasn't even thinking about what kind of horse someone would be.

Nichol raised his eyebrows, while he waited for me to speak, as if my noodle was loose. I got it tightened up and jumped in. "Where would a body, you know, pass off some steroids and such?"

His eyeballs about came out of their sockets.

"You want steroids?"

"No, looking to get shed of some."

"What are you talking about?" Nichol folded his arms over his chest, facing me.

"Forget I mentioned it," I said.

"Do you want me to forget my business was broken into?" He waved an arm around the office. "This office wasn't just vandalized. Stuff was stolen."

"Really? Like what?"

"Like drugs."

"Oh," I said, "Oh, shit. Oops. I mean, oh—"

"Can you be more articulate?"

Obviously not. What's the matter with him anyways? Can't he see this is as articulate as I get when I find out drugs were stolen from the vet's office and there's some in my pocket? I reached into my jeans and yanked out the baggie of vials.

"Were these them?"

Nichol leaned forward and took the baggie, eyeing me and it with equal care. "Could be, but the lot number is scraped off."

"Why would the lot number be scraped off?" Maybe I'm not such a hot horseshoeing detective. "To make it harder to trace?"

Nichol nodded.

"Part of the drug name's scraped off, too," I said.

"But there's enough there for me to know it's testosterone. And if the person in possession plans to use the contents, there's no reason to leave part of the name on the vials. It would actually be a liability since these are a controlled substance."

"So why would someone leave part of the name on?"

"To prove the contents, in case you wanted to sell the drugs." Nichol cleared his throat hard. "Where'd you get these?"

"From the Harpers' tack room, the day we were there for Spartacus's laminitis."

He whistled. "We saw a little 'roid rage then, I think."

"Maybe in the horse, too." I didn't want to think about how Junior had scared me that day. "That stud's got problems."

"That makes sense. Steroids could provoke laminitis."

"And give fertility problems and make it harder for a minor wound to heal?"

Nichol nodded. "I rechecked the horse this morning. Spartacus never had a change in food, stress, anything like that before Ted noticed the front-end lameness. The horse is doing better now and we'll need you out in a few weeks to reset those shoes. Same goes for that other emergency horse we did, the old pet. They'll be needing another visit from their favorite shoer."

Did he forget I'd been fired from the Flying Cross? For a change, I didn't want to talk about horses' feet. To my way of thinking, other itches needed scratching. I pointed to the baggie. "What are these used for except to beef something up?"

Nichol tapped his fingertips together. "A vet would prescribe them to a debilitated horse to increase its vigor and appetite."

"But people use them too, right?"

"Yes and people abuse them. But other than obtaining them illegally—"

"Stealing them?"

"Or knowing a dealer," Nichol said. "Other than illegal methods, you'd need a prescription for them. At least, you do here."

"Here?"

"Anyone can buy them in any farmacia south of the border."

I pondered. The south border is over a thousand miles away from the heart of Oregon. "Unless the Harpers have a prescription—and I've never written them one—they shouldn't have these. I doubt the police can do much, since it's third-hand and the bottles are damaged, but I'll talk to them." He held out his palm for the drugs.

I handed the evidence over, happy to get rid of the drugs. The police and the Harpers could sort it out with Nichol.

"Did the police ask you to give blood?" I asked, surprising Nichol.

"No. Why would they?"

Why not, I wondered. They've tested everyone else's. "Did you think I'd broken into your office?"

Nichol gave me a good long looking-at and shook his head. "I think you're a nut. A very cute nut. And I knew that you were at the Rocking B when my office was burglarized. I heard you left late. I heard young Mr. Harper left early."

"So, if young Mr. Harper were to have his blood tested. . . ." Impressing myself with all I considered, I allowed right out loud that maybe I would turn into a detective, if this shoeing business didn't work out.

But Nichol shook his head. "The effects of steroids last beyond usage. It's perfectly possible for a relatively recent user to test clean while still feeling the benefits of the drug."

I let that bit of news run around my brain cells for a minute.

Nichol's smirk was at the ready. "They didn't teach you that in horseshoer detective school?"

Well, no, they didn't.

His smirk sort of dissolved into a genuine grin. If I didn't know better, I'd have thought he was flirting with me. Maybe I didn't know better.

The thing of it is, is I've never been a guy shopper. Heckfire, my first two so-called fellas ranked as disasters. I hadn't wanted or needed a third. Things just sort of fell into place with Guy when I started living in his garage.

Nichol gave my shoulder a squeeze as he opened the treatment room door for me.

The problem with guys is they leave a gal wasting time thinking about them. And I've no thinking time to spare. I barely remembered to check that the thrushy horse was current on its tetanus. "There's all these loose ends. And I'm wondering why anyone would steal the Solquists' horse." Then I had to explain, since Nichol hadn't heard about the missing mare.

He asked, "What does that have to do with anything?"

It was exactly what people should have been asking.

* * *

After my next shoeing, I went to the Langstons' place and found a fretty-faced Abby playing hooky, noodling around her little back-of-the-house pasture. The kid looked fit to be tied and was none too full of sense when I asked her what was going on.

"Liberty," she cried, too near tears.

"She looks okay."

Liberty stood munching hay. The horse was the biggest part of Abby's life, her thoughts, her reasons, her breath. She had dreams of and for her horse, I knew. I'd dreamed Red, the minute he came sliding out of his mama as I'd watched him, gangly-legged and slick. Glory and future, I reckoned, is all Abby saw when she looked at her horse. Every possible thing she could accomplish, every experience she could notch on her belt, counting coup.

She's told me all about this fire, and I felt it in my bones, same as just before I was an idiot, fat teenybopper who lost her way and got drunk one stupid night.

I stroked the little gray mare, thinking.

Abby's told me how she'll do hundred-mile races someday, do that running and riding combo sport. She wants to try racing and jumping and competitive trail riding and, of course, breed Liberty someday and continue the legacy. She sees herself eighty years from now as an old lady riding Liberty III or IV or V. I know. When I was ten years old, I saw the same dreams for Red and his kids—kids he'll never have, mind, since he ended up properly gelded as a long yearling.

I smiled, but Abby couldn't with her chin aquiver.

"What if he comes back?" she cried. "What'll I do?"

Then Abby bolted.

Chapter 23

I FOUND ABBY ON HER FEED room floor, squashed between a few bales of sweet-smelling orchard grass and a sack of alfalfa pellets. Her arms wrapped tight around her shins, hugging her legs to her chest, face planted on her kneecaps while she bawled.

"You'd better start talking, young missy."

She howled and covered her head with her hands.

I wasn't having any of that and snapped my fingers in her face. "What exactly are you so scared of?"

Hiccuping sniffles, the kind that keep a girl from talking, seized Abby.

Thing is, it's no use glowering at someone who won't look you in the eye. Waste of a good glower. I stepped to the doorway of her little feed room, looked at her horse, then back at the kid. "Who's Liberty bred to?"

Abby clapped her mouth shut so hard, breathing was put away, then she double-sealed the hatch with both hands.

I was getting nowhere and slowly with this kid. "What's going on with your neighbors?"

"Really, I don't know anything about them. I'm just scared."

There was no real reason for the Solquists' missing horse to scare her. And the missing mare had nothing to do with how Abby's mare got pregnant. The Solquists had a gelding and a mare, no stud.

So how did Liberty get in a family way?

Abby didn't have much money, worked for what she did have, foots most of the horse bills, except feed. Her daddy isn't raising a slouch. But I was starting to guess he'd raised up a little thief.

"You take something didn't belong to you, kiddo?"

Her face colored like an instant sunburn, tears leaking out.

"Speak up," I said.

"I rode over to . . ." Sniffle, sniffle.

"Wherever it was you rode Liberty to, I'm guessing it's been many months." I sighed. Pregnancy can sometimes be a bit hard to see in a maiden mare.

Abby nodded, turned away and looked beat. I let her think I was a little smarter than I am, hoping she'd come clean and not make me keep playing twenty questions. But I do love it when my brain finds its overdrive. Probably the gear's in such good shape because it's seen so little use. I could have looked up, I reckon, and seen a light bulb hanging over my bean. With one hand on each of Abby's shoulders, I turned her to face me and the truth. Then I waited until she tipped her head back and looked up at me before I said it, not really asking because I was pretty sure I guessed right. "You rode her across the highway, over to the Flying Cross."

"Yes." She breathed her answer through a quivering chin.

"When she was in season," I said.

Abby nodded and blinked her wet eyes.

"And you let her get mounted by Spartacus?"

She froze.

"Abby, you stole."

Abby looked away, like she considered getting fresh, then thought better of it. I decided her face was too scared for having been caught naughty. I crumpled, took a seat on the hay-covered plank floor. After a bit, the girl sat beside me, our shoulders against each other, feeling every breath.

"The way it works is," I said at last, "is you pay before you own." I folded my arms. "Where'd you get a fool idea like stealing a breeding?"

"From you," she said in a tiny, earnest voice.

"What!"

"From one of the books you gave me. *Thunderhead*."

"Huh?"

"*Thunderhead* is the story that comes after *My Friend Flicka*," Abby explained.

"Oh, for mercy's sake," I snapped, "I know which one comes when."

It had been a long time since I'd read those novels, but yeah, I guess I remembered now that Ken rode Flicka over to a neighbor's ranch and got his mare bred to some hotshot stud. And when Thunderhead was born, Ken's daddy had known right away it wasn't his stallion's get, but it all worked out in the end because Ken managed to hang in there and train Thunderhead and—

What in the name of horse pucky is the matter with me? How can I remember stories I read fifteen years ago and I can't remember to give Schram the bute for Weatherby or of the name of that daggummed detective? I frowned, and not to waste the grimace, turned it full bore on Abby.

"You stole." I wanted her to say it, and she fairly wilted under my words.

"Yes, ma'am." Abby studied the dust between her shoes, looking scared.

More scared than she should have.

A glimmer of some not-yet-formed question tried to spark in my brain innards. "And what else happened?"

"He saw me as I rode away. I think he might have guessed."

"Mr. Harper?"

She shook her head.

I nodded. "Mr. Harper's son."

"I've been so scared." Abby's chin crumpled again.

"Because you think the Solquists' mare may have been taken accidentally by someone who was actually trying for Liberty."

"Yes!"

"By Mr. Harper's son, Junior." I wasn't the only person to think the missing mare was key. I was second. But Abby couldn't tell anyone her secret. She'd stolen a stud service—a baby to be—and someone wanted the baby back.

Not that that's such an awful secret.

I've got worse.

But I wanted to help this kid, so I sucked it up and went to the Flying Cross to talk to my ex-clients.

* * *

As I pulled up to the Harper house, I heard father and son on the far side of the garage, deep in a hollering match. The racket of one of them running a chainsaw died down. The short side of the garage had an extra-long eave for semi-dry storage underneath. The wall was burdened with a stack of plywood on edge, rakes and shovels hung on hooks, then a wheelbarrow scattered with wood-chips that had sprayed from the long side. All stuff that had been there before, unnoticed by me.

Junior was saying he'd get it dealt with. Senior was saying to fix it and move on. The chainsaw had covered the sound of my diesel truck arriving. I stood by Ol' Blue, trying to decide whether to make noise swinging the door shut or not.

Junior's voice got louder. "What do you mean, move on?"

Don't yell back, Mr. Harper. Don't push that mean son of yours. I wondered if the chainsaw was still within reach and which man was closest to the weapon. Junior had sure looked ready to brain me with a horseshoe when I'd last seen him.

"I mean you have to leave," Mr. Harper said. The widower sounded like he'd been down irresponsibility roads with his boy before, given how he sighed. "I said you can have the Suzuki. Did you already wreck it?"

"No! You always think the worst."

I bet not. And I held my breath, wondering whether to turn on my boot heel and skedaddle.

Junior was still snotting off. "I want what's mine."

I pictured one thing leading to another, a pushing match, the weaker one going down. No good. I slammed Ol' Blue's driver door hard and stepped toward their side of the garage, wishing I'd grabbed a hammer or something heavy.

"Tonight," Harper said, looking up at his son. "Midnight."

Seeing me standing behind the old man, Junior gave his daddy a quick glare and stormed off down the long driveway past the house, toward the back cottage. I hoped the cops were wrong and the worst possibility wasn't true, hoped no one had hurt Patsy-Lynn. That she'd accidentally taken her own life. Such would be the simplest explanation, and the kindest.

Old Man Harper turned to me. "Can I help you, Rainy?" He seemed so much older since his wife had died. The confrontation with his son had left him a little steamy-eyed, too.

"I'm here about one of my clients, a kid. She did something stupid and it kind of involves you . . . and him." I pointed toward the long driveway his son had disappeared down, past the big house.

Harper motioned me to his front door and I followed him inside to the room with the Colonel Sanders sculpture. I remembered mentioning the statue to Guy, him saying it was a bust of Brahms. Brahms would bust a gut howling if he knew what passes for music with this crowd. Mr. Harper had twangy stuff wafting around the house from a high-end stereo.

It couldn't be too comfortable to be Harper, caught between his live son and dead wife. I remembered how sick I'd felt the last time I'd been here, at the funeral reception, half scared the old man might think I'd hurt his wife. I took a breath and started talking.

Harper took quite a spell to absorb what I told him—that his son scared the daylights out of Abby Langston when she was trespassing at the Flying Cross on Liberty. He took it with a grimace and finally allowed it wasn't his boy's first lapse in judgment. He faced the mantle photographs of Junior in his football uniform. I bet Old Man Harper had seen a lot of what my report cards used to call *not meeting potential*. I thought about Junior wanting what was his, and figured he'd planned from the get-go to take back the baby that Abby tried for. I wondered how much it was just Junior's nature to be so contrary and how much the old man had made him rotten with spoiling.

His voice was gravel. "They had a file on him at the college. He was asked to leave and he did. And that's what's going to happen now, too. Your young client has nothing to worry about. My son is leaving town, leaving the country. He will not bother the little girl or anyone else." Harper moved for the front door like he couldn't look at those photos another breath.

I shook my head as he held the door for me. "I don't understand."

What I didn't understand was a long list of things, but I was going to start simple as soon as I got Harper's attention again. Now, I followed him out past the wood pile where he picked up a chainsaw. Apparently, he still did plenty of his own outdoor work when he wasn't doing whatever businessman-type work kept him occupied elsewhere.

More than anything, I wondered where exactly his son was right that minute. It's not that I was scared, but the willies were moving in on me.

"Sir, I heard tell that you have some tools missing."

"My son should check the old barn, way out back. Calls it his man cave, didn't want Patsy-Lynn around it. I don't go there myself."

My ears pricked up. "Huh. I thought your wife and son figured that Mexican fellow Manny stole some tools."

Old Man Harper smiled. "He's from Montana. Ted is teasing when he calls him Manny the Mexican."

I took a pause, then allowed, "I'm an idiot."

The old man went to fiddling with the chainsaw, slacking the chain, inspecting it, then asking, "Do you, by chance, have a bastard file?"

"A bast—" I choked a bit.

"Are you all right, dear?"

My mind screamed for anything else to talk about. "Where, uh, where's your son going?"

"He's going away."

It sounded so final, the way he said it. I looked at the old man, trying to understand. He looked away, only offering thin words. "He has to go away for good. I told him."

What a bad feeling that scrap of news gave me. "But why, sir?"

"He's my son."

That about finished things for him. I still didn't know what else to say about his son or his wife, and I'd talked my piece about Abby, so I said good-bye.

* * *

Ol' Blue and I started crawling down the Flying Cross driveway.

The old man said his son was going away. He said it like it was his choice, not Junior's. And the why of it? Because *he's my son.*

The wrong words could make me insane. I gripped the steering wheel hard enough to hurt. Glancing back at Harper's fancy barn, I reckoned it was more than clear why Spartacus still had that scrape on his leg, a bad attitude, and why he went laminitic. I'd have to go hit my textbooks to get an A on the particulars, but there was another score I could settle sooner. If the person who took the Solquist mare hadn't been meaning to get her, but instead meant to get another little gray with stolen seed in her womb, well, it could account for a few things. I thought back to that map at the sheriff's office. And I thought about things coming full circle.

He's my son.

A couple drops of sweat beaded up and ran down my spine, tickling in the most heebie-jeebie way imaginable. My ponytail needed a good twist, so I gave it three or four.

He's my son.

Why did Harper have to go and say a thing like that? Before Patsy-Lynn was in the picture, I guess Harper's last wife gave him a child and what clinches things for him is that boy.

He's. My. Son.

I wiped sweat and fresh tears away, mad at the world. There wasn't a whole passel of time. I had a late afternoon shoeing at the Thurmans, but if I hurried, I could fit in a quick hike and satisfy a bit of curiosity that noodled me.

The place where the backcountry riders had been training, it called for inspection.

West of the highway, the main access road through the Forest Service land has few private owners, the main one being Donna Chevigny, way back at the big old Buckeye ranch. She was widowed some time back and has been trying to keep her spread going by herself. Her husband had done his own shoeing. Word was, she was trying to stay on top of it herself now. In the worst way, I wanted to be Donna Chevigny's shoer, have that ranch account, but, as Dixon Talbot pointed out, it didn't seem right to go and ask.

A shoer, like a girl wanting to go to the prom, needs to be asked.

Not taking the forest road as far back as the Buckeye, I turned Ol' Blue onto the second spur road and parked at the trailhead where people usually trailered their horses. This is where the endurance people started their conditioning rides. All the better trails are in the standing forest to the west of Stakes Ridge, above the first valley. That first spur road, going up Dry Valley, is logged out and rockier country to boot.

Talk was, a horse had been heard screaming out here somewhere.

Horses scream when they're unhappy or excited.

And they get unhappy and excited when they're moved.

This screamer was new here.

At the prep school, they showed us a movie about Ethel Kennedy. She got arrested for horse thieving when it was still a capital crime. But Mrs. Kennedy, she was rescuing a miserable horse, just like I wanted to do. I got my mecate off the floor of the passenger side of Ol' Blue, coiled its length in big loops, and started my hike up the ridge.

Either way, I was set. If the horse was there, I'd have a way to ride her home. If the horse thief was there, I'd have a way to hang him.

Chapter 24

FROM THE TOP OF STAKES RIDGE to the bottom of Dry Valley stands a long lonesome stretch of scrubby pine that could hide a little horse if it wanted to. Thought I heard a glimmer of a distant whinny. Sound shoots around the land and there seemed no better option than to get high. On the climb up the ridge, I definitely heard a horse holler, indignant and stressed, but I couldn't make out exactly where the call came from.

The afternoon was turning unaccountably hot. Upon reaching the ridgetop I was a sweaty girl. Good thing that I, like plenty of shoers, carry extra shirts in the truck. Sometimes I go through three shirts a day. I pulled my shirttail up and bent to swab off my forehead.

The right position makes the difference. A glint caught my full attention. Sunlight sparkled on something down at the far end of the other valley, up over a little rise.

I squatted and squinted, making sure it wasn't some pond kissing the sunshine back. Nope, the glimmer was man-made, a metal-roofed little barn. Tracing a finger in the dirt, I made a map, then felt steeped in stupid as I recognized the lay of the land.

My dirt drawing was almost full circle and made sense now. I glowered at my dusty index finger, wishing it'd made things clear to me much earlier.

That property with the metal building was the way-back of Harper's land. It had to be, just up and over that low rise. I remembered the map in the sheriff's office, the forest road, curving, curving, as it skirted private land to reach all the trees it could. Everyone rode land west of the Stakes Ridge, because the first service road—to Dry Valley—had such rough ground in parts, it wasn't much fun, and it had been recently logged, so was less pretty. If I'd walked toward the Flying Cross from that first road, I might have reached a screaming horse who'd probably been led in from the ranch, then abandoned a few miles south of the Harper property. Now, I didn't have time to hike on before my shoeing appointment.

* * *

Harper, Harper, Harper, my mind harped as I hiked back down the slope to Ol' Blue. Mercy, now one question sparked, an inquiry so obvious even I could think it up.

But I couldn't exactly go ask Harper Junior the same thing the police had asked me right after Patsy-Lynn's funeral.

Right after they found the rasp.

The thing of it is, is a gal who knew Junior, that is, knew him in the biblical sense of the term, would also know if the man belonged on the scratch and dent table.

All the sudden, I wanted to talk to Cherry Edelman. And that was a first for me.

How to start the conversation was a pickle.

Then I realized the same questions the sheriff's department wanted to apply to me or Guy or any of Patsy-Lynn's help—the questions I was trying to apply to Junior—ought to be applied to Cherry.

Cherry Edelman wanted to be a rich guy's wife. Did she create a job opening for that particular position? It made sense, good sense.

Cherry had been all about the new vet. She could easily be all about turning into the next Mrs. Harper, choosing Junior instead of the Old Man as a passport to Patsy-Lynn's easy life.

And I was probably the only one in Cowdry who could see Cherry as a suspect.

Hunting Cherry up in town would have to wait until my work was done for the day, but driving to my last appointment, I put in some pondering on how best to put the question to her.

* * *

Jean Thurman was giving her young 'uns a good bawling-out when I got to our shoeing appointment. Every seven weeks, it's a long afternoon for me at the Thurman place, three or four to shoe and some trims besides. He works all day and she works in the mornings, so I can't get started earlier. I fix feet fast as I can while Jean holds the horses and hollers at her kids. Blessedly, they had a new gelding pony and he was all I had to shoe today.

After I had the pony half done, the Thurmans' youngest got ahold of his sister's braids and tried to use 'em for reins. When she wouldn't giddy-up, he gave her hair an almighty yank and hollered, "Ho!"

By the time Jean got the boy's hands off his sister's hair and the girl's hands off her brother's throat, the little horse I was working on got good and spooked.

He started behaving like the Anti-Horse. I considered blessing the water in my cooling bucket and heaving it over his head for a quick exorcism. A screaming kid wasn't helping matters. I gave his mama a look to say so. The little nipper was packed off to the house to think about mending his ways and we had no more of that hair-pulling business.

"It just makes you think about retroactive birth control," Jean sighed. "You think that stock tank's deep enough to drown 'em?"

I looked up. A ten-foot metal circle, two feet tall, it was deep enough, all right. I winced and told myself the heat was getting to me. Cowdry could now and again act like it was a hot place to live and the temperature would spike twenty or thirty degrees compared to the day before.

Whether it was Jean's poor choice of words or horse flesh or little punkins, I wasn't very happy when I left the Thurmans. It was hard to get in the right frame of mind to see Cherry Edelman, but I was ready to tangle, if need be. She might have taken Patsy-Lynn down, but I could flatten Cherry. Still, I had to go in sly. If I could nudge her to talk to me a little, I could get evidence, an admission, if I could be sure she was being truthful, if, if, if.

If Cherry was the devil, had gotten into a spat with Patsy-Lynn, I could handle her. But how could I prove that Cherry had been on the receiving end of a swung rasp?

Thinking about where I was headed, I cleaned up a bit, I'm not proud to say. I don't know why I felt compelled to wipe the horse off myself. Anyways, I keep a big bottle of cheap lotion in the truck. The trick is, all kinds of crud can be cleaned off without soap or water if slathered with enough lotion and then wiped off with the cleaner parts of my most recently shed shirt. I polished up my mitts, picking under my nails and pushing at the cuticles 'til the dirty parts pretty well fell away. I looked and smelled a lot better from the elbows down, and I slid on a fresh T-shirt to boot.

Never before had I been to Cherry's home, but I found my way there. It was an old house, with a semi-kept look, resembling its owner's. The closed single car garage hid whatever vehicle she drove and I wondered if it was a truck. There was no answer to my knocking, but scratchy hip hop was playing out back, so I chanced to walk around.

She had cold frames back there protecting tomatoes, zucchini, broccoli, and cauliflower. Nice rows of veggies basking out behind the house and the vegetables weren't sunning alone. There was Cherry, lying face down on a chaise lounge. Late in the afternoon, yet the moon was out, Cherry's moon, that is.

She peeked over one shoulder, rolled herself on over—treating me to a flash—then slid a towel over the girl-goods.

"Hey, Rainy." But there was a question in her voice, as I'd never before come calling.

Cherry paid attention to things I didn't. She calculated.

One thing could have led to another. She and Patsy-Lynn had a tiff. One shoves the other. Patsy-Lynn loses the catfight with the much younger woman, ends up with her head conked. The car's running. Cherry leaves.

Patsy-Lynn dies.

I still wanted it to be an accident. Not evil. Not murder. I wanted to make excuses. And part of me didn't want it to be Cherry who was responsible for Patsy-Lynn's death.

Seems like I'd noticed at some point Cherry worked retail, tending a cash register at some crappy store. I was sure Cherry wanted a life of leisure and nice things, like Patsy-Lynn had, but maybe Cherry didn't outright kill to get it. Maybe she just didn't help Patsy-Lynn when she should have.

Like me.

"Hey, Rainy," Cherry said again, louder, like I was a deaf mute in her garden.

"Yeah, hey." I realized I hadn't seen a mark on her body—and I'd gotten a good view of the whole of her. If she'd been smacked with a rasp hard enough to draw blood and snag flesh in the rasp teeth just last week then a wound should still be there.

So then, Cherry was in the clear and there was a whole 'nother direction to consider. I could think of plenty of ways to phrase it badly.

Say Cherry, that fellow you bonked during Patsy-Lynn's funeral reception. Oh, which one, you ask?

Hey there, Cherry. How are ya? Busy? Sure. Been to the clinic? Understandably. I was just wanting to know if you'd happened to notice an owie anywhere on a particular man . . . Oh, not how you pick 'em, is it?

Um, Cherry. Here's a question. When you and Harper Junior were in your birthday suits, did you happen to look above his waist at any point?

"Hello?" Cherry spoke to the air, then gave a little snort, the kind usually coming out of thirteen-year-olds who are fed up. "Pass me that tea, m'kay?"

A plastic mongo tumbler, ice clunking against the sides, sweated in her shadow. Looked like good tea. I handed it to her like that was my reason for being. Maybe I wasn't there to pin a murder on her or her one-afternoon stand after all. Maybe I was wrong about everything.

Finally, I got to it. "Um, you know Harper's son?"

"Win? He's Winston Junior, you know."

I guess when you bonk a guy named Winston Harper Jr. at his stepmother's funeral you get to call him Win.

"Okey-dokey." I faltered, but she was off to the races, needing no reason to blab.

"He's going to Mexico. I'm going with him this time." She said it like it was a real prize.

Mexico. Needing another trip to the farmacia, I'd guess. He'd run out. And if he'd stolen steroids from Nichol's office and had them in his tack room, well, he didn't have those anymore. But when his daddy said Junior was leaving, it sounded permanent.

So, Cherry was going with him. With Junior. With *Win*.

All the sudden, I was her protector, but she didn't know it.

What if Junior got crotchety? What if his mean mood had been any uglier when I was dealing with Spartacus's laminitis and Nichol hadn't been there? Cherry wouldn't have a big veterinarian around if she went on a road trip with Junior. She wouldn't have my muscles to make herself safe.

"Don't do it," I said. "Don't go anywhere with him."

Cherry adjusted her towel with a lazy hand in a silly gesture of pretend modesty. "Come again?"

Heckfire, this just wasn't working out at all. She probably thought I was jealous or an idiot or just bad-tempered, 'cause that's what I sounded like, even to me. But Junior was a toady-bully and I reckoned it was up to me to tell her. "I think you should stay away from him. He's a bad apple."

"You know, Rainy, you catch more flies with honey than with vinegar."

I never understood why people say that. Who wants to catch flies? Maybe someone like her who opens her mouth and legs more than she ought to.

"I know you don't think much of me," I grumbled.

"Aw, Rainy," Cherry said, maraschino-sweet. "Except for you being so foul and bad-tempered, you're quite nice."

She popped her gum, dismissing me with a bye-bye wave.

* * *

By now, Guy should be near to finishing his day at the diner, thinking ugly thoughts of his own about the Cascade Kitchen and wishing he was working in his own restaurant instead of suffering with the over-salted greasy grub that got handed out when he wasn't able to stop it. Bad chow aside, the reason for me to be in that diner was to get me a sounding board.

Guy smiled. "What have you been up to?"

"Investigating. I talked to some folks."

His eyebrows climbed. "Investigating? Who did you talk to about what?"

"Cherry Edelman, Mr. Harper, Abby," I said, counting back on my finger, then working the other direction, from the day's push-off. "Dixon Talbot came to the house after you left this morning. And I talked to Nichol."

Guy made a big frowny face and his jaw ratcheted forward. "I'm not wild about Neal."

Blank, I was. Why did Guy throw me curveballs? "I don't know who that is."

He froze, then relaxed like he'd slipped into a warm spring. His shoulders smoothed and a beamer of a grin spread across his face. "You don't even know his first name?"

"Whose first name?"

"The vet's. Neal Nichol."

"Oh. No, guess not. Why?" There is a reason I get so almighty distracted. And I choke down this demon every single day. Down.

Don't think about it, even though I did it again last year, last month, last week, yesterday, today. I'll do it again tomorrow. Gah!

Guy said, "I'm not enchanted with his interest in you."

Enchanted? I didn't want to think about Nichol right then.

"There's something going on, something not right. There's these people, the Solquists, whose mare went missing and—"

"I'm the one who told you about that horse being missing. Remember? That was me." Guy shook his head, looking slightly miffed.

"Okay, I think I know where the horse is, up Dry Valley, off the first spur road. I went up the Stakes Ridge and heard a horse, but I had a shoeing appointment and didn't have time to go back to the first road and I want . . ." I stopped. Guy looked distracted.

The diner owner, Dennis McDowell in the corner booth with some other good ol' boys, eyed us over coffee.

"Oh?" Guy said. Then he whirled to deal with a delivery truck that came to the Cascade Kitchen's back door. I followed him through the swinging doors to the kitchen area, not letting this drop for Guy or his boss.

Guy hefted a big box from the deliveryman and made for a high steel shelf to unload. He shoved the box onto the shelf with the side of his chest like this was his habit. Guess that's why he changes aprons and chef shirts—he goes through shirts as much as I do—so often, 'cause that crate left quite a mark on the one he was wearing. He paid it no mind, all his attention back on me.

I balked.

"Rainy?"

So, Guy's a man who can take a shot in the ribs and not worry about it, I'll give him that.

"Rainy, what's bugging you?"

"We'll never go riding," I said, plaintive without meaning to be.

"The fact is, I'd love to go horseback riding with you."

Would he quit calling it *horseback* riding? There's no other kind of riding. I sighed at the futility of it all.

It was past time to get to things that could be dealt with. Just enough light was left in the day to get to that horse out in the hills. Since I'd be bringing her home in the dark, I swung by the house to grab my good dog and maybe a flashlight and some trail grub.

One of Guy's water bottles was on the kitchen table. I turned to fill it and tripped over Spooky. We were both offended by the encounter.

What else, I asked Charley, scratching my blockhead while I ran the tap. Maybe bandages, just in case? He wagged, saying he was ready, didn't need to pack a thing.

Tap, tap. Goslings pecked at the back door. I saw Guy's goose pen was near done. He'd strung wire mesh from it to the house so they could run around by the backdoor.

The little baby bird home looked real good. It would need a top enclosure before they got too old, but Guy'd done a bang-up job on the goose house, made it sturdy and respectable-looking.

I'd sold him short on his skills.

Charley's got skills, too. He wanted to go out back and herd birds. But then he cocked his ears. Somebody was out there, at the back of the house.

I love Charley, truly I do. Yet I wished right then he wasn't Australian, but instead a German.

Charley yipped, sure, let me know that someone was there, something was wrong.

The door flung open and a huge silhouette of a man took up the whole doorway. Beyond cornering the goslings that wandered in the open door, my dog was fresh out of ideas. The baby geese were busy, getting away from Harper Junior, then obeying Charley.

Junior looked ready to take someone apart.

Right then, I had the wrong kind of shepherd.

Chapter 25

SPOOKY PEEKED OUT FROM THE EDGE of the couch, trying to pick the worst threat: me, Harper Junior, or the geese huddled in the corner behind Charley.

"You shouldn't let them wander around like that." Junior sneered at my good dog holding the goslings. "A working dog ought to work or be in a kennel."

Thank the stars he was giving out free advice. I'd have never seen my way to paying money to hear him jabber. I'd thought at first he was talking about the geese wandering around, then realized he was talking about my loose dog. Figures a guy like Junior wouldn't understand a working dog could be a friend, too.

He rocked on his toes, bulging his shoulders like anger burned under his skin. One fist gripped a medium paper grocery bag and a jacket I thought I recognized from somewhere. The jacket was way too small for him at any rate and I'd no clue what was in the bag.

"So," I said, clearing my throat, "nice of you to stop by. I've got stuff to do and I'm sure you're a busy fella—"

"Busy." He snorted and moved the stuff he was carrying to one armpit, freeing both his hands. The thing in the bag was hard, a big thick tube, like a can on steroids. "Yeah, you think *I'm* busy? *You're* busy."

Well, sure, I'm busy. I could list up to twelve and a half things I'd have rather been doing. Talking to him wasn't even in the top twelve thousand. And Junior seemed unsettled no end, edgy, like he wanted a tense chat.

And I remembered that Patsy-Lynn had an edgy, wanting-to-hang-around type attitude the last time I saw her.

Right before she died.

Right before someone killed her.

Notions glimmered. The credit card receipts hadn't panned out. The sheriff's man probably hadn't pressed the Harpers for them until after the funeral so the old man had the weekend to figure out that his son's alibi didn't hold up. It would have been mighty handy if my brain would fire off a little faster in the future.

I started getting a true hankering for a future of my own.

Harper Junior seemed to get a hankering to chat about the past. He gave a sharp little headshake. "You know football?"

When they started having Monday night football on Thursdays as well, that was when I'd had enough. And I don't even try to wrap my mind around this idea of fantasy football. I shook my head.

He draped the jacket—Patsy-Lynn's barn coat, I realized—over one of the dinette chairs. My heart started to go pitter-pat.

"No," I said.

Junior spoke through his teeth, saliva flicking off his lips, looking agitated, like he was dying to make me understand something. "I was great."

Mmm. Many, many fresh-mouthed replies leaped to mind, but I kept my lips locked, good as gold. Mmmphh.

"Lots of guys did it." Junior shrugged. "Some of it's legal. And the rest . . ."

So he knew I knew. And I barely knew.

Thinking hard, I tried to figure out what exactly I thought I knew.

Nichol said people had to know a dealer to get steroids, or they had to steal them or buy them out of the country. Junior didn't know a dealer around here, I decided. He was the dealer.

Of one thing I was dead sure. Junior was at the Flying Cross when Patsy-Lynn died.

I saw Patsy-Lynn's jacket again and felt sick enough to puke on my boots.

Twisting my ponytail, trying to think what best to do under Junior's pure annoyance that looked ready to foam, I didn't stare right at him but didn't quite look away. Seemed like he was a pot getting ready to boil over.

Spit burbled at one corner of his mouth as he demanded, "What did she tell you?"

"Huh?"

"You heard me," he sneered.

Sure, but so what? Hearing and understanding, not the same thing. And he must have decided I wasn't a good enough actress to play dumb because he elaborated.

"That day. You know. Look, she told me you were coming back, just went to get some more supplies, shoes or something. And she said she'd told you about, you know, me helping the stud."

Six shades of stupid, that's how I felt. All kinds of bad. Shame, really, when I thought about how Patsy-Lynn had wanted me to hang out. She'd wanted me to be there when Junior came home. She knew he was going coming back. She was nervous about being alone with him. And I'd left her. She'd known he was doping her horse and maybe she was scared of his rages.

And when he got there—right after I left—the poor woman had bluffed that I was coming back. I'd left Patsy-Lynn on her own when she was scared and needing someone in her corner.

The thing of it is, is I am someone who swore: I will never leave someone who needs me. Never again.

Of course, I hadn't wanted anyone to need me. Nobody at all.

But Patsy-Lynn had needed someone and I'd gone about my afternoon.

Sick to my stomach, I wrenched with worry. What had I done by failing to do?

I saw my guilt plain, plenty of it. I saw Guy's kitchen, clean and tidy. Beyond the scrubbed surface were beautiful condiments pushed back on the counters, above was the rack I'd built. Those spices and things meant something to Guy, he produced with them. He had oils and about twelve different kinds of salt, and cardamom whole in pods. They were things folks used with horses, too. They were pretty, before and after Guy used them in the kitchen.

Was I seeing this sight for the last time?

"You're a little busybody," Junior said, his voice full of hate. "You're a little bitch."

Well, he was a bully and I don't cotton to being bullied. What was he going to say next, that I was fat? I cocked a leg back, making ready to groove his gonads with my boot toe.

Junior shoved me down so hard and fast my wind went out and my teeth deepened themselves into my jawbones when I smacked my chin on my knees. Charley chuffed in the corner, scaring his geese, which made him go back to tending them.

If someone who was already strong abused a drug that exaggerated his strength, impaired his judgment and his ability to control aggression, how many bad things could happen? He could scare the hooey out of a little girl who stole a stud fee. He could dose and overdose a studhorse with steroids to make more muscles.

He could kill his stepmother if she objected—maybe not on purpose, just in a fit of 'roid rage, but that didn't change her being dead.

And he could decide it was a good idea to get a ride to Vine Maple Lane and pull out a pistol.

Junior leveled the gun right between the points in my T-shirt as I stood up.

I hate the way a gal's body wants to tell the world when she's excited. I swallowed, trying not to look like I was gulping.

"Tell me if you're going to kill me. I won't be mad, just tell me."

"Mr. Harper," he said.

"Huh?"

"You'll address me as Mr. Harper."

Like cold hell I will. I was stirring up a good growl when I came to my senses. I swear, sometimes Red's planet tries to order me around. I don't want to die. Mostly I don't, anyways.

Got-a-Gun-I'm-a-Big-Man seemed to want me to say something.

I made it meek and squeaked a little, "Mr. Harper," like an apology. Was I supposed to curtsy, too?

But this was my home. Mine and Guy's. I could have had a decent life here. Could have had.

Truth was, a part of me was ready to die, had been for nigh a decade.

Junior took a hard step toward me. I let him close the distance without flinching, playing chicken. Clearly, I was supposed to cower, give ground, back up.

Oh, his anger spiked in a hurry. He lunged, grabbing at my waist with one hand for the do-all in its scabbard on my belt. Quick as a snake, he had my tool in his own pocket. He waved the gun toward the table and I took a seat like I'm the kind of gal that hops to whenever a guy points. Next he'd be wanting me on my knees, scrubbing the floor with a toothbrush and I'd tell him to take a flying leap from—

Whoa, Red's planet must be sending me orders. I needed to stick my head in a bucket to block the signals, but there was no bucket handy at the dining table.

Guy's fancy tape measure was there, next to a pile of cooking magazines and his bottles of vitamins. I let my hands rest near it. I reckoned I could stomach whatever was going to happen, but it'd be nice if someone else knew what Junior had done.

It would have been good, I realized in a flood, if someone other than my folks knew what I had done.

Guy was the person I wanted to tell.

But I had to pick between clearing things up about me or about Patsy-Lynn.

One smart, good thing waited for me to do it. And I owed her.

Here I come, Smart Good Thing.

When I fidgeted one hand on Guy's fancy tape measure gadget, Junior didn't get much madder, so I did it, pressed the record button on the tape measure, and cut to the chase.

"But why'd you kill Patsy-Lynn, Mr. Harper?"

Junior did throat clearing that would send most dogs running for cover and didn't help my nerves one lick. Then he allowed, "It just happened. I didn't mean to hurt her, but she made me so mad."

I looked at the tape measure and wondered if it had recorded what he finally said or if it had run out of recording space back when he was working his tonsils and sinuses.

"Put that down," he ordered.

Of course, I obeyed. And when he cocked his wrist toward the door, using the pistol to tell me what to do, I headed outside without a word, still wondering what was in his paper bag.

* * *

So this was how things were going to end for me? Turning Over a New Leaf aside, this wasn't my plan. My plan was I'd make it on my own, be nice, be good and responsible and try not to muck up anyone else's life, ever again. What was this now, payback?

This would not be a good time to bawl, but I sure felt put upon.

Outside, he motioned me to Ol' Blue. "Let's take a ride," he said, his voice so low and measured I started to sweat.

Really, really bad, I didn't want to take a ride. And it made me wonder how he'd gotten there in the first place, being as there was no other vehicle in the driveway. I wondered really, really hard if I'd done that stupid tape measure thing right.

Charley knew I was scared and he gave little growls as he followed us toward Ol' Blue, but all Junior had to do was cock an arm back like he was throwing a rock. Charley kept his distance. And Red, he's not the kind of friend who goes to bat on this kind of a problem—someone taking me for a one-way ride. I'd never had this kind of problem before.

That silly tape recorder measuring gadget was right in the middle of the table. Guy would have to see it. He'd press the button. He'd hear Junior confess to killing Patsy-Lynn. And then Guy would call out the cavalry or some such.

Wouldn't he?

Or maybe Guy would record that he wanted to cut a board about two feet long for a lid on the goose pen and my last evidence would vanish.

Chapter 26

R ED MET MY GAZE, A HORSE question on his face. I had no
answer to think back at him. It had taken so long to track him
down, to recover the horse of my ten-year-old's heart. The journey
had taken me here, to Cowdry, here to Vine Maple Lane. With
my ponytail screwed around one thumb, I didn't think any better.
I twisted it the other way, but still couldn't wring a worthwhile
thought out of my muddled mind.

"Quit fucking around like that," Junior snarled.

My hands dropped to my sides. Mama never put it to me that
way. Maybe if she had, I wouldn't have this little hair-twisty habit
thing going on.

He was still staring at me, breathing hard, looking like he
wanted to hurt something.

"Okay," I said, real ready to not play with my hair anymore.

"Okay, what?" His voice was full of suggestion in the most
school-me way imaginable.

Oh, it hurt. But he had all the marbles, so to speak, even if he
didn't seem to have his own. "Okay, Mr. Harper."

He looked mighty well pleased with that comment. "Get in the truck and start it up." He motioned with his pistol then gave me a look, like an answer was needed.

"Okay, Mr. Harper." I hated this form of Simon Says. I climbed in behind the wheel and turned my key enough to get the glow plugs to start warming.

"I said start it up," Junior snarled.

His agitation was a bulging thing. I didn't need him any more menacing. I said very softly, "It's a diesel. I can't start it yet, got to wait for the glow plugs."

By then the batteries had done their job and I was able to comply with Junior's demand just as his tiny brain realized I wasn't being a mule on sheer principle.

And then he did the strangest bit, he set his paper bag in his lap and pulled a little plastic baggie out of his pocket. There was a bloody hanky in it that he shook right into Ol' Blue's glove box. From an inside pocket, he flicked out a baggie of greenbacks, twenties, I think. He stuffed the cash in my glove box, too.

The grin he gave me was not of this species.

"Where to?" I asked with a good gulp. Then I added the Mr. *Harper* title to keep his Lordship happy. And while I was wondering, what's with the "Mr. Harper" crap, I shook with the sudden realization that Guy might play the recording on his fancy measuring tape and think I was talking to the real Mr. Harper, this idiot's old man, which would leave things boned but good.

Junior cleared his throat again, looking straight ahead. Twilight was dropping and it made him look creepier. "What's going to happen is, you're going to write a note explaining everything. Once we get to where we're going, you're going to do that."

As interesting as this bit of news was, I couldn't manage to get excited, being as I didn't know what he was talking about. I kept thinking about how Mr. Harper—the real Mr. Harper—seemed to think his son was okay enough even though it seemed he knew the boy was a cantle short of a decent saddle. He wouldn't break with this no-good stinker he'd spawned. Maybe if he had, his wife would be alive and I wouldn't be heading for the hills with the world's biggest chunk of walking human beef who bore the world's biggest idiocy and inferiority complexes, with both meters pegged.

I drove Ol' Blue down Vine Maple Lane and took a right when His Excellency ordered me to.

No doubt about it, I figured, Old Man Harper should have gotten shed of this kid of his long ago. He knew, part of him knew anyways, that his kid was trouble.

Once, I'd started to tell my mama that you couldn't break with your own child, but I realized how stupid I, of all people on the planet, would sound saying such a thing. After all, just because I was now a decade past being thirteen when Jesse, the seventeen-year-old liar who was my supposed boyfriend . . . And my folks, well, ten years and change didn't make that friendless situation set any better with me.

Just where did my so-called friends think I was that near-year that my daddy told everyone I was with my mama and my mama told everyone I was with my daddy?

Anyways, it'd need more than a decade for forgetting.

On the highway, Junior kept the gun pointing at my ribs then had me drive the gravel road into the Forest Service land where I'd been earlier, this time taking the first spur road, the one that goes up Dry Valley.

He graduated to pointing the gun at my head, maybe just because there was no traffic. With no one to witness his assault on me, Junior could get away with it. Just like a bully.

He looked like a man with a plan and I realized one thing I should have asked Dixon Talbot that morning was where he'd picked Junior up. I bet it was around here. Maybe Talbot had been going up to the Buckeye ranch, snooping around for a job, then on his way down the forest land, he came across Junior, afoot.

If Junior had been slipping off this trailhead—definitely the road less traveled—it made all the difference. I knew where I was going now.

The road got narrower and rougher. When I saw the stranded Suzuki Samurai, I slowed Ol' Blue. Junior picked up my appointment book and his paper bag, then motioned with the pistol that I should stop the truck. I wanted to burst out of Ol' Blue, make a run for it.

My eyes went to the Solquists' mare, Misty, thirty feet away. She whinnied at our arrival, mournful, no longer the indignant screams I'd heard before.

Junior ignored her, looked at the flat left front tire on the Suzuki.

Misty was tied to an old high line that ran between two trees. She stood in the remains of a beat-up bale of timothy that was trampled into the mud of a little spring feeding Grass Creek.

Junior grabbed my mecate reins off the truck floor, and a tiny speck of hope fired up within me. Even though we'd driven twenty-odd miles to get here, we were probably only five miles straight south of his daddy's fancy house, even closer to the old Harper cottage out back of their main outfit. This old dirt trail probably ran straight to that cottage. Ol' Blue wouldn't fit any farther down, but the track looked to be drivable with the Samurai.

Things might be okay. Maybe Junior just wanted help moving the horse or needed a lift because of his flat. I could see how he mistook the Solquists' mare for Liberty in the dark, one little gun-metal gray Arab mare for another. Misty was chunky, but not pregnant. I figured Junior had put the plywood over the cattle guard at the end of the Solquists' driveway and just led Misty from the vehicle, tied her to the bumper or led her from the window as he drove right down the Flying Cross driveway past the old cottage and beyond, straight to this hideaway camp.

It didn't use up too much of my imagination to picture Junior getting a flat tire then hiking out the short way to the forest

road. Then Dixon Talbot had chanced upon him and given him
a lift.

Junior grabbed my day planner off the dash, killed Ol' Blue's
ignition, then turned on my headlights, which I hate, because hey,
my truck batteries—

"Get out."

Get out is what I did. It was better in the early evening air, looking at a pretty little horse, not cooped up in my truck's cab with
a whackjob and his pistol. He threw his paper bag at me. I wasn't
sure whether to duck or catch, but I caught it and found a can of
flat tire fixer. Apparently I had chores to do.

I attached the nozzle to the left front tire stem of his Suzuki,
pumping it up with the can's compressed air and sealant. The
moon would be full, but it had not yet risen above the dying day,
so the headlights helped. Junior just grunted while I fixed his flat
tire. The man was built to have servants.

"Look, I know your dad said you're leaving tonight."

He chuffed. "My dad is making a mistake with his heart pills
tonight."

My mouth opened, but my tongue came up with nothing to say.
Turned out he had another chore for me anyways.

"Start writing. Use some of the paper in the back of this thing."
He threw my appointment book at me along with a pen from his
shirt pocket. I waited like a little secretary ready for the boss man's
dictation.

As if.

"Write that you're sorry you killed her, you didn't mean for it to
happen, things just got out of hand and now you're going to make
things right by . . ." He licked his lips, wily poetry failing, his brains
steaming to come up with choice words. "Write that, write what I
said so far."

So I was to be offing myself? I nodded and just about couldn't
stand the irony. Ten years ago, I'd wanted to do it, but didn't come
up with a purpose and plan and poise and—

"Write it!"

I got to writing, held up the pad with the half-finished sentence for him to see.

"Good. That's good," Junior said. "Write that you're making things right now. Scratch out 'by' and write 'now.'"

I did it and sat there looking at my supposed suicide note.

Huh.

Ten years I'd been waiting for inspiration or a lightning bolt to come strike me down, since I never had the gumption or initiative or nerve to take care of things myself. I wasn't ready to believe Junior was any sort of divine intervention, but it was a bit comical that I was only now going to be getting around to what I'd sworn I'd do back when I was thirteen and fourteen.

Broken promises are the sorriest kind of troubled thought.

The three rules I'd come up with as a way to run my life afterwards weren't figuring on redemption, just on knowing I ought to try.

I'm a teetotaler. I don't partake because I was drunk when I . . . that time. I got tough and grew quite a mouth on me next, couldn't hardly form a sentence without saying fuc—. Oops. Anyways, it's true. I used bad language everywhere, as a compliment, as a verb, an adjective, an interjection, just every way to speak we were ever taught. I used it as a way to be as ugly as I felt. I was poisonous. And I knew it. So, slowly, after I got off the streets, got in and out of a really bad idea of a marriage, saw my way clear to shoeing school, got a dream, I tried to Turn Over a New Leaf. Rule two, I quit being a potty mouth.

But most important, I didn't need anyone and for damn sure—I mean for sure and for certain—I didn't want anyone needing me. Ever.

"Get up on that stump."

Once, it had been a decent tree. Not a skyscraper, but respectable, with a trunk that was a couple feet across. A big maple tree had taken over the nearby light after this evergreen was cut. The three-foot-high stump was right under a terrific maple limb.

Junior took my mecate and pitched the beautiful horsehair reins of my handmade hackamore across the limb, flipping them to get them hanging closer to the pedestal he wanted me on.

He set my note on the ground and weighted it with a fist-sized rock.

He pulled my do-all from his pocket and threw it on the ground.

He cocked his revolver's hammer back and touched it to my nose.

There really didn't seem to be a lot of options. Get up on that stump or get shot in the face.

I climbed up on my pedestal sick with a realization.

I would never, ever be able to make things right if I died now.

I got it then, why I'd never done myself in. It would have taken away any future chance to fix the past. Even though I'd long fig-ured it couldn't be fixed, there was the chance to try, to make an effort, but if I died, that chance was snuffed.

Red, Red, Red. Why did I . . .

Nope, now I'd never have a chance to make amends.

Hope was the biggest thing Junior or anyone else could have taken away from me.

When he snugged the noose around my neck, I couldn't stop my hands from grabbing the mecate. A slow strangling from a horsehair rope is a bad feeling.

He hauled on his end of the line and I took a breath like I was jumping off a bridge into a river. Now I was on my tippy toes, the rough mecate pressing hard into the sides of my neck, tilting my chin up high as it pushed on my jugulars. I could only see the early stars. I heard Junior tying off the other end of the mecate, then his little Samurai started up and motored down the shortcut to the Harper place.

I tried to untie the noose, but his knot was iron hard, and there was no slack to speak of.

It would be tough, but surely I was strong enough to climb a rope, right? So I climbed right away, before I got weak, pulling myself up the rope arm over arm, then realized of course there was no way for me to hold on with the hand I was swinging from while untying the knot at my neck with the other hand.

The effort used me up. I barely got my toes back to the stump. My face was cold where the tears—stress, I suppose—washed down.

After who knows how long, I'd get tired and not be able to stay on my tiptoes. I'd slip down off my pedestal.

I was going to die that night, I could see that plain enough and I didn't have too awful many regrets. One wish screamed, though, just screamed. The thought I took with me as I started graying out, was sorry. So, so, sorry. I wished I'd been better, done everything better. Wished I'd tried to fix things and say how sorry I was.

If I could have had one thing, I would have wanted to *know* that he knew he was loved. I hoped beyond everything that he was all right, he'd somehow landed on his feet.

I just wanted to know my son was okay.

Chapter 27

GUY WAS PANTING AND SWEATING LIKE he'd been used up for the night.

Guess he could see me for a good half-mile or more as he ran up the hill. I was on the far side of woozy, sagging on my noose. Dim awareness of Guy grabbing me, picking me up to get my weight off the rope, filtered in as I got my first good breath in a while. He held me with one arm while using the other hand to try untying the mecate, but there was no untying that knot with one hand.

Zing! We were airborne. Guy's new plan, apparently, was that our combined weight would break the branch. The second time he kicked us off the stump, we twirled around until the limb gave with a crack. We dropped into the dust and the big maple branch slammed to the ground at our feet, bouncing the mecate still tied around my neck.

I rolled to my side, a better position for puking. It was mostly dry heaves but disgusting all the same. The urge to purge had been with me so long, years and years, but tamped down. Let loose, I gagged and spread my jaws for an almighty retch.

Guy reached for me. We stared at each other for a minute. I'd never felt so caught. It was time to confess.

"I never even tried to make it right."

"God, I saw you silhouetted there as I came up the hill," Guy said. "I can't believe what you did. Are you all right? I just want you to be all right."

The blackest of thoughts gummed up my mind. For so long, I'd tamped this thing down, but it burned in my brain as I strangled and begged to know if my little boy was okay. And worse, much worse, was my shame at not tracking him down, not checking on him ever, not getting him back.

Because I had done all that for my horse.

I didn't mean to cry, and I know my face looked all twisted. As twisted as my priorities. My cheeks and mouth were so scrunched up, I could hardly shriek. What I managed was a whimper.

"I couldn't tell you. I just couldn't."

"What?" Guy asked.

"I'm sorry. I'm just so sorry."

"What? What are you not telling me? What's happened?" Guy sounded a little panicky.

"It was 'domestic infant.'" I winced, feeling a smidgen better for the ugly truth to be out. "'Closed.'"

"I don't understand what you're saying."

"I gave away my baby." I bawled like I was going to die. "And then . . ."

Mewling for the better part of five minutes didn't accomplish anything other than getting Guy's shirtfront all wet. I tried to push myself back from his chest, but my stomach clenched up and my nose faucet turned on and hey, who wants her guy to see her face like that?

Guy kept stroking my back and kissing my hair. "You had a baby? And you put it up for adoption? When? When did this happen?"

"Ten years ago. He's ten now." And that set me off for another good while of making animal-type squalls, my shoulders shaking.

I would make Guy see how bad I am. Guy deserved to know, to get it. "I . . . I went looking for Red. Found Charley on my way."

Guy was soft, letting out his breath. I could hear him doing the math in his head. Rainy gave away her baby when she was four-teen. So she was thirteen when she got pregnant. That wasn't the worst of it.

The worst of it made me howl. "I got my horse back. I never did a thing for my baby."

Who does that? Takes better care of a horse than a human? I did a bad, bad thing, getting Red back.

I just wanted to be twelve again, in Texas, dreaming about riding Red, my young horse. But then Daddy sent me to Mama in California for another switch-off year.

Guy caressed my face. "Do you know anything else about your child?"

I shook my head.

"It wasn't an open adoption?"

"That's where you call up a number out of an ad in the person-als," I muttered. Oh, I'd seen those ads. Read a lot of them. *Loving couple would cherish your child, expenses paid, call collect. Professional dad and stay-at-home mom will give your baby blah blah, consideration given, call anytime.* I choked and couldn't help being bitter as I said the rest. "And you sell him to some couple, right?"

"Well . . ."

"I didn't do that. I didn't take money for him."

Fear has a taste and a texture if it's bad enough, which it was by the time I was nine months pregnant. I'd been plenty scared before. When I got drunk, when I did it with Jesse, when my period was late, when I fessed up to the folks and when they packed me off to the home in Oklahoma for girls in trouble. And when the strangers finally pushed me into a delivery room.

By then, fear was oozing in my pores and crudding up my mouth. I couldn't get clean of it and just hoped against hope that I'd be purged when the baby was out. By delivery time, I was breathing like a smoker on account of the weight pressing on my belly. Hardly able to see my feet 'cause a seven-pound human being was inside me kicking whenever he felt like it.

It was, and still is, the most scared I'd ever been in my life.

I'd been sure the baby knew all about me and hated me for everything. I'd been horrible to him so far and was going to get worse. And of course, I couldn't get away from him, I had to wait him out, let him kick me and hurt me.

And that namby-pamby counselor the clinic sent in for five seconds, she was a piece of work. Felt called to say that a lot of teenage girls have babies so they'll have someone who loves them.

As if I needed someone to love me.

"I think what you did was very brave," Guy said, after my story was out. "Maybe I'll go look up this Jesse character and speak to him about responsibility."

"But I was responsible for what I did, for my irresponsibility."

"Have you been flogging yourself for a decade? When were you going to stop and say whatever you needed to say so you could go on? You're here now. You're with me now—"

"But I got my horse back, made things right with him. I didn't do anything for my real baby. What kind of a person—"

"A good person."

"I tracked Red down for months, for over a thousand miles, across half the western states."

"You did a good thing."

Could it be okay that I got my horse back? I'd wanted Red back so bad. It had felt so good to find him at last, to touch him and hear his nicker. Good, but guilty. I sniffed. "Guess I'm alive thanks to you."

"God, Rainy, I can't believe how close you came to taking yourself away, away from me and our life."

"The heck I did." I stood up but a headache banged away inside my skull. Guy looked confused as he rose with me. I didn't want him making my throbber any worse, asking idiotic questions. Besides, I had a question of my own. "What are you doing here?"

"Helping you. I came to help you search for the horse." He looked past my shoulder. "I see you found her. But then you . . . We'll get you help."

"Did you play the measuring tape recorder thingy?"

"Huh?"

He sounded just like me! It was yelling time. "I didn't hang myself. Harper Junior strung me up."

A more confussed face never was made. How can a man with such an honest face be any good at poker? Guy pulled my arms as I tried to hug myself, inserted himself into the embrace and slid his arms behind my back again, squeezing me against his chest.

Thump, thump, thump, went his heart. It's the noise I always imagine Charley's fluffy stub tail would make hitting the walls and floor if it wasn't a two-incher. Guy's heart's no stubby model. It pounded his face crimson when I told him about Junior trying to kill me.

"Harper Junior is trying to make it look like I killed Patsy-Lynn and then killed myself. He put cash and a bloody handkerchief in Ol' Blue's glovebox and he put Patsy-Lynn's jacket in our kitchen." I could see Guy's paying attention, six kinds of shock tromping over his face as I explained. "I think his daddy told him to leave town tonight, for good. A big part of Mr. Harper realizes Junior had something to do with Patsy-Lynn's death, but no part of him realizes his kid's going to mess with his meds tonight. Junior's setting up his old man to die."

Guy looked purely agitated in all matters. I lurched to start Ol' Blue. I was going to stop that bully.

No, I wasn't.

Never leave an old diesel's headlights on, especially if it already has old batteries. Turning the key in the ignition only produced the clicking sound that means the truck's a three-quarter-ton doorstop. Ol' Blue didn't have enough juice to warm the glow plugs.

"Guy, how'd you get here?" There were a lot of holes I had to fill in.

He looked like his brain cogs were whirling, too.

"Rode up on my scooter, but got a flat down the road. I saw you silhouetted, hanging, and I just ran." He jerked a thumb over his shoulder and his mouth did a wry twist. "These forest roads are murder."

I holstered my do-all even as Guy hovered protectively over me.

"Say," I asked, bright-like, feeling good enough for a quick taunt, "'fore you came after me here, did you do something real intelligent, like call the po-lice?"

Guy wiped his forehead. "I didn't tell anyone I was coming here. I just rode up because it was the only place I could think of. Dry Valley, the end of the first spur road. You said you were coming here to look for a missing horse. That horse, I suppose?"

Guy pointed at Misty, who stared back.

"No one else has paid much attention to this mare being stolen," I said, "the whole idea of her being missing, I mean."

I gave her attention now, went to her, murmured and rubbed her swiveling ears.

"Pretty little thing," Guy said. "Why's she tied up out here?"

"Long story." I shook my head. "Look, for sure and for certain, Junior's skedaddling on this shortcut for home, then messing with his old man's pills, then leaving town with Patsy-Lynn's blood in Ol' Blue."

"And her jacket at the house?" said Guy, paling up as he got it. "It really will look like you killed her."

Would the police believe me when I told them Junior had planted that stuff? Did I handle that recording tape measure right?

Was Mr. Harper already dead from some foul-up with his heart pills, all arranged tonight by his son?

Would Mr. Harper still let his son spirit out of the country if he knew all his kid had done? Would he battle us if he knew that

Guy and I were going after Junior? Because we were. I could feel the notion burning.

Guy checked his cell phone, but had no reception, which was par for this backcountry. He paced, his jaw set.

Using my teeth, I unknotted my mecate.

The mare and Guy both looked interested in my doings when I slipped the bosal on her. Ol' Blue was dead and Guy's scooter had a flat, blast these rocks. We were a good twenty miles or more from help in town unless we chanced on someone coming down from the Buckeye ranch. But if we went straight north on the Jeep trail, we were probably only a few miles from the Harper house.

Walking was put away when horses were invented. Too many folks gave up riding after Henry Ford came along. Besides, these boots were not made for walking, I don't care what that song says.

And Guy's a sprinter.

There's exactly one fast way to move two people with one horse, but those two people have to be awfully motivated. Lighting a fire under Guy about anything but cooking has always been a challenge.

I explained this sport little Abby's wild about.

"The way it works is two people leapfrog each other on a trail, taking turns riding and running." It's the original hitch-and-hiking, 'cause the person ahead on the horse ties the pony up after a piece then commences to go afoot. Once the other runner gets to the tied-up horse, he rides all the way up to and past the first runner, then ties the horse up and hikes or runs more. I guess folks can move at track speeds in the wilderness this way.

Guy was so good looking, listening to me there in the low light, his face, the way his jaw and cheekbones almost kiss out of his skin. And the lanky build thing he's got going. He is one nicely put-together fella, he really is. He's a runner, a Thoroughbred. I gulped as he reached for me and had to lean back a little to not get swallowed up in a hug that could lead to all sorts of mischief.

"It's called Ride and Tie," I told him.

"What is?"

"This thing we're going to do to get ourselves out of here, to catch Harper Junior. I'm betting he's nearly back home. His dad is not safe. The Flying Cross is straight north of us, maybe five miles tops down this Jeep track."

Guy looked down the dirt trail, several kinds of puzzled crossing his face.

I swung onto the mare's back.

We'd have to race the moon to stop Junior.

Chapter 28

I NUDGED MY CALVES INTO THE wild-eyed horse and Guy took off running. I soon cantered past him. Minutes later, in steep stuff, I slowed her to a trot and a couple minutes after that, I figured I'd ridden my spell, so I pointed Misty at a likely tree. It felt clumsy bailing down from her off side to avoid the tree. If it wasn't for the not-being-good-at-it part, I'd be good at this sport. Tying Misty and jogging away made her nicker a question. I promised the mare that Guy would be along to untie her in a few minutes.

I ran fast as my breath let me keep a steady pace, picking it up a bit every time the footing allowed, even when hoofbeats pounded up behind me.

Guy was all business, sitting up straight, his legs long down Misty's sides, relaxed and balanced, his back and hips perfectly loosey-goosey. At ease riding bareback, he was a natural. Once ahead of me, Guy hollered, "How far should I go?"

"A few minutes," I said on an exhale, not breaking pace as I ate his dust.

He and the mare were gone and I was running alone again.

Almost every thought in the world galloped through my mind while I ran and rode through Dry Valley that night. There was a shoeing job I'd done last week, a big spoiled Appendix-bred horse that tried to show me something, but I didn't know it at the time.

Why is it people think they can breed two horses that each have a few good points and a few flaws, yet they think they're going to get offspring with a combination of both sets of good points? For crying out loud, these clients bred a sensitive, too-hot, rangy, crummy-footed Thoroughbred to an over-muscled Quarter Horse with solid little feet like the cold concrete he probably had between his ears and they expected to get a nice, big, calm, sensitive horse with good feet. Why don't they expect what they got, which is a nervous nellie dumb-butt with thin hoof walls who's not suited to do anything real well? Zenith was always going to be a goofy gelding and he had a rude habit that I especially hate: getting overly relaxed when I worked on his feet.

Dangling his lily in my face.

"Put that away," I'd said, popping Zenith light-like on the belly. He did, which seemed sympathetic.

Getting Zenith's old shoes off, I use my nail cutters and my crease nail pullers, though I don't with every horse. Zenith is a wuss who needs tender loving care on his tootsies. I six-nailed him, of course, though that took some convincing of his owners, who'd always had him handed back from their last shoer eight-nailed. It's not like I'm trying to save two nails per hoof out of a shoeing, but even punching my own holes I couldn't fit four on a side, his walls are so thin in the heel quarters. Plus, if I place nails too far back, then hooves can't expand as the weeks wear on. Main point being, everything needs room to grow.

The point I'd explained to that gelding in my head was about having two mismatched parents. And Zenith had the attention span of a bucket so I thought-explained it to him several times. I should have paid attention to the lesson from his feet instead.

Room to grow. Now I explained it to myself, because my attention span's no better than Zenith's. I didn't like what I'd done when I was thirteen, and I liked less what I'd done when I was fourteen. I made one huge mistake after another. After shoeing school, after internships, my first best idea was to find Red. It was good, I decided now, that it had been so hard and taken so many months and miles to track Red down to Cowdry. I'd found a good dog on the way. I'd found a chance here in Oregon. I'd met Guy, who gave me all the attention a gal could handle. More than I could handle.

Guy was a good man, a novice riding bareback under a full moon because we were going to go stop a killer.

I ran on.

It's a quiet feeling, remote and peaceful and a little scary, running a trail under moonlight. And I thought, this Ride and Tie is what life is like. It's being on your own, but being a part of a team. Pulling together, but doing your part. I ran like I was running for more than myself, and was winded when I saw Misty pawing under a pine tree. I'd probably only been alone on the trail a few minutes since Guy rode by. Not to be accused of dilly-dallying when I ought to be pulling my load, I untied and hopped on Misty in one leap, sorting out the mecate as she trotted off under me.

Bless her, the little mare had it all figured out now. Catch Guy, lope past him a ways, and when I slowed her, pick a tree that looked like a nice place to rest.

It occurred to me that this Ride and Tie thing is a type of race more natural to a horse than anything else we ask of them. These beauty beasts are built to run a piece and rest, run a piece and rest. They were never meant to run three or a hundred miles straight, or tussle with steers, or blaze around barrels in an arena, or jump five-foot fences thirty times in a row. Folks have made horses do a lot of nonsense.

Some pretty hard riding was required to catch Guy, and I wasn't on the ground very long during my afoot spells. Realizing that he was making more mileage running than me, I swore under the moon that next time I hit the dirt, I'd make Guy ride his heart out to catch me.

"Go a bit more," Guy said, arms pumping when I rode by him.

I pressed Misty up a wicked hill that topped out on a plateau of scrubby grassland. We picked the last shrub and she dived for it at the first hint I was asking for a stop. A tough competitor, this mare had gathered up all there was to know about being a Ride and Tie pony. She should turn pro.

So should Guy, who soon loped past as I ran my best.

If I'd thought Guy city-soft, I was learning my lesson. He could take a licking, cowboy-up and get to riding where it counted. And there was something else, something he was trying to tell me when we flew by each other every five or ten minutes.

The next time I rode past, Guy called out, "What can I get?"

I reined in and yelled over my shoulder, thinking he was exhausted and needed the horse right away. "You want her now?"

He waved. "Ride on. I've got a half-mile sprint left."

It was ground to fly on, good footing, firm and not too rocky. I pointed Misty down the slope. In a piece, I swung off, tied her, and ran solo.

When Guy rode up on Misty, I was clean winded. He tumbled off her right side and I went to haul my sweet self up on her left. Abby's Ride and Tie heroes would call this strategy using handoffs and flying ties to maximize our speed while keeping tight. Getting tired, my mounting attempt failed and I needed a second try.

I gripped the mecate and put everything I had into vaulting on for what might be my last spell astride.

Sound carries in the canyons. I heard Guy through the boughs, around the rocks, and hoped no one else did as his voice echoed, "I love you."

Misty galloped us past him. The wind made my eyes water. It can reset a gal's whole whirling brain for a guy to say something as wide as Texas right before the last leg of a Ride and Tie for life. It can make her consider the facts.

Guy hadn't done anything but care about me. I ought to decide there wasn't anything wrong with caring about me. He's never weak, not in any sense. Things only went downhill with Guy when I was a stinker.

I didn't push Misty anymore. She'd worked hard and didn't need to have her legs run off. We walked an awful steep descent. She was blowing, deserving this slower pace. Besides, it gave me a chance to ask this good gray mare a question.

"What the devil d'you suppose he meant by that?"

Truly, Guy's asked me for a life together before, but I'd discounted the notion, partly on account of him joking. Mostly because considering a real life together had been unfair. Back then, Guy hadn't known how ugly I am, what I'd done. And what I'd left undone by getting Red back, but in no way checking on my child.

But now he knows. He knows and he's saying he wants to be with me? Didn't make sense.

But he's tired, I pointed out to the mare's right ear, which came back for a listen on my deliberations. She was waiting, I think, for me to get to the good part, the part where I figure out the whole deal.

I rode at a walk and trot to settle the little mare. This was down-hill trail, so I let Misty pick her way, sliding her hocks in the dust as we got off the valley's shoulders.

Before when Guy mentioned us as a permanent thing, he hadn't been serious, right? I sure hadn't taken the idea seriously. We'd been so far from each other, too far apart even when we shared a table.

Suddenly, the whole idea of Guy struck me, made good sense. Usually, when I get struck, it's a sunrise or Charley playing with a frog, or good old Red blowing howdy, or a hawk in the sky.

I'm silly, I guess, the way I sometimes get struck by things that aren't of the greatest importance. At that moment in my life, the most important thing was stopping Harper Junior. And living through the deal, should we come to it.

But instead I thought, this is beautiful. It's just beautiful.

The night was stark wondrous out there. The moon cast so much pale golden light on the rocks they glowed. I saw my hand, reaching up to pat the mare's neck, and my fingers looked beautiful. Grace and sweaty strength showed as her muscles flexed under a short hair coat. Everything was wondrous to behold. The creak of my leather boots when I flexed my ankles. The dull thud of Misty's concave hooves muffled in the dirt. The extra clink and spark every time her steel struck rock. These sounds were chords of life to me. As Misty breathed, I swear I felt in my guts the flare of her nostrils while she did the trail-trotting job she'd been asked. Willing and working, this horse covered ground because it was what she was built to do. She'd tied well and quit crying when she was left alone at a tree. She'd caught on to the task, to move us all north, at speed. At that moment in the history of the world, she was the candidate to partner with Guy and me. I was in love with the mare's wits and heart, nearly as much as I'd ever loved anything.

Nearly anything.

The Scotch broom reached onto the rough trail and sprayed me with yellow flowers when my thighs knocked the swaying boughs. Thistles and stinging nettle were coming up with a fury in the logged ground, but that's the way of it. Some plants hurt us and others help. Most do both, like the spike-thorned wild roses. These were budding out, making the air smell so sweet it gave strength to anyone breathing. Running and riding this hard, I used a lot of air. I felt alive, maybe because I'd almost been killed, maybe because I was sharp enough now to kill Junior if need be. I felt more alive leapfrogging down the trail with Guy than I'd ever felt.

This was ground that hardly left Guy behind. I heard him bounding down the slope, panting a good clip while I let Misty get her legs back under herself.

I could live, I thought, if I can respect this Misty mare as I do with this breath, if I could love her enough to keep going. And I'm going to give her back to her real family. Tonight. I am strong, I really am. Strong enough to love, even though I could never love anything as much as I'd needed to love the baby boy I gave away.

It scared me, how much I loved him, love him still.

I'd held him once, just one time.

And then I let them take him away.

I'm sorry, son. I did it for you, not to you. I gave you away so they'd give you to people who would do better by you. Please forgive me, please try to understand. They promised to give you to good people. Two good parents. I had to trust them. You have to trust me that I didn't have it in me to do better.

When I went looking for Red, got him back, of course I thought of you first. I always think of you. You're why I'm so distracted.

You're so special. I promise you that there's good, even for a boy whose mama handed him over. There's good and there's beauty. Please see the beauty of the world. That's what I most want you to see, not to see me and mine. I want you to see the beauty. Please, son.

And I thought he might, he might see the beauty, this son whose name I'll never know.

Why these thoughts came to me, where they'd been for the last decade, I don't know. What made everything smell so crisp, every sound amplify, every moonlit sight stronger and sharper than human senses were normally capable of noticing?

Maybe it was because my eyes were so well adjusted in the dark. I saw Junior's Suzuki Samurai beside the Harpers' old metal barn. We'd caught up to my would-be killer. And maybe we'd done so before he'd hurt his father. Now what?

Chapter 29

THE OLD METAL BARN WAS A simple windowless square, with a light glowing inside, and a small lean-to on the near side that sheltered scrap wood and old tools such as a rusty compressor, a welder, a chop saw, and more. The barn doors were huge—half of the whole front end of the building hung from head rollers, and they were slid open, which made temporary walls jutting out beyond the corners. The design would have provided easy access for loading hay by the ton. I figured it had been the Harpers' main storage before the big fancy barn was built nearer the main house. And just this side of the first door and the lean-to sat Junior's Suzuki, its back hatch open, ready for packing something from the gaping barn.

Fifty or a hundred yards farther, the road improved all the way to the little dark cottage. I remembered catching a glimpse of that original homestead when I was at Patsy-Lynn's funeral reception. When I'd hiked up the Stakes Ridge looking for Misty in the early afternoon, I'd glimpsed sunlight reflecting off the old metal barn.

Guy ran up wiping sweat from his brow and joined in my look-see at the layout. We both put quieting hands on Misty's neck, me still astride, her body heat warming my thighs. We were awful close to salvation or big trouble. Harper's main house was just down this gravel driveway and beyond it was the big barn with Spartacus and other horses. If the home herd got wind of us, heard hoofbeats, they might call out to the strange horse that just rode up.

What if Misty whinnied back, announcing our presence?

Clanking noises came from inside the barn. What Harper Junior was doing in there, I couldn't hazard a guess.

"You ride on," Guy said. "We'll keep going, get to a phone."

"But Junior's in there now. And I think the deal with his daddy is that he has to be out of town by midnight."

Guy shook his head. "We'll go on past the main house, out Oldham and onto the highway. It's not much further to Keith Langston's place. We'll use his phone."

"But what if Junior drives away while we're headed to Langston's house? At least let's ground him here so he doesn't slip away." I slid off and tied Misty to a hemlock, passing my hands over her face to plead.

Please, please, don't nicker, don't paw, don't create a ruckus. I tried to mind-talk the mare, then left her in the shadows.

Cutting into the dark area between the lean-to and the Suzuki, Guy and I inched closer to that gaping barn door and the sounds of Junior banging metal around inside. A case of the creeps descended upon my shoulders but good. What the oops was Junior doing in there?

The pistol Junior had put in my face was on the Suzuki's dashboard. I twisted my do-all into pliers, clamped onto the tire stem of the off hind tire, and yanked. Hissing noise. Instant flat tire.

"Well, fine," Guy said, his voice lower than the whooshing air of the tire. "I see we're not planning on borrowing this car and driving down to use a phone somewhere."

I paused at the next tire. Why hadn't I thought of driving off in the Suzuki as a way to strand Junior? I'd just been thinking about grounding him, but now we were going to have to hold him somehow.

And no, I wasn't going to call him Mister.

Creepy-crawling my way into the barn seemed like a good idea at the time, but looking back, I guess plan B would have made more sense from the get-go. Guy and I closed the distance quiet as we could, but I was sure my pounding heart was going to alert Junior.

He was right inside, boots sounding nearer as he carried something that gave a hollow clunk when he set it down in the open doorway less than twelve feet from us.

Gas cans. It's a long drive to Mexico. Time to nip down there for sun and steroids, wait for things to cool off here.

When Junior turned and went back for something deeper in the barn, I whispered to Guy, "Let's go get him." Plan A, two against one, seemed like decent odds if I didn't put any more thought into the notion.

Guy looked truly appalled. "That's a pretty bad idea, Rainy."

I gave him my new look. It's the I Should Have Gone With the Big Veterinarian look.

Guy straightened up into tougher posture, like someone to go into battle with, then walked right into the barn like he owned the place.

That impressed me a good lick and I only paused long enough to wrap my mitts around the stoutest board I could in a quick grab at the lean-to's scrap wood pile.

Good thing, 'cause Winston Harper Junior boiled after Guy in an instant fury that was to be reckoned with. Hands on each other's throats, they whirled, Junior kneeing Guy and generally slamming him around into an old tractor, boxes of gear, a tool bench. Guy's quick, and big enough, but he was locked up with a man who had about a hundred pounds on him.

"Hey!" I hollered, "Stop that!" I kept yelling, almost adding "no fair."

Just in case I was fixing to calm down, Guy yelled, "Get out of here, Rainy. Run."

I didn't run. I did what comes natural.

Cocked back my weapon, and when Junior's back was to me, I whacked him right in the cheese wheel.

He went down, hands on the back of his head, squealing like a girl. I ran outside quick as a bunny and Guy backed out of the barn a bit slower. No sooner than our breathing got less gaspy, a shadow grew, darkening the doorway.

Junior looked even bigger when a light was behind him.

"Guy, I think he wants a rematch."

"Well, fine. Go talk to him." Guy bumped me in the ribs with his elbow and glanced toward the scrap pile.

"That's your very best plan?"

He nodded and nudged me again.

Like a boss, I walked into the barn and this time noticed plenty of tools that Manuel Smith from Montana didn't steal. A hedge trimmer. A leaf blower. There never had been stolen money, but Junior could probably blow through some serious cash during an easy night in Portland.

And Junior didn't look best pleased to see me. A demo list of expressions bounced across his face. I was shown surprise, effort of thinking, anger in several levels, and then his most interesting, fixing to kill.

"Hi there, Mister Harper," I said through gritted teeth. When am I ever going to manage to keep a promise?

"I'll take your head off!" He charged.

I ran.

Guy's plank cracked against the side of Junior's skull the split second I cleared the door.

This left Guy beaming at his handiwork, the board in his fists splintered to kindling. He said to the mumbling, semi-conscious Harper Junior, "I know somebody who needs a nap."

I felt much safer under the night sky than in the metal barn with the whackjob, even when the whackjob looked down for the count.

Guy slid the metal door shut, looked unsuccessfully for a way to secure it, then started picking through the scrap pile again, hefting one two-by-four then another, like a pinch hitter choosing the best Louisville slugger for his final at-bat.

"What's your plan?" I asked.

"Oh. I'm going to bonk him over the head again just before the next time he tries to kill us."

Like, he was planning on making a night of this routine?

And this boy says he wants to spend his life with me?

Maybe he was figuring on that life being about another two minutes long. I snorted to let him know what a weak idea he'd brained up. "That's quite a plan."

Guy shrugged. "Well, I haven't worked on it long. I might have done better if I had more time."

What and all with Junior moaning inside and maybe back on his way to being frisky, Guy didn't have time to finish explaining this swell plan of his.

I looked to see what ideas the tools in the lean-to might serve. If we could just lock the barn door on Junior somehow. The thing with sliding barn doors is you have to jam both halves together at the same time for a lock, as well as lock them to the main wall, otherwise a person can just slide the works away.

Guy frowned at the black boxy thing I pulled out of the lean-to. As I plugged it into the barn's outdoor power socket, he blabbed nonsense. "Rainy? Sweetie? Hon? Whatcha doing? What is that?"

It was a MIG welder, 80 amp, 120 volt. A handy little machine, especially given there probably wasn't 220 power out there. And what I was doing was welding the metal barn shut.

The little wire feed unit had an accessory bracket with a brass brush and slag hammer, but I wouldn't be prettying up my work. A rush job is not my favorite kind, but I've got to take the bad with the good.

With a few hasty, ugly welds, I was going to stop Junior, really stop him. Stop the guy who'd killed Patsy-Lynn and hurt her horse and tried to kill me. I told Guy, "Grab me that mask, will you?"

I scraped the barn's door handle with my do-all to get a good contact and clamped the ground line to it. About ready to rock and roll, my habits still made me take a safety glance around. There was an awful lot of tinder about. It's called hog fuel, the rough shredded bits of bark and scrap slash left over from logging operations. Horse folk use it by the truckload to meet the Oregon mud every year. And gas cans weren't the very best thing to have lying around while welding either. I'd just have to be careful, quick, and keep checking where the sparks landed.

"Guy, there's just the one piece of eye protection here, so—"

"I'll use these." He pulled sunglasses out of his shirt pocket.

I shook my head. "Not good enough. And what about Misty? Go to her, keep your back to the welder, and put your hands over her eyes."

There was no reason to blind the hardy little horse who'd carried us down the trail in the dark.

There was no reason to hurt anyone who didn't deserve it.

It wasn't an auto-darkening eye shield, so my first squeezes of the welder's trigger were wild apple guesses. I flipped the visor up and down a bunch, peeking and adjusting the scrap metal I made part of the barn, turning the metal door into a permanent wall.

Welding to that metal building wasn't easy, given its thinness.

The impossibly bright arc was a flicker of hope and a promise of strength. I made it work, ignoring the sparks flying at my body, letting them burn themselves out on my jeans and singe carbon pits into my boots. I checked my progress, welded, checked and welded. This was a long few minutes.

When I finished, a flame danced on the metal, the paint burning off. I blew it out.

Guy started singing "Come on Rainy, light my fire."

Junior started kicking inside.

I picked up the slag hammer, fixed to do battle again if Junior broke my welds, thinking a weapon with longer reach would have been a more inspired notion.

Big as he was, though, Junior wasn't a big enough man to test my metal. My welds held and it sounded like Junior dozed off again, weakened.

I'd made metal anew. I had real strength. I'd earned it.

Junior hadn't earned his. Muscles and moods and zits on his mug, that's what his steroids got him.

An inability to make babies or heal a simple scrape, plus tender feet after his system got screwed up metabolically, that's what excess steroids got Spartacus. Too much size, not enough sanity.

And what did it get Patsy-Lynn?

A dark truck drove up, very slowly, from the direction of the big house.

Guy took a step to stand between me and the approaching truck. He faced it, giving me his back. "Is that the pickup that drove by when we were talking at the old pizza place?"

"Dixon Talbot's rig?" I leaned around him to stare at the big black truck in the night, dual rear wheels, judging from the width. The trees blocked my chance to see if there was a shoer's box in the back. Was I wrong about everything, always? "Let's get out of here."

"What's the problem?" Guy asked.

"Just come on." I turned for the backcountry trail we'd run in on.

Guy grabbed my hand, held fast. "Rainy, what's going on?"

Junior's daddy's voice creaked from the driver's window. "Rainy? Is that Rainy Dale?"

This was the truck I'd seen on Oldham lane after shoeing for Patsy-Lynn that last time. Now I placed it as her towing truck, one she only used hauling to shows.

I bet Junior'd borrowed it that day she died and she'd known he was coming back.

I bet his daddy came to understand this in the days after the funeral, too. The sheriff's men would have talked to him about my seeing a truck coming up Oldham lane. Junior had said he was hundreds of miles away when Patsy-Lynn died. A road trip is provable, but the credit card statement showed what poor Patsy-Lynn had already known. Junior was home early. And then he'd taken the truck, but she knew he could be back any minute, so she wanted me to stay with her. At some point, Old Man Harper had figured out for sure that his son was lying about being hundreds of miles away when his wife died. Maybe he studied those non-existent credit card transactions before handing the records over to the police. Junior's story fell apart with scrutiny.

I stood fast, like Guy, willing to have a go at Harper Senior. He needed to make right by his wife. I needed him to.

However else was I going to let go the guilt of not being Patsy-Lynn's friend when she'd needed one?

Guy had a question. "Now what?" He still held my hand as he looked across the gravel at the oncoming truck.

But Mr. Harper stopped, shut his engine off, and just sat in the driver's seat. Headlights of other cars turned into Harper's driveway, searching the night.

"Now we call the po-lice and Junior goes to the pokey. We'll talk to his daddy. I bet even early on, a part of the old man wondered if his son had an outburst and hurt Patsy-Lynn. Maybe Junior didn't mean to kill her. Probably he didn't mean to. But she died at his hands. And that must have been pretty hard for Mr. Harper to face. And he loves his son, like natural. So, sending his kid away was his best solution."

Guy snapped his fingers. "That's why the old man wouldn't give a blood sample to the police. Being the father, his DNA would have been a close enough match to the DNA on the rasp that it would have strengthened suspicion on his son. He's smart enough to know that. And that's why the police asked Keith and me for samples, trying to make it seem to Mr. Harper like, hey, they're asking everybody, just give a sample."

Since I'd just found out Guy was smart enough to guess the reason why Mr. Harper refused to give blood—and the reason had never dawned on me—I was sort of impressed with my man.

And there was that part about Guy saving my life, which started just because he was coming to help me find a missing horse that was none of my business, but bugged me all the same.

We only caught Junior 'cause Guy was willing to do an instant Ride and Tie with me in the dark on a strange horse. Bareback. Without a bridle. Turns out the guy can ride.

And Guy is the only person I know who'd walk into a dead-end barn and go toe to toe with Winston Harper Junior.

Besides, he can run like the dickens and sometimes that's as good as standing to fight.

"I figured out some things," I said. "From the sheriff, I realized not everything was related. They made me think about drugs. I think it was Dixon Talbot who snapped off my hood ornament and I bet he throws my business cards in the garbage. But it wasn't his truck coming to the Flying Cross the day I left Patsy-Lynn. If the deputies go talk to Talbot, I bet they find out he gave Harper Junior a ride right after Junior left Misty up in the hills and got a flat tire."

Guy tried to cut in like a fellow on a dance floor. "Rainy—"

"And it wasn't a shoer who broke into Nichol's office. I'm sure that was Junior. And he stole steroids."

"You almost got killed up there," Guy shook his head, closed his eyes, and wrapped his arms around me.

But I was on a roll. "See, I guessed that Abby'd bred Liberty to Spartacus. I started to think about why Spartacus got so big and nasty and suddenly had sore feet and his scrape didn't heal and he had trouble breeding. That's all problems from getting overdosed with steroids. And I thought about why Patsy-Lynn might have a problem with her husband's son. After I got Abby talking, I guessed that Junior took Misty, but he meant to get Liberty."

He'd wanted the baby back, the baby Abby tried to make and take.

Guy rubbed the used little horse's face. Misty was almost home now. We could lead her there, avoiding the cattle guard by going through the Langstons' pasture. The Solquists would be glad to have their mare back.

Junior would have had a long wait expecting Misty to drop Spartacus's baby. And Liberty and Abby were safe from him now.

"Misty," I told her, "you did great. You need water, a rub down, and some good feed."

"*Hay Misty for Me,*" Guy sang.

"The singing doesn't actually help," I said, trying not to encourage him with a smile.

"Every little bit helps." Guy grinned.

"Like I got a little bit from Talbot and Nichol and Abby and the sheriff and—" I stopped because he waved. "What?"

"I'd just like to get this nailed down," he said. "Will you marry me?"

Yeah, I'd figured out some things.

I love Guy. Love him.

Chapter 30

BEFORE MIDNIGHT, JUNIOR WOKE UP AGAIN and started trying to open the door, but my welds held.

The sheriff's car and two deputies rolled up, parking right on Old Man Harper's heels. Watching this, a bit of tenderness crawled into my heart for Old Man Harper. Calling the law by midnight had been his deal with himself and his son. He had kept his promise.

After we speed-explained our end of it to the police, Guy and I talked more to the real Mr. Harper about what his son had done and why the old barn was welded shut.

I cut the welds for the deputies, but stayed wary of Junior 'til they got him handcuffed and in the back seat of a patrol car. They brought out an ambulance so his head could get looked at, but the handcuffs stayed on for keeps.

After that, Sheriff Magoutsen and his men wanted to hear details.

I told him all about welding the barn shut in the first place, the little battle we'd had in and out of the barn. About the chase through the woods before that. Junior's abduction of me. The evidence on the kitchen table back home. And my destruction

of evidence, from when I'd found and cut up the plywood Junior
had used over the cattle guard near the Solquists' road. I asked if
they'd want my new tool box, since that's what Junior's plywood
had become.

Mr. Harper, the real Mr. Harper, the aged man, cried. His shoulders shook and he mumbled in defeat. "At first, Win didn't tell me
anything and I couldn't understand her death at all. I mean, why
would she kill herself? And why was she injured? Her face was
bruised."

I swallowed, hearing for the first time what else had happened
to Patsy-Lynn, picturing her stepson belting her across the face
like my ex had done me.

"Win said we were missing cash, but now I think he just said
that to distract the sheriff and me." Mr. Harper shook his head.
"The sheriff's men were trying to figure out the rasp, knew it
wasn't unrelated to Patsy-Lynn dying, but we didn't know what
to think. Then I checked the credit card statements the sheriff's investigator wanted and I realized my son wasn't on the road
when he said he was. When I confronted him, Win finally told
me he didn't mean to hurt her, that he was in the garage and she'd
already started the car, she'd been about to leave. He told me she
was mad at him about some mare he'd brought in, and about who
had control over the stud. He said they argued and maybe pushed
at each other and she hit him with the rasp, then he pushed her
down and left. Win said he hadn't meant to hurt her. He said she
must have passed out. And my Patsy-Lynn died of carbon mon-
oxide poisoning."

Magoutsen nodded. He'd known—all the sheriff's men had
known—medically, how she died.

Guy and I looked at each other. I reckon we were both thinking
that Junior could have saved Patsy-Lynn. And I bet I knew why
she was mad at him in the first place. She didn't like some strange
Arab being at their Quarter Horse place with no explanation. She
didn't like him messing with her stallion.

But she wouldn't have hauled off and hit Junior with a rasp, starting that fight.

She wasn't a dummy. She wanted to live. I bet he pushed her long before she swung her weapon.

He started that fight and he finished it. She was already afraid of her stepson and that's why she wanted me to hang around.

I wished I had.

Patsy-Lynn, I am so very sorry. If I had it to do over again, I'd be a friend. I'd stay with you.

I'd be a better person when someone needed a better person to help out.

And I bet Junior knew real clear what he'd done after he laid his 'roid rage on his stepmama.

Mr. Harper was realizing too, that there was more to the story. Now he'd learned from me and the police that his son had tried to kill me and tried to make it look like I'd killed Patsy-Lynn. I told the sheriff about Junior planning to tamper with his dad's pills and he gave me a severe nod that meant he'd take care of this, too.

Harper looked shell-shocked, leaving me thinking about all he'd lost, all he thought he'd had.

A good son.

I never had one except when he was inside me.

Guy says some lucky couple has a good son only because of me.

* * *

Come morning, Guy got my mama on the phone and he made a lot of things plain. He got my daddy on the phone and did likewise.

Nobody but me had held a grudge against me all this time. Guy gets the past, but he's all about the future.

Within another day, I said yes to him. We got all the folks back on the phone again to tell them we were engaged. Guy was mighty delighted-looking with having a fiancée.

"How'd I manage to persuade you?" he asked.

I thought, just for a minute, about giving him a look to indicate he should make himself clear, but I could well enough guess his meaning. Maybe making Guy work so hard at it, at me and at us, wasn't too becoming. Finally, I did my part, understood him. He wasn't talking about a goose pen or his restaurant dream, he was talking about me.

I spoke slowly. "I think it was you being a good guy who really cares about me." And I reckon I went red from my toes to the tip of my ponytail.

"Well, fine," Guy said.

* * *

A few weeks on, Guy and I kept stiff upper lips when Keith Langston made his daughter sign a contract that she owed Mr. Harper for the stud fee and she would have to give away Liberty's baby to boot.

"I can't have her profit from what she did and I have to have her pay for what she took. I'm trying to raise a winner here."

Abby wailed at the double whammy, looked to me for some sympathy, but Guy and I had already talked about the wise severity of Langston's thinking.

She washed dishes for Guy, and I put her to work as a helper on Saturdays. She says she's going to be a vet someday, but a horse-shoer first. I turned her back over to her daddy after one long day where we'd worked a rodeo and I couldn't stop smiling.

Abby had cleaned up the pulled shoes for me, held horses, fetched stuff, and acted all big and important when I let her light my forge. We were dirty and needing showers 'cause I'd been running the fire all day.

But come nightfall, Guy answered a phone call from Langston. Could we help with Abby's horse?

"Well, sure," we said.

* * *

Liberty's groans were typical of a maiden mare. I remembered making similar sounds.

Her eyes were wide with fear and wonder. Sweat soaked her body to a darker gray than her clean coat. Now Liberty was a gunmetal gray-black that was a lot closer to the slick dark nose of the colt who came into the world with my hands on him. With one palm on the foal's forelegs, Guy guided the baby's head toward the ground. At the last second, Liberty rose to her feet again. Since we didn't want the little guy to take a header on his first introduction to the world, we got wet and sticky letting him slide over our arms.

The baby wasn't solid-colored. He had big splashes of white. His mane and little squirrel tail were bi-color. Spartacus's bold paint colors on Liberty's delicate Arab frame. He was a looker, this little horse baby. A lot of folks pay decent dollars for these half-breeds, calling this Quarter Horse-Arabian mix a Quarab. Throwing pinto coloring in the mix can add value, though breeding for color isn't a good idea.

Abby pulled the amniotic sac off the baby's shoulders. Liberty nudged her colt to standing in minutes.

My eyes let loose like busted faucets.

We were in love all over again, stroking that doe-eyed, fresh, wet foal, loving it with Liberty. I was awed by his sudden presence, a new life in a little barn. Guy called him a little beanie.

"He's yours, if you want him," Abby said.

Guy and I stared at her, this good girl managing to give away her Wonder Mare's firstborn in its first minutes of life. What was she thinking? And she saw this question on our faces.

Speaking with the most worthy maturity, Abby said, "I want a really good home for him. If you take him, after he's weaned of course, I could still see him every day, watch him grow up."

I looked at Guy. "You want a horse?"

He nodded, looking struck silly.

Abby cleared her throat. "Then you get to name him."

Was there no end to her growing up tonight? I wondered if Guy appreciated this honor. When I looked up from wiping my eyes,

Guy was hugging Abby. They turned loose of each other and she hugged her daddy, who was standing in the stall door, nodding approval at it all. So Guy took up hugging me.

"I'll have a horse," he said. "Red will have pasture company. We'll go . . . riding together."

When he let go of me, a tiny part of me went Uh Oh 'cause he looked terribly tickled with himself.

Guy turned to Abby. "How about *Pinto Bean?*"

Oh, mercy. The kid was laughing. I was impressed that Guy apparently had paid attention to the names of horse coats of a different color.

Pinto Bean got the goods from both parents and a christening that could make anyone smile.

"I'll call him Bean," Guy finished, like that helped matters.

Maybe it did. Maybe every little bit helps to nail things down.

THE END

Acknowledgments

So many people gave so much wondrous support and feedback as I wrote *The Clincher*. I'd like to thank Mark Gottlieb (my agent and the best advocate a writer could have), Barry, Rob, Sandy, Corinne, Molly, PJ, Monty, Edwin, Jessica, Judy, Margaret, Katherine, and, of course, my editor Lilly Golden for so many contributions to the Rainy Dale Horseshoer Mystery Series.

DEAD BLOW

Chapter 1

DYING FROM A HIND HOOF GETTING run through my skull would smart, at least for a minute. If this big old girl didn't learn some manners pronto, I'd be finding out if the noggin went numb right quick or if maybe it kept stinging as I flopped around in the barn aisle, landed-trout style.

Or Sandy could behave herself, that'd be an idea.

She and I were on the near side of needing to take a Pay-Attention-and-Act-Like-a-Lady walk. The barn grunt was off cleaning stalls. He'd just put the mare in cross-ties—I hate working with the horse in cross-ties—before scuffing away without a word. Wasn't his horse and he was probably paid a shovelful less than dirt, so he wasn't about to do extra, like mind this mare who was due for a full trim. Now I was left with a horse stomping, pulling away, and swaying like we were in a hurricane.

I'd had more than I could enjoy.

The horse stood nicely for the two seconds it took me to get back in position under her haunch, then she snapped her leg into me and twisted away, hopping on her other hind leg and throwing me onto my toolbox. I got up mad but let that go for now, because anger and horses don't mix well. I gave Sandy a stink eye. She gave me one right back, indicating maybe she hadn't caught up on her kicking quota.

Then something just wonderful happened.

Whatever saint is supposed to keep watch over horseshoers woke up from a nap and cast a quick spell on Sandy. She stood like stone and I finished that hoof like nobody's business. Well, nobody else's business, what and all with this being my whole business. And business was fair near booming. I still broke out in the grins thinking about the phone call this morning. Couldn't wait to go grab dinner with Guy and tell him about my new account.

When the Widow Chevigny rang and asked me to shoe for the Buckeye, it suited me fine. This was a ranch account and I wanted to be Donna Chevigny's shoer mighty bad. Word is, she's been needing a shoer. Her husband had done their shoeing but he died last year, around the time I moved to Cowdry. Being new, I learned about the accident—rolled his tractor, is what I heard—in bits, over time. I've been needing a larger clientele, but hadn't wanted to pound on a widow's door asking for a job.

"I want rim shoes," Donna told me on the phone. "Getting some of my ranch horses shod for a herd dispersal sale. They've been keeping themselves way off at the back, by the grazing lease." This brought a big sigh and I knew she was thinking about how it'd take her time and trouble to bring the horses in. Guess the area where her excess herd was hanging was too rough for driving to, or she'd have been telling me how long it'd take us to get out there with trucks or four-wheelers or something.

Brimming with my new possession, I allowed as to how I could cold shoe out in the tooley-weeds, without need for my anvil and stand. My fellow's folks had gifted me with a Pocket Anvil as an engagement present. What gal wouldn't be completely swept off her boots with such a bonus? That nifty gift selection was Guy's doing, I reckon, because I can't imagine how his parents would have thought up sending us a Pocket Anvil and a pasta thingy for engagement presents.

Still, a decent shoe inventory would be quite a ball and chain to pack to the far end of the Buckeye ranch, so I asked, "Do you happen to know what size feet you got out there?"

"They're all ones." Donna sounded like a woman who was certain. "All four feet on all twelve horses."

"I won't be shoeing a dozen in a day, ma'am." Gulp. I mean, yeah, stories go around about old-timey ranch shoers whupping out fifteen and twenty shoeing jobs in a day, but I've never known a sure shoer to manage twelve on a short day where the work site was remote, needing an hour's ride to get to and from the string. Lots of steel to pack. Chances were, some of those front feet were supposed to be size 2, and some of those hinds were aughts, anyways.

"I thought you'd try for half one day, half another." Donna told me the brand of horseshoes she favored. Regular stuff. I had a fresh box in Ol' Blue, my truck.

Thrilled with my new tool, I told Donna all about the Pocket Anvil, this portable gadget that lets me shape horseshoes in the backcountry. Getting by without an anvil would let me ride out to shoe in remote country. Without my forge, I wouldn't be hot-fitting the shoes, of course, but I'm not above cold shoeing when circumstances demand.

"A Pocket Anvil? Goodness, I've never heard of such a thing." Donna sounded floored, then hopeful. "I wouldn't have to bring the horses in?"

"Nope. We could ride out to them as long as you scare up some saddlebags that'll freight my gear. Just the regular hand tools, a couple dozen shoes, nails, and my Pocket Anvil." *Just*, ha! It was still no small chore. And I'd be shoeing without my good hoof stand all day. Whew. On the plus side, without my anvil, I wouldn't be striking steel with heavy hammer blows, so my ears wouldn't be ringing after I worked at the Buckeye.

Donna's appreciative exhale let me know she was considering my offer. "It sure would help me out an awful lot if we ride out to the stock instead of me having to bring them in the day before."

"We'll do it," I promised. I already had my appointment book out and found a free day that worked for both of us. I used to worry about not having my work weeks scheduled full, then came to find that they fill up just fine. Too awful many holes in my time was not a thing.

Donna worked all the hours a day sent, too. "Is six too early for you to be here? I'd have my horse tacked up, with the heavy packing saddle bags, if you're sure we can handle everything you'll need to haul."

Given that it was fall, we'd be riding out in the cool dark morning at that time, which sounded kind of wonderful. "I'm sure. Um, the horses needing shoes, they handle all right?" I didn't exactly want to be battling broncs in the backcountry.

"They all handle fine. We won't have any problems with them out in the rough, and there's an old pole corral there. Goodness, Rainy, it will save me hours of pushing stock and eating dust if we can just ride out to where they're pastured."

"You'd need to give me a mount," I told her. "My Red's a good horse and I'd love to ride him at your place, but I don't have a trailer."

"I can put a good horse under you," Donna promised.

* * *

Soon as I finished trimming Sandy's big tough mustang's feet and nodded to the barn guy, I went to get something under my belt. The restaurant I go to in town is an outfit that's gone from a good place to get a glass of water to a whole bit better thanks to my Intended.

If Guy's not there, the Cascade Kitchen is just a diner and that's what it always looks like. Lots of orange caps and vests at the counter come hunting season, sometimes a tractor in the parking lot if a trucker hogs the dirt road out back when the fellow who farms the adjacent hundred acres comes in for a hot lunch.

Today a living quarters horse trailer hooked up to a dually four-door F350 truck took the five-plus parking spots that a rig that size demands. The pickup's custom paint job read *Paso Pastures*. I didn't know who owned the truck and trailer, but horse people are my tribe. Folks are getting used to seeing me ride Red into town for an ice cream. If the Cascade Kitchen's owner put a corral, or at least a hitching rail, behind the restaurant, it would suit me fine.

Walking in the back door like a boss, I grabbed the mail stuffed in the wall tray to give it a gander. Guy and I started using the Cascade Kitchen for mail after our road mailbox got baseball-batted. Sizzling scents made mail sorting a pleasure.

Way too many cooking and spice catalogs, then the mail pile got good. A horseshoeing supply catalog, an ad for glue-on shoes, another horseshoeing supply catalog, a tack catalog, a different horseshoeing supply catalog, a couple bills, and some official-looking fat letters. Envelopes for Guy and me from the fifth judicial district, whatever that meant, which apparently pulls up a chair in Clackamas County. We're in Butte County, but this fifth judicial deal also claimed to be from the State of Oregon. How many people get mail from their own state? Too early for Christmas, so these would be . . . subpoenas? I thought those got handed out by seedy-looking creeps who tracked you down when—

Whack-whack-whack, whackety whack. Guy's rangy, almost six-foot frame stood at a metal counter in front of a cutting board piled with red peppers. His right arm moved like it was demon-possessed, powering a butcher's knife, whacking peppers into long strips.

Only I could break the spell. "Hey."

Guy's smile melted off and the knife got quit on the counter as he squirreled his arms around me. "What happened to you? Are you okay?"

I followed his stare to my dirt-covered legs. I'd forgotten about doing a tango with the last horse and taking a spill. "I was working on Sandy's hinds. She's from the Riddle Mountain herd, a big Kiger mare—"

Guy broke in with a solo. "I've got a . . . *Kiger by the tail it's plain to see.*"

Never sings the right words, Guy. Bursting into song is one of his things, like he breathes and eats and sleeps. He knows a gajillion and six songs, but he adjusts the words quite a bit. We'd talked at the house this morning about me going out to work on some mustangs. New clients have a pair of these beautiful, stripey-legged tough duns with the hardest feet any horse ever thought of growing. True Kigers, that band of barefooters, born wild in Oregon's southeast. I'd been tickled to become their shoer—okay, their new trimmer—and tickled to tell Guy about the job.

He tickled me, snaking his arms all over as he dusted me off and went for free feels.

It's a little embarrassing to be fussed over and it'd be best we not get started in the kitchen. I mean, in our kitchen at home, that's fine, but not here at his work. Wasn't bumping on the counter some kind of food safety violation? Man in his line of work ought to know that kind of thing. I pushed him away.

"Well, fine." Guy kissed me like he meant it, smoothed my ponytail, then brushed again at the dirt on my jeans. "Anything broken?"

See, here he was gathering points. He knows I'd prefer a How's-the-Kit question when he can see plain enough that I'm still standing.

"My chaps," I said. "I've got to cut a long, thin strip of leather to replace one of the leg straps."

Guy grinned and used his knife to scoop up slices of red pepper. "Julienne leather?"

Oh, he seemed to think he was clever with this little . . . was it a joke?

I am new at julienne jokes.

New at a lot of stuff, actually, like a fella feeding me love. New at making my way in Cowdry, this town I've called my own for the better part of a year and a half. Sometimes it's too good to be true, like I can't believe this is my life.

Customers seated at the tables and booths and counter gave me a glance as I went through the swinging doors to the front with Guy. I like to act all cool as I go to my spot at the very end of the lunch counter and rack my boots on the rail. That last twirly stool is as good as mine.

As the man who wants to marry me fetched up a tall iced tea— not sweet, no lemon—and put out pie for folks in the far booth, I blabbed bits about me getting a go at the Buckeye ranch account.

The Buckeye ranch is a cattle operation with a few good ranch geldings sold on the side, making little more than enough hay for its own use. Trying to keep the Buckeye ranch running on her own was going to be the death of Donna Chevigny, I feared. More work than a body can do. I didn't know how she was fixed for money, but I knew that even if her hiring me as a shoer strained her pocketbook, it would take strain off her back. And she picked me, the New Girl, as I'm known to horse folk here.

Hadn't asked for the title. Hadn't asked to be Donna Chevigny's shoer, come to that. I'd bided my time and didn't sniff around for the job like Dixon Talbot, one of the other full-timers in Cowdry. Plenty of part-timers would have liked to land the Buckeye account, I reckon. There's generally enough shoeing jobs to go around. All through the warm weather, we work our butts right off. It's fall now and soon things will taper down. People ride less in bad weather, and hooves grow more slowly up here during the north country winters.

Guy raised his eyebrows and made the right noises, especially at the part about me telling the widow that I could do remote shoeing with my Pocket Anvil.

"Well, fine, you'll like that, hm? Riding out to shoe with this woman?"

"Donna Chevigny," I told him again. "Looking to get some tuck now."

"And that would be?"

Having done my formative eating in Texas and California, my palate, such as it is, doesn't know what to do with itself with Guy in its life. Hope in my heart, I asked, "A burger?"

He rolled his eyes, as he is wont to do with my cuisine choices. It's not like the Cascade Kitchen is some upscale eatery with wine guys and cheese courses anyways.

"With mixed greens?" Guy suggested. When I gave him a Look, he moved on with, "Fries or potato salad?"

"Tater salad." I winked. He gave me more iced tea, then bumped through the swinging doors to burn me a burger. But something gave me the heebie-jeebies. Eyeballs bore into me from somewhere, quivering my skin like Red's does when he's knocking a fly off his back. In the mirrored part of the wall behind the counter, I saw a gal with a wolf's watch studying everything.

Somewhere. I knew her from somewhere.

Well, from around town, most likely. Cowdry's not too awful big and it does seem like the same people are the fill-ins at the post office and bank and grocery store and all that, so probably I just—

There she did it again, checked me out in the mirror. Now both of us knew we were looking at each other and had half a mind at wondering what the other was up to.

She looked a tad younger than me, probably barely drinking age, in sneakers, shorts, and a bright, synthetic T-shirt, with dark hair not prone to summer streaks like mine is. Her build could have helped her make it as a horseshoer—strong-looking but not too tall, and no gut to get in the way when squatting under a horse. But probably, horseshoeing wasn't her career choice. It startles people when they find out how I earn my living. Every time, their surprise makes me grin.

More motion in the mirror distracted me from remembering where I knew Wolf Eyes from. A couple rose from the booth right behind me. This woman's clothes were my kind, broken-in jeans and an open plaid shirt over a cotton tank top. Her hair dangled in her face, not properly tucked behind her ears or in a ponytail. And him?

He was a big guy with a Fred Flintstone haircut. Something about big beefy boys leaves a bad taste in my mouth, probably because the last one I dealt with tried to hang me with my own rope.

Flintstone wore perfect, too-clean jeans and a yoked blue western shirt with white piping. His cowboy boots were shiny, with no scuffs and no caked pucky in the inner corner where the heel meets the sole.

Not a real horse guy, just someone with a costume in his wardrobe.

"Doll, let's go now." He slid a hand across her patooty and gave the left half a squeeze.

She ignored his command and grope, so at least she had that going for herself. When he dropped money on the table and headed out, she turned her tall self around and strolled the other direction, toward the powder room. I just knew she'd be in there a good long spell while he cooled his boot heels, but I guessed her payback would be wasted on him.

Like a horse or a dog, a fellow ought to know when he's being punished for turdiness.

Doll, he called her. Jeez Louise.

She didn't much look like a doll to me, but what do I know about dolls? Dolls and me broke up as soon as I discovered horses. I don't know how old I was exactly but it was before figuring out how to read. Way, way before boys.

The Tall Doll brushed aside long brown bangs hanging shaggy over her eyes and winked at me as she passed by on her way to the ladies'. Older than me by half a decade, she wore those packer-style, lace-up riding boots that gave her extra height and let me figure her for someone who spent time in a saddle, since the boots were scuffed in all the right places to show stirrup wear. This gal was horse people. Obviously, she used someone other than me for a shoer, but maybe she was from elsewhere in the county since I didn't think I'd seen her around town. And I'd been thinking lately, what with growing new roots here in Butte County in general and

Cowdry in particular, that a friend would be a nice addition. Guy and I need people to invite to our wedding, which we're not planning yet, since I'm not there yet, but it's coming, sure enough.

A real friend, a girlfriend, that's something that might be a good thing to have.

She'd have to be a rider, of course, to be my new best friend.

In the mirror, I saw Fred Flintstone out in the parking lot. He opened up the big Ford truck, letting me view the *Paso Pastures* sign on the door as he opened it. And I realized Wolf Eyes took it in, too. Something in her shoulders relaxed. She slid onto the empty stool next to me and hitched her chin in greeting.

"Melinda. Melinda Kellan."

I'm five-foot-six on a tall day and I'd say we measured the same. This Melinda's muscles probably resulted from lifting lead, not honest-earned by hefting an anvil and shaping steel.

Guy set a meal in front of me and headed off with a couple of vegetable sides for another table. I wanted to get after my new job—chowing down—with a good businesslike attitude, but then I recollected where I'd seen this Melinda Kellan before. And I bet now that I remembered, I was blanching like Guy's vegetables. I sure felt smart as a carrot.

Melinda Kellan was the police clerk who took something from me during that unfortunate misunderstanding a while back.

My fingerprints.

"You work at the sheriff's office. The little one out here in Cowdry. You're the one who fingerprinted me." Butte's a small county but Cowdry's a pretty good ways from the county seat, so there's just a small deputy force out here, with office space in the strip mall near the grocery store. I've been needing to check in with them, to see if I'll have to testify. I can never remember the investigator's name. I always thought of him as Suit Fellow.

Melinda Kellan squinted at me all this time I jabbered and recollected. I figured she ought to be able to help me out.

"What's that guy's name, you know, the one who . . . investigates stuff?" I waved my hands to help her guess the rest.

She smirked, said a name that went in my left ear, sprinted across the open prairie of my mind, and fell out my right ear. Then she nodded. "He's retiring soon."

Huh? I hate it when people answer a question that didn't get asked, not lingering on the one that wanted good answering. Do I really have to see Detective what's-his-name and will he make me go to court? But instead of hollering all this at her, I kept my mouth very shut.

"Will you do something for me?" Melinda Kellan spoke like she wasn't asking, more telling. "Will you let me know if anything, anything at all, strikes you as not fitting while you're at the Chevigny place?"

Just made me itch to say something like, "Sure, I'd be happy to spy on my new client—a widow at that—for you, you bored little clerk." Instead, I gave her more of a studying, trying to get my eyeballs and brain moving since my mouth wasn't working much. Melinda Kellan wore running shoes. She's not horse people. I turned away from the little inquisitor, bit my burger, and made eye contact with her through the mirror. "You ride?"

Kellan shook her head.

"Ever make hay?"

She grinned. "Not in the way you mean."

Bristling like a porky-pine, I nodded, turning a little red and not liking her little sin-uendo at all. It figured. Figured she didn't ride and didn't get, just didn't get, how tough and dangerous the work of making food is. I don't mean making food like Guy, in a kitchen. I mean making it like Donna Chevigny does, like her departed husband had. Making feed for cattle and tending those cattle 'til they're ready for slaughter and—

"So, I don't ride. What about it?"

Like she was looking to start something.

Then Melinda Kellan went quiet as the tall rider sauntered back from her powder, taking the long walk across the restaurant in her sweet time.

There's horse folk and then there's everybody else. With plenty of people, I can peg 'em for what kind of horse they'd be if they'd been blessed born. Guy, for example, would be a Thoroughbred, though a palomino. Sometimes I can tell more than the breed, I'd know how good the legs and feet would be and what kind of an attitude is in the eye. It's not always a good thing, this gift of mine. There's some people I don't take to, but everybody I cotton to shows up in my mind as a horse. Not Melinda Kellan though. She wasn't one of us, not tough enough.

Tall Doll and I made eye contact in the mirror as she passed behind me this time. I winked. We had an instant connection. She would be an Appendix Quarter Horse, with good feet, if she were a horse. My new near friend paused and said, "Watch that you don't turn your back on that Chevigny woman."

I stared in the mirror at the Tall Doll, taken aback. Saying bad things about people in Donna Chevigny's position is like drowning kittens, kicking puppies, and slapping orphans. Bad form. It's just not done, talking trash on widows behind their backs. I really should mind what I say and how loud and who's around when I blab to Guy about my new shoeing accounts.

Turning my stool all the way around, I faced Tall Doll. "Missus Chevigny's a widow."

She made a wry, friendly face, then dropped her tone low enough to keep it between us. "She caused Cam's funeral. And you could end up in the ground just like he did."